I0520163

Protectors of the Black Prince

Book I:
Victory, Slaughter, Capture, Escape

a novel series
by

Curtis Stephen Burdick

Cover design by Jeff Burdick

To Dolores,
my wife and best friend

Also by Curtis Burdick

Novellas

Discoveries at River View

Sorceress

PROLOGUE

"Archer, ready thy bow!" yelled a tournament official from behind Michael Costwain, an eighteen-year-old master archer, who, had his face been seen, would have been mistaken for a boy.

Michael appeared to aim at the heavens as he drew back the tightly twisted, thin strands of oiled leather that formed a bowstring until the spike-tipped arrow reached the longbow's bone handgrip.

Breathe in with the pull, out after release, were the words that always went through Michael's mind with the first arrow. The voice in his head was not his, but that of George Bainty, or 'Baints' as everyone called him. Baints was the renowned veteran archer in the company of Sir Godfrey of Hampstead, Michael's company as well, who had trained him since the age of eleven. Baints had been the perennial Hampstead Longbow champion until Michael began his remarkable reign.

The back of Michael's right thumb, pressed on the end of the arrow's ash shaft, touched his cheek. He held the maximum tension, while quickly lowering the angled, six-foot bow, two inches taller than he was, carved from English yew. He sighted the arrow tip on an elevated trajectory that experience and years of practice had taught him would hit its intended target, while allowing for the slight breeze that swept the field.

"Only a tickler of a wind from the right, lad," called out Thomas Curry from behind.

Michael heard the distinctive, gravelly voice and knew at once it was his company's sergeant. Curry was Sir Godfrey's long-time and trusted leader of his legendary company of longbowmen.

Years previous, Curry had saved the young knight's life at Londaghen, during one of the most vicious and bloody battles ever fought against the Scots. Curry's father and grandfather before him had all served the illustrious, noble Hampstead family as master archers.

Michael's lean, angular face had not even the slightest hint of stubble, and though attractive, this made him appear far too young to be one of England's most celebrated archers. But his eyes, large and intense, did not at all reflect youth, and his sight, as was the case with all expert bowmen, was exceptional.

His hair was cut short in a circle all around his head and just above the ears in the yeoman's style. He had a jagged, two-inch scar above his right eye, the reminder of a flawed bow that had shattered in use. He was taller than most archers but exceedingly thin of frame, a frame that belied the enormous upper body strength he possessed and that allowed him to also be exceedingly swift of foot. His ability to track a wounded stag on the run and score the final kill at full speed was marveled at and celebrated by fellow archers.

Michael was dressed in the manner bowmen appeared in battle, gray leggings made of coarse linen and tied with strings over a codpiece. These extended down his legs to the tied tops of wool sock-boots, the soles of which were stitched layers of leather. Over his torso was a jerkin, a loosely woven, wool shirt covered by a short, thin but tight, green archer's tunic, which allowed great freedom of movement and bore, on its front, the coat of arms of his knight and lord, Sir Godfrey, Earl of Hampstead.

But Michael was hardly engaged in mortal combat this day. His target was not a feared, barbaric Scot or marauding Norseman, or even a poacher on his lord's vast estate, but two bales of resin-soaked and dried hay, tightly compacted together with leather straps, and positioned on a stand, one hundred fifty yards in the distance. It was painted with concentric circles in black pitch and crimson, the outer ring being exactly forty-two inches in diameter, then alternating inward with the very center a bright royal red circle, twelve inches across.

His intense concentration now blocked out all distraction, including the din of noise, although restrained, in the background from the thousands who crowded the open fields of Leeds for the annual Royal Tournament of Champions, pitting expert archers from all over England and Wales against each other. All contestants had won a local competition during the past year in one or more of ten official archery prize categories. The tournament had grown enormously in recent years, as spectators—nobles, knights, and clergy alike—had begun to travel from all over Christendom to watch the greatest of the renowned English and Welsh longbowmen compete, universally acknowledged as the greatest archers in all the world.

"Time!" the tournament's officiator, Farley Creasy, yelled down from atop a makeshift tower, simultaneously turning over a modified hourglass. Creasy was a sixty-one-year-old, elf-like, London tax magistrate with bushy eyebrows and bulbous nose, known for his incorruptibility. He wore the bright-red vest of tournament officials that bore the embroidered insignia of a longbow and sheaf of arrows.

Immediately, Michael's right thumb, and fore and index fingers, relaxed their grip on the arrow shaft's deeply notched end and released the arrow with no discernible movement in any other part of his body. The high-pitched twang of the taut bowstring was instantly followed by the whooshing sound made by the arrow's three gray goose pinion feathers that quickly became a whistling whine as it spun, accelerated, and then arched down on the target. The string scraped the leather brassard on Michael's left forearm, worn to protect the skin from being rubbed raw and bloody after more than three or four arrows.

The first shaft was quickly followed by others, pulled from the leather quiver high on his back over his right shoulder, remarkably fourteen in all, two more than most contestants, until Creasy yelled, "Time expired!" signaling that the one minute of sand held in the converted hourglass had exhausted itself.

The first arrow had hit its mark, a red center impact, but on the margin, with the second and third striking nearly dead center, followed by three more, two in the adjacent black ring and one totally off the mark, hitting outside the first outer ring, just as Michael let loose the last of his arrows. He was pulling a fifteenth arrow out of his quiver when Creasy's shout stopped him.

Successive arrows hit the target with dull thuds, if the sound could have been heard, and a precision that brought forth a building chorus of astonished awe from the crowd, even among the other archers, which quickly became thundering eruptions of wild cheering and then turned into chants of, "Michael!, Michael!" as the last arrow hit the now-crowded, red center mark, shredding a feather and shaving ash off one of the other arrows. Of the fourteen arrows that had been unleashed, all save one hit within the target's circles, with eight in the bright-red center, four in the adjacent black ring, and one in the first crimson ring. Michael's expression revealed excited satisfaction as the results were yelled in relay from one official to another, until Creasy yelled down the official results to the suddenly hushed crowd.

"Forty and six of fifty! A new record tally!" Creasy bellowed twice. Instantly the building anticipation of the crowd, till now kept restrained, was unleashed and erupted into another round of wild cheering.

But Michael's elation was not at all about his astounding feat of marksmanship, but rather, over the effect he hoped it had on Lady Mary, the fourteen-year-old daughter of his lord and knight, whom he secretly loved so fervently it scared him at times. His very soul seemed to ache with the thought of it, for it was an unrequited love. Unless he somehow became a knight, as impossible in probability as his becoming a noble, she would surely be given to another, and yet, he could not imagine living his life without her.

Michael's gaze scanned the reviewing stand, packed with nobles—English, Welsh, and foreign-born—royal emissaries of King Richard the Lionheart, who could not attend due to brewing conflict with Philip Augustus in Normandy, the Archbishop of Canterbury, and other important clergy, but he took little note of their attendance.

His eyes fixed solely on his heart's love, Lady Mary, a radiant, exuberant beauty with smooth, white skin and golden hair that seemed to shine in the sunlight like a halo. She was seated between her mother, Lady Elizabeth, and her father, The Knight and Earl of Hampstead. Michael was certain her eyes at that moment were as intently focused on him as his were on her. It was a magical, heart-pounding moment. He felt sure something passed between them at that instant.

Mary stood then, took a white-lace face cloth from her sleeve, and began waving it—*waving it at him*! He was sure of it now. Lady Mary was waving her cloth directly at him with one hand, while motioning with her other hand for him to come to her. Her fingers were pointing directly at him, Michael Costwain, who loved her more deeply than any knight or noble she was assuredly destined to wed could ever possibly hope to . . .

Victory

Chapter I

"Sire! The ground Christ himself walked upon, the coast of the Holiest of Lands, should soon be visible!" the Genoese captain yelled down in French to Richard the Lionheart, King of England, who, sea legs steady, anxiously paced the bow of the *Trinity*, the huge, four-deck, bursa transport that led the massive but scattered Crusader fleet.

Richard's pacing ceased immediately, and he moved to the rail, where he peered out intently across the deep blue-black undulations of a Mediterranean Sea, much calmer now in the aftermath of the storm that had surprised them during the night. His eyes squinted and strained at the horizon, to get a never-before-experienced glimpse of the first, faint indications of the sacred, biblical coastline.

The rising sun had just begun its first hint of what would become a spectacular explosion of fanned color across a clearing sky in the east. The warm, humid air carried the pungent smell of life distinctive to the sea and was increasingly filled with gulls signaling that land was indeed near. The sound of their steady calls, the strains of stressed rigging against bellied sails, the rhythmic splash of thirty oars slapping the water in near unison, the sound of water violently sliced by the bow, and squeaking, ill-fitted planks that had been hurriedly assembled and thinly sealed with cypress pitch filled the air.

Richard wore no crown or head covering of any kind, and his long red hair was blown about by the crosscurrents of a wind that did little to cool him, since he was fully dressed, save for armor, with chain mail completely covering his torso, under which was a heavy linen bodice that caused him to sweat profusely.

His right hand gripped the hilt of his sword, resting in a magnificent gem-encrusted scabbard attached to a belt of iron links plated in gold and cinched tightly around his waist. This was tightened over a red outer tunic that was trimmed with an exquisite crisscrossed pattern of gold and silver thread and prominently displayed, on its front and back, the thick white cross of the English Crusaders.

He had always possessed the regal, arrogant bearing of a king, even as a youth. He was taller than most, an inch over six feet. His taut but pleasingly proportioned facial features, accentuated by a thin growth of meticulously trimmed beard, were both handsome and hard-edged, and perfectly accentuated a look of rage or fierce determination when angered, easily inspiring terror in anyone his gaze landed on, without even the utterance of a single word.

Richard was strong, fearless, even reckless in battle, and lacked the slightest hint of compassion or empathy for others, which allowed him to make life-and-death decisions without pangs of conscience or remorse. Richard slept best after executions and battles. His courage was revered by all, and those closest to him feared him the most. Yet he was deeply religious, devoted to his mother, Eleanor of Aquitaine, who had helped him plot against his father, Henry II, to gain the throne, and his only fear was that of eternal damnation. This all combined to make him the perfect pawn for a Church and Pope bent once again on recapturing Jerusalem and the Holy Land—lost in a series of monumentally humiliating defeats four years earlier—and restoring the glory and influence of an institution in significant decline.

The calm was shattered then by the anticipated, excited shout from the toothless lookout atop the main mast, with arm and hand outstretched and pointing. "Coast sighted! Palestine ahead! The Holy Land!"

Moments later, Richard, stretching himself now over the bow, was finally able to discern the faint outline of the signal towers of the city fortress of Acre, silhouetted against the emerging sun, and then the scrub-brown and yellow-white hills to the south fronted by miles of unobstructed beach. This would be the place of their landing, the culmination of a journey that had marked the start of the Third Crusade in England well over a year earlier.

The sight of a land that had for so long dominated his dreams and prayers galvanized him into action. Richard rushed up and down the deck, shouting, "On your feet! The Land of Christ beckons us!"

A few, those not still retching or otherwise incapacitated, began to stand and will themselves to obey the royal command. "We must offer up our benediction to The Almighty!" Richard barked out as he kicked at those of his royal entourage lying on deck, who still had not stirred.

Simultaneously, oars were pulled in, and the rest of the scurrilous-looking Genoese and Cypriot crew began to emerge from below deck to trim sails and slow the ship as they closed on their anchorage.

"The Holy Land is within our sight! We shall soon have the sand of Christ beneath our feet!" Richard shouted repeatedly, continuing to rouse his personal entourage and other comatose knights above deck, with them quickly doing the same in turn to their retainers below.

Soon those able to stand were before their illustrious monarch, most unsteady, swaying slightly on the open center deck. Less than half of Richard's royal knights and archers, personal men-at-arms, and other retainers were physically able to heed his call. None of the clergy accompanying them were able to do so. In addition to the king's royal knights who did manage to gather before him, was the remarkable English vassal knight, one of Richard's favorite and most trusted, Godfrey, Earl of Hampstead, expert of both sword and bow, whom Richard had summoned to have the protection of his renowned company of champion archers, and Gerard de Seucre, a French knight and baron of stupendous height and width.

Gerard had been delayed in his departure by the demands of raising the necessary funds to mount his campaign and was unable to join the French King, Philip, when he departed. By chance he had met and joined the English expedition as it awaited the lengthy process of provisioning in Marseilles before setting sail for Sicily, then Cyprus, and finally the Holy Land.

Godfrey and Gerard discovered they had distant Norman ancestral ties, and had gradually become good friends, a fact that had also impressed Richard and lessened his concern about the presence of a French knight in his inner circle during such a long journey. Camaraderie had also developed between many in their respective companies, especially among the archers, some of whom now slowly made their way up the ladder from the third level, the deck below the clergy, royal archers, and retainers, to join the assembly. If it were not for the stiff breeze sweeping the deck, the foul odor that clung to them all, impervious to the perfumes some employed, would have overpowered even the heavy smell of the sea.

Godfrey was thirty-eight and stood five foot, eight inches, average for a knight, but he was unusually strong and powerfully built. His fair skin, blond hair, now turning white, and blue eyes seemed to betray a Nordic influence in his genes, although it could have also been Germanic, and he had little growth of facial hair on an otherwise handsome face. He was descended from a noble Norman family with lineage to William the Conqueror, yet his ancestors, especially his grandfather, were held in relative esteem by the Saxon peasantry. His grandmother had actively worked behind the scenes to get the nobles to fund the beginning of the expansion of the cathedral—that had only just recently been completed—and fought to ensure fair prices and low taxes for farmers and tradesmen during market days in the village square.

Though a reluctant warrior, Godfrey was an exceptional one, and had fought courageously in many campaigns alongside Richard, especially against the Scots, but had not participated in the most recent Frankish campaigns, remaining behind, at Richard's request, to protect the king's interests in England. But, when the call to Crusade came from Pope Gregory VIII, Godfrey was one of the few resident English nobles asked to accompany Richard, who considered himself French rather than English, as were most of his royal knights and personal entourage.

Godfrey's expertise with a battle sword was legendary, and he was also an archer of skill, especially from a horse, unusual for a knight. Of equal consideration was his company of longbowmen, who were legendary in their own right, and the most expert and lethal in all of Christendom.

But unknown to their kings, Godfrey, like his father and grandfather, who also fought the Saracen Infidel, harbored a personal skepticism and simmering distrust of the Pope, his real motives, and the trappings of power and political intrigue that seemed to have overwhelmed the Roman Church's religious mission.

If truth be known, Godfrey dreaded the very idea of this Crusade that required a journey of unimagined length, the distance of which was measured in months, the duration of which would most likely be years. Having to leave his frail, sickly wife, Elizabeth, his daughter, Mary, and his two young sons—the only boys who survived infancy, after three others had not—left him ill at ease. He was haunted by premonitions that, even if he survived, he would never again see his beloved wife alive. But Richard was his liege lord, and Godfrey had no choice but to follow him into battle wherever that may lead, for battle, after all, was the real focus of a knight's life.

Godfrey stood before The Lionheart on the swaying deck and helped his giant friend and fellow knight, Gerard, steady himself after a night of continuous retching and unending seasickness. The effects of his long night made the large man look almost child-like, with his head down, shoulders slumped forward, barely able to stand, and wearing a tunic badly stained from the journey. Gerard used every ounce of his strength to obey the command of the great English king as a point of French pride and honor, regardless of how desperately sick he felt.

"I am steady now," Gerard whispered hoarsely in French to Godfrey, wanting to stand on his own before the great English king.

"Are you sure, my friend? You still do not look—"

"Merci, but I can stand alone," Gerard interrupted, absolutely determined to hold himself erect without help. Godfrey carefully let him go and admired the French knight's will and pride. Such fierce stubbornness would surely be needed where they were going.

Gerard had always taken his immense physical size and strength for granted. He was a year younger than Godfrey, stood two inches over six feet, and seemed to tower over everyone except The Lionheart. His face was not handsome, but its countless scars, most from battle, some from tournaments, and his close-cropped mustache did give him a dangerous and dashing quality women found attractive. Until now, he couldn't even remember when he'd last been sick. But he'd never been on a ship in a storm. As far as he was concerned, when the fighting was over and the Saracen defeated, he would return home via the overland route through Constantinople, rather than ever set foot on a boat again.

Born to a family of minor nobility, his size, strength, and ability with a sword and his courage on the field of battle had quickly brought him to the attention of Philip Augustus, to whom he pledged his allegiance. After being crowned the Frankish King, Philip himself had given him the lands of Seucre and its magnificent castle, for helping him attain the throne against the forces of Raymond of Aragon. Gerard, though, was forced into heavy mortgages to raise the funds to crusade, not unlike Philip himself. Like Godfrey, he also wondered what would become of his once-vast estate under his wife and mother's inexperienced management, with only their daughters and the remaining elderly overseers and serfs to assist them. His wife had been under a spell of malaise ever since King Philip had summoned all his knights to announce his commitment to the Pope. Gerard carried his worry within, constant, like the ache from a deep, to-the-bone battle scar.

As critical a strain on Gerard's finances as the Crusade had been, and the concern for those he left behind, he was still greatly excited about the prospect of such a monumental clash between the forces of good and evil, and his participation in it. It had been far too long since he'd been locked in significant mortal combat.

Fighting had been the part of his life in which he truly excelled. It had brought him honor and position beyond any his family had ever attained, or even expected. He truly lived to serve his king, whom he felt trusted him above all others. And nothing could match the exhilaration he felt in battle; the feeling of a glory earned in the moment of realized victory after vanquishing all who took up arms against him.

Those who distinguished themselves in battle, more than any other, earned honor for their family names, and title and wealth bestowed by the king himself. He had worked hard and sacrificed much to be among the elite of Philip's knights, and had survived to reap the rewards. Fighting was what he did best, and, in truth, it was his passion in life. He relished every moment of it.

The Lionheart withdrew his ancient, battle-scarred sword from the ornate scabbard, put the point to the deck in front of him, and knelt. Instantly, his action was duplicated by all, although Gerard was the last to do so, and only with help from Godfrey.

With one hand pointing skyward, Richard called out, "Join me, all of you, as we give thanks to our Lord and Creator the Father, His son, Jesus Christ, who died for our sins in the land we now see. And we thank the Holy Spirit for guiding us to our anointed, divine task to return this most holy of all earth, and its precious shrines and sacred relics, to Christendom. We do this for His greater glory and in the name of His bishop on Earth, his holiness, Pope Gregory VIII!" Then he added with a dramatic flourish, "God wills it!" to which the entire group yelled in unison, "God wills it!"

At the oval-shaped stern, opposite the royal entourage that included the king's personal retainers, archers, and knights on the forward deck, and to either side of the helmsman, were a mixed group of English and French archers from Godfrey and Gerard's companies. They were among the few who had not suffered the debilitating effects of a storm-tossed sea enough to keep them in the muggy heat and stench below deck.

Unlike knights and nobles, they were not fully dressed. They wore only under-leggings, short, tight pants that were laced at the waist and extended to mid-calf, and jerkins, loose, coarse linen shirts with sleeves, open from breast to neck with their string ties hanging undone. They were easily identified as archers, since each wore a brassard on the forearm that held his bow. An archer rarely, if ever, took his brassard off, day or night, and when he did, usually to change jerkins, it was off only momentarily. The long, narrow piece of leather was as much a part of an archer's bow arm as the fingers on his hand.

Once King Richard returned to the bow, most sat back against the stern gunwale, relieved after the effort of kneeling on the rough-hewn cypress planking, and enjoyed the comfort brought by the salty sea breeze blowing over them. Others stood and gazed out reflectively at the land of their imaginations or the expanding brilliance of a sunrise that now laced the sky in blended shades of yellow and orange, one of whom was Michael Costwain.

Now nineteen, Michael had won every archery award and contest in the south of England, then went on to win six of ten events in the Leeds Royal Tournament the year before and had, at the unheard age of fourteen, won his first major competition in the prestigious Hampstead Open Tournament. He was both excited and apprehensive, like many in the company, about the fact that he would soon face real battle in a foreign land for the first time.

Michael had grown up a part of Godfrey's household, and then earned the right to be one of his personal men-at-arms. Michael idolized the knight, who had treated him and his mother more like an uncle than a lord. The Crusade was his chance to repay Godfrey, using the skill God blessed him with, to help bring his knight glory and victory against the infidel. Of equal importance to him was to fulfill a seemingly impossible fantasy, one he knew only extraordinary courage and achievement in battle could possibly bring about.

He desperately wanted to be made a vassal knight in service to Godfrey. Only a king or prince could anoint such, and all knew King Richard prized courage in battle above all else. It was a rare occurrence, to be sure, but had happened before. Only then could he ever be truly happy, for then he could court and wed Godfrey's fifteen-year-old daughter, Lady Mary, whom he felt was enamored of him also, although no words of this ever passed her lips. But she had given him her embroidered cloth after his stunning performance at the Leeds Tournament over a year ago, the last held since the announcement of the Crusade. It was his obsession. There was nothing in the world that he prayed for more than to become a knight and make her his wife.

"By the sword of St. George, I thought I'd never see the glories of a sunrise again!" said Basil Martin to his lifelong friend, Whittler Will, but loud enough for the others nearby to hear and smile or nod in agreement.

Martin lay prone on the deck, breathing heavily, after having pulled himself up the ladder from oppressive confinement below deck. Basil was short for an archer, but strong and skillful. He and Will had joined the banner of Godfrey together when word had gone out to Hampstead's surrounding villages that their knight was following King Richard to the Holy Land in crusade against the heathen. It was said that he was in great need of archers, but could offer only meager pay in return. Their expert skill with the bow was complemented by their talent to shape wood into all manner of necessities and novelties, and especially into bows from the unique wood of the English yew tree. But their mastery of the knife went well beyond just carving. They were also extraordinary experts in the use of knives as weapons, and could throw with lethal accuracy from sixty paces. They had also devised an ingenious way to carry four knives on their belt and thighs to be ready for quick use.

"Aye, and if ye retched on me one more time last night, ye would have seen the glories of the Pearly Gates," responded Whittler Will, smiling at his friend and provoking laughs from the others, a knife and chunk of English pine already in his hands.

Will, unlike his best friend, was tall and thin, and, together, they looked the part of juggler and tumbler vagabonds, who traveled through villages providing entertainment. The rough wood in his hands would soon be fashioned into the image of the Virgin Mary and given to another of the archers for protection in battle. The bachelor pair were in their early twenties, had never seen battle beyond tournament competition, and looked upon the crusade as the adventure of a lifetime.

George Bainty, or 'Baints,' as everyone called him, eyed the carving being fashioned in Will's hands, never tiring of watching the magic of wood being transformed into an intricate religious icon.

"Amazing what the lad can do with an old splinter of rotted pine," Baints said up over his shoulder to Michael, who continued to stare out, but no longer at the sunrise. He had turned facing in the direction of home, England.

Baints was the oldest in the group at forty, had a weathered, leathery face that bore the pockmarks of disease, and was the only archer of both the English and French companies who was a Crusader veteran. He had served as a young archer under the renowned knight, John of Andover, in the garrison of Jerusalem for three years, when the holy city was still under Crusader control. The revered knight had died of a minor, seemingly inconsequential cut that became infected and slowly drained him of life. Baints, like most Crusaders at that time, saw limited action, and the long stretches of inactivity, and other circumstances beyond his control, resulted in him learning much about Islamic culture and language. This was a knowledge he kept to himself, though, for it would serve no useful purpose to give voice to his radical views.

Baints served in the capacity of the archer's sergeant, unofficially assuming the role when the veteran, Thomas Curry, died suddenly one night of a violent seizure on their way to Marseilles. Baints neither asked for nor wanted the departed Curry's position in title, and Godfrey left the arrangement undisturbed, but told Baints he'd receive Curry's share of plunder nonetheless.

"It is a valuable skill, for sure," responded Michael. "Can serve one well to garner a decent wage when the bow is finally put down," he continued with a seriousness that surprised Baints. He pushed himself up from the deck and joined the young warrior at the rail, where their talk could be more private.

"Ye suddenly talk with a wisdom beyond thy years, lad. In a way, it greatly saddens me. Being away from home has made ye too serious, I fear, or ye had visions of meeting thy Creator in the storm last night."

Baints tried to lighten the mood with his last comment. He had taken the remarkable young man under his wing long ago, when Michael, then only eleven, surprised him and the other archers in the service of Godfrey one day as they practiced, with his request to draw string with them. He had learned later that Michael was only a child of five when his father, a barkeep, had been killed in a tavern brawl. His mother had told him that shortly after, the great young knight, Godfrey, in a surprising act of noble charity, had brought them to his manor castle to work on the household staff.

Michael, assigned work in the stable, often was able to watch Godfrey's archers practice and engage in contests of skill. Secretly, he had practiced the grueling exercises they taught apprentice archers. He held a heavy yew branch out with his left arm and tried to keep it perfectly steady for hours at a time, then bend it a hundred times in a row over his back to the point of breaking. Finally, he had boldly asked the archers to allow him to take a turn at their practice and amazed them all with his remarkable skill for a beginner. He lacked speed of release and expert precision, but he demonstrated a natural eye and extraordinary athletic ability, not to mention his passion to learn and excel.

Michael's gaze remained fixed on the horizon as he spoke more to himself than Baints, "King Richard leads us on a Holy Crusade in service of Christ himself . . . "

Baints continued in an understanding tone, "When thee are young, the mind is easily consumed with the thrill of glorious adventure in distant lands. This I know all too well, lad."

Michael continued as if ignoring Baints's last words. There was intense passion in the young man's eyes now. "We *must* save the Holy Land, Baints, wrest it from the infidel grip of the Saracen. Father Clovis and the Abbot himself gave the Pope's blessing after our contrition. Shall we die in such noble service, we will enter heaven in glory without wait."

Baints's expression hardened, and he said, "Remember, it is the soil of *their* homeland we fight on."

Michael became indignant in his surprise at Baints's pointed words. "It is the land of *our* Christ! They defile its holiest of sites and revile its sacred relics."

"Who is it that attests to the defiling of our holy sites?"

Michael's expression turned incredulous. "Father Clovis, Bishop Barkham, the Abbot, His Holiness, *everyone*—King Richard himself, who obsesses over the Relics of the True Cross!" Michael exclaimed. "Baints, by all that is holy, what has gotten hold of thee? Why have you journeyed, then!"

Baints laid a hand on Michael's shoulder. "Lad, I-I speak out of turn, misunderstand not. I never waver in my belief in the Father, Son, and Holy Ghost, that there is a place of eternal peace and happiness or fiery damnation in His judgment. But, lad, I am here only to serve my knight. I swore to follow him. I know not the truth or motive of clerics and kings. As I advance in age, I—"

Baints abruptly stopped himself from further comment. Michael was at a loss for continued argument as he pondered Baints's words. His confidence in his holy cause had been chipped at, and it was clearly unsettling to him. Baints was not only his mentor, but as much a father as he ever had.

"You should not let others hear you speak thus," Michael finally responded quietly.

"I say this only to you . . . and should not have done so, lad," Baints said contritely, shaking his head.

"It is the sight of the land again, for me a return to emotions felt long ago, of great conflict within, of which I have never spoken. But I speak with honest heart to you, as I always will. Michael, I do implore, you should always be of your own mind in these things. As for me, I have trust only in our knight. Beyond that, I can summon little passion or conviction for—"

"Baints, you need not explain further. I am sorry. I-I have great anxieties. I know that what we will soon do will not involve shooting at targets for sport or ribbons or prizes of silver coin. I pray for the steadiness of nerve to draw straight and aim true, and not disappoint those around me. Baints, more than all else, I *must* distinguish myself in ways to come to the king's attention," Michael said with a hushed passion, staring even more intently out across the sea.

"I know, lad. First of all, we all fear the unknown and the cry of the infidel in our mind, but I've no doubt you'll distinguish thyself, as will the entire company. Alas, I had the very same anxieties myself many years ago, in my first skirmish with the Scots."

"What happened?" asked Michael curiously, turning to Baints.

"I did my duty, but not for king, England, Lord, or even myself, but for the bowmen, my friends, on either side of me."

There was a pause between them, and now they both peered out across the vast expanse of the rhythmic movement of the Mediterranean. Michael finally turned to Baints, a look of steely determination in his eyes.

"I have more than friends to spur me on. I must do far more, though, than just my duty. For in honesty, Baints, there is more in my emotion than my, my proclamations of piety. I must admit to you, I seek glory more for my own aims. I *must* excel on the field of battle in such a remarkable display for my repeated courage and actions as to come to the attention of the king himself."

Baints put an arm around the young archer and patted his shoulder.

"I understand ye heart, Michael. I know it is her cloth you keep inside your jerkin. Being reckless or foolish will gain ye nothing, lad. I doubt The Lionheart is one to dismiss bloodline, no matter what the deed."

"Then I fear I will die for the trying, for I cannot bear the thought of returning only to have her given to another."

"Aye, returning . . . " Baints replied gravely, but let the words hang, uncompleted.

A moment later the relative calm was interrupted by the humbled but still distinctive voice of Mighty Morgan, slowly pulling his weakened, massive body up the ladder from below deck.

"If I'm to die soon . . . I will not . . . do so in, in the-the stench below deck!" he lamented comically, although unintentionally so, as he forced himself up the last step and actually crawled to an open space, made ready for him by his older cousin, Portius Bundage, where he collapsed.

Bundage, the next oldest at thirty-eight, was Godfrey's chief huntsman on his estate, and a deadly shot at moving targets, especially fast-flying quail, Godfrey's favorite dish.

The group couldn't hold back their laughter at the sight of the gentle, young, blond giant reduced to crawling on deck. Morgan earned his nickname because he used a bow twice the thickness of others and could shoot an arrow farther with reasonable accuracy than anyone in England had ever done, but struggled with targets close in.

Somewhat of a simpleton, pleasant to all, devoutly religious to the extreme, and fiercely loyal to friends, Morgan was watched over by Bundage, who felt a great affection for the young archer that transcended his family tie.

"You'll soon feel better up here, cousin. You'll not expire this day, I assure thee," said Bundage sympathetically, with laughter in his words as Morgan slowly curled up in the fetal position next to him.

"I hope it is truth you say . . . but I fear ye . . . wrong," Morgan said weakly, and forced out a plea to his friends: "Someone go back . . . look upon Two-String and Cletis. I-I could not stir them." With those last words, Mighty Morgan drifted off to sleep, comforted by the breeze and his cousin next to him.

Bundage uncorked a leather bag of water and poured a short stream on the head and lips of the man-boy, who moaned in appreciation as Whittler Will and Basil Martin heeded Morgan's request and went down into the hold to check on their other friends.

"That was me in Marseilles, when I had the fever," said Henri Desuer in French to his friend DuClair, while pointing to Morgan nearby. The few French who had made it up to the deck sat or lay together opposite the others.

Henri was a sixteen-year-old French archer of considerable skill and had to beg Gerard to take him over the objections of others in the French company. Henri's father, a champion archer and former Crusader, had fought in a minor battle near Tripoli ten years earlier, but had the misfortune to be captured. He was released in a prisoner exchange, but only after having his thumbs and string fingers cut off. He vowed that his sons would avenge him, trained them relentlessly, and Henri was the first, just barely of age to fight.

Gerard finally accepted the young archer, primarily because the father agreed he would join without pay. After arrival in Marseilles and joining the English expedition, Henri caught a fever, as had many others, before they were to sail, and was nearly left behind with the most desperate cases. He recovered sufficiently in time to be taken and became friends with Michael, who was one of those who took pity on the boy and volunteered to tend the fair-haired, handsome, boy-archer in shifts, during his ordeal.

"Owee, I thought you would be left, never to see you again," said DuClaire, who looked more haggard than any in the group, though this was not unexpected, as he looked that way on the best of days.

DuClaire had languished in debtor's prison for two years, until Gerard, who knew his family and was desperate for experienced, veteran archers, secured his release in return for a promise to apply DuClaire's pay or plunder to his debts upon his return should he survive, a not uncommon arrangement during Crusades. Gerard also insisted that he become Henri's shadow, a guardian of sorts, to which he reluctantly agreed, but then had grown to genuinely like the naive but skillful lad.

DuClaire himself was a cunning archer, educated, fought with Gerard in the campaigns at Flanders, skilled at trick shots, on which he unfortunately gambled compulsively, and was remarkably effective when not drunk. Somewhat of a loner, and seemingly perpetually despondent, he had immediately tended Henri, even before they knew his fever was not lethal. DuClaire felt responsible, for after winning money from the English archers, he had taken the virgin lad to one of the seaport's many brothels that clung to its waterfront like barnacles, and introduced him to the pleasures of the flesh, where, he was sure, Henri had contracted the fever.

"We should go back down and bring Robere and Gesault up here and check once again on the sergeant. They were the worst of any during the night," commented Henri, still looking at Mighty Morgan curled up like a child.

"Robere? That priss! Let him lie in his vomit," DuClaire said disgustedly. "Why Gerard brought him along—he must have owed the old knight a fierce debt. The boy's all but useless. He'll not last long where we go. I just fear he'll be the cause of others, maybe us, departing this life with him! And Gesault, there's one for the exorcists! Those fits of mumbling to himself and making the sign . . . by God, though, he's as sure a shot as anyone I've drawn string with. I'll surely look after him. You wet nurse DeGraise. The sergeant never abided me anywhere near him."

In the next instant the ship's scowling, dangerous-looking bearded captain was shouting out orders, as if in a panic, and a sudden whirlwind of activity erupted on deck with the ship's crew scurrying about, climbing rigging and reducing sails to a minimum to further slow the great galley. They were within a half-league of the coast, which was now clearly visible. Everyone was up, standing at the rails, looking solemnly at the land in which Christ was born, lived, and died.

When they were within an arrow's reach of the beach all sails were struck, oars were redeployed, and the great galley was slowly brought in closer, as one of the crew constantly checked the depth from the bow with a knotted, weighted rope. They anchored in clear sight of the desolate coast and its narrow beach that was lined by a band of rolling sand dunes, behind which were the gradually sloping, scrub-covered hills of Sidon. Less than two leagues to the north lay the sprawling, Muslim-held fortress-city of Acre.

Then it began. The enormous job of unloading one hundred ten barges and galleys, with two hundred knights, their retainers, horses, arms, and other equipment and supplies, twenty-five hundred archers, footmen, and laborers, together with dismantled siege engines and catapults, pots of Greek Fire by the dozens, wagons, livestock, foodstuffs, and countless other provisions. Each ship carried several small skiffs to assist in the task.

Richard, his retainers, knights, and bowmen from his ship, came ashore first under the protection of archers positioned on the closest of the other ships, accompanied by the only bishop able to summon sufficient strength to accompany the king, and who immediately and swiftly conducted a benediction on the beach and blessed all who were the first to set foot on the sacred earth of the Holy Land.

Once they secured the shoreline, the workmen and carpenters, guiding massive floating timbers and hewn lumber, which had been lowered into the water, came ashore to begin the task of assembling a makeshift dock. This would hasten the unloading of all supplies an army on the march, in June of the year 1191, required.

Chapter II

The news that Richard the Lionheart and his army had finally landed nearby spread with near euphoria throughout the exhausted camp of Guy of Lusignan. Combined with the recent arrival of Guy's sovereign, King Philip of France, it not only further buoyed their spirits, but, for the first time, actually gave them confidence that they were going to decisively turn the tide of the stalled siege.

The few priests who remained alive or survived the grueling journey with Philip immediately held impromptu Masses of thanks at various sites throughout the sprawling camp. For over a year Guy's battered force had bravely and tenaciously maintained their siege outside the earthen and sandstone walls of the fortress-city and castle of Acre. They had been reinforced by small remnants of scattered Crusader forces, including a German contingent that had been decimated in an earlier battle near Antioch, in which its leader, Prince Otto, had been taken prisoner and was being held for ransom. Finally, just two weeks earlier, they were joined by Philip and the leading elements of his Crusader army, which had landed two months previous near one of the few remaining Crusader strongholds, the French-held coastal fortress of Tripoli, far to the north of Acre. Philip's arrival broke a recently mounted siege there by a small Turkish force. Tripoli was one of the few Christian enclaves that had proved impregnable and not important enough for the Saracens to divert significant resources to destroy, and as a consequence had easily been re-supplied by the French from the sea.

The Muslims were aware of the landing but had underestimated the progress Philip's army would make. Unlike other Crusader monarchs and nobles, King Philip, and his disciplined forces, had not been distracted by conquests or plunder en route to their destination.

That Guy and his meager forces had managed to maintain the siege, much less survive, was a tribute to the military resourcefulness of the noble and knight, and the religious idealism of his now-growing force. But the besiegers of Acre would soon face the possibility of becoming besieged themselves, trapped between the castle's walls on the west and the leading edge of the army of the great Muslim leader and military strategist, Saladin Salah ed-Din Yusuf, moving in quickly from the east. It was headed directly against the unprotected extreme right flank of Guy and Philip, closest to Richard's landing force. Saladin had planned and led the annihilation of Crusader forces in 1187 at Hattin and the eventual recapture of Jerusalem and most of the surrounding Crusader kingdoms, and had united the disparate Muslim factions as never before.

Messengers soon informed Richard of the approaching danger, and he quickly marshaled as many of his knights, bowmen, and footmen with lances and pikes that had already landed and quick-marched them over the short, thin ribbon of coastal hills to protect the right flank of Philip's army. Among this group were Godfrey and Ge'ard, and those of their companies who were well enough to land. They deployed so quickly that the groups were mixed together. They had no time to regroup into their own units once ashore, for they immediately found themselves directly in the path of the Saracen's surprise attack, led by scimitar-waving horsemen on magnificent steeds, followed by camel-mounted lancers.

"There's no footmen leading or archers to protect them! They'll be butchered," an unsteady Gerard yelled over to Godfrey in surprise. Both were mounted, but on unfamiliar horses.

"There's much about these pagan heathens I fail to understand," Godfrey answered, and then yelled, "Archers, hurry! To the ready!"

Godfrey's unarmored war-horse bayed loudly from the excitement as Gerard followed with a similar order in French, while fighting angrily to keep his unadorned horse steady. They had taken whatever horses were available on the beach. The English and French archers ran a short distance past them and formed a line in front of the knights. Michael had led the group of archers running to take up positions. The young French archer, Henri, ended up on his right, with the ever-vigilant Baints pushing in to make room on Michael's left. Moving into the space on Henri's right was an out-of-breath, DuClaire. He nodded to Michael and Baints. The excitement of actual battle, the first time for many, produced enough adrenaline to clear their heads and overwhelm the weakness and unsteadiness still plaguing most of them from the voyage.

Mighty Morgan finally lumbered onto the line, delayed not by his sickness—that had begun to pass once he landed on shore and was able to eat and drink something—but because he was helping his cousin, who limped. Portius Bundage had been injured long ago by a deer buck he'd shot and thought mortally wounded; when he had closed in on it, however, it had suddenly kicked out with a futile last attempt to right itself, shattering his kneecap, which had never fully healed. He had joined regardless of his injury at Godfrey's request, when, after his call to arms, the knight remained critically short of experienced archers.

They took positions at the very end of the almost completely formed line. Footmen followed behind them and began massing behind the knights and archers. They had been collected together from scattered elements on the beach and rallied forward by The Lionheart himself, aided by his own royal knights, and who now joined the line farther to the left of Godfrey and Gerard.

The English and French bowmen used nearly identical arrangements, immediately planting a dozen or more arrows in the sand at their front foot for instant retrieval, and each readied one across the long, thick bows of yew. The French bows were a foot shorter but no less lethal within one hundred fifty yards.

The Saracen horsemen bore down on them fearlessly. The magnificent horses were colorfully adorned with *jadudalas*, headpieces decorated with silver and gold balls of silk that hung on either side of the horse's head. Their leather bridles were also wrapped with thin strands of multicolored, dyed cotton cloth. Tassels called *sandelas,* made of dried berries attached to thin strips of leather, were also tied just above the horse's ankles. The riders sat on *quedais*, saddles fashioned out of woven reeds, fitted to the rider after being thoroughly soaked in water, and then dried and covered with thick, stretched, tightly woven, white cotton cloth.

"Aim!" Godfrey yelled, as his order was all that was needed for both groups. The archers assumed a sideways stance, spread their legs wide, and pulled back on strings of thin, tightly twisted leather, bending the bows to maximum tension and holding steady. Their aim was for the horses, just under their necks. Horses were bigger targets than their riders, and not only did it more effectively stop the charge of cavalry, but the headfirst fall off the horse often seriously injured or disabled the rider and left him open and vulnerable as well.

"It will be such vile cruelty to destroy animals as magnificent as these," whispered Michael to Henri. Michael took aim at the lead white stallion with no reservation or doubt about his task or the outcome. He felt a strange calm facing the defilers of the Holy Land. It was because God was with them, he thought assuredly.

"Aye, but with heathen upon them, they too are heathen, and pitied not to be," Henri answered, with fear clearly evident in his words of halting English. The language had been taught to him by DuClaire, who had learned the 'crude tongue' in jail from an English cellmate, and then from Michael, with each of them teaching the other their language during their long journey. Surprisingly, Michael had found that he learned the French language quickly, a fact that Baints was also impressed by.

"God wills it," Michael responded more to himself than Henri.

"Dues lo volt," repeated Henri in French.

"Dues lo volt bon amino le servant!" answered Michael excitedly.

Once the lead riders were within one hundred yards of the Crusaders, Godfrey nodded to Gerard, and they both yelled the order to shoot. The twang of released strings and high-pitched buzzing of arrows was followed seconds later by the death whines of horses tumbling headfirst to the ground and the interrupted battle cries of their brave Muslim riders. The carnage was near total to the front ranks. Within a minute each archer had unloosed twelve arrows and readied more from their extra quivers. Muslims not disabled or under horses were struck by arrows until they fell. The scene was the same up and down the entire flank.

The Saracen lancers wisely turned at the stunning sight of annihilation in front of them. Three brave infidel souls, apparently determined to meet Allah that day and ascend to paradise, welcomed by seventy virgins, continued to charge straight for Godfrey and Gerard's line and would not be denied their wish.

Baints stepped forward out of the line, a signal the veteran was preempting the other archers. They understood and lowered their bows. But it wasn't for himself he did so, for he immediately motioned for Michael to come forward and take the shots. Without hesitating, Michael moved out, quickly tucked two arrows into the sand, kept one on the bow, spread his feet wide again, aimed, and released three times in remarkably quick succession. Within seconds all three riders were prone in the sand behind their slowing camels, each with an arrow through either their chests or head. A wild cheer erupted from the entire line at Michael's feat, including the knights and King Richard, who took note of the young archer and raised his sword in acknowledgment at the astounding triumph. Baints patted his shoulder, bursting with the pride and awe he felt in the young man, who, in a way, was like the sons he lost long ago.

"Mon ami, there can be none better than my friend, in all the world," Henri said in amazement.

Michael looked at Henri amid the cheers and felt elated. He had passed his first test.

"St. George be praised! The Lionheart himself took notice! I saw him raise his battle sword to thee, Michael," Baints said excitedly, while they readied more arrows in case there should be another assault, as well as to provide cover for the knights, led by Richard himself, who now charged the field.

Only a handful of Muslim fanatics offered any resistance and were quickly dispatched with broad swords that brutally slashed them to pieces. Few prisoners were taken. Gerard, still greatly debilitated from the severity of his sickness at sea, could barely wield his sword with any effectiveness. Godfrey made a point of riding close to his sensitive and severely frustrated French friend, to offer assistance if needed.

Footmen quickly followed the knights and moved among the bodies, stripped them of valuables, and gathered up the heathen weapons, especially the prized, jewel-laden scimitars and daggers, all to be packed in chests that would later be divided by the nobles who participated in the fight. Next to recapturing the Holy Land for Christendom, plunder was their most important priority.

Godfrey and Gerard, like nearly all the Crusader nobles, depended greatly on the recovery of treasure to ensure their families would not live in poverty while they basked in heaven, as promised by the Pope, should they die in battle. And if they did survive, they surely didn't want to live destitute after their return home.

Richard the Lionheart had quickly and decisively won what he proclaimed the first battle against the forces of the great Muslim military commander and ruler, Saladin, but, in reality, it had been only a minor skirmish. Guy and his men were heartened by Richard's swift victory, but Guy knew Saladin had sent only a small part of his massing army to test the renowned king and disrupt his landing. A real battle had yet to be fought.

Michael, Henri, and the other archers waited for the footmen to finish, then solemnly walked among the dead and dying, retrieving arrows from man and horse alike. Some shafts were lodged firmly in bone and were left behind. Footmen had mercifully killed any animal critically disabled, but executed only those wounded riders who motioned for them to do so. After the Crusaders left the battlefield, Saracen slaves would be allowed to remove the dead and wounded. When viewed up close, the carnage they had wreaked was awesome. Michael and Henri had never viewed anything like it. Henri felt himself getting sick and didn't mind admitting it to Michael.

"My insides are turned worse than on the ship in the storm."

"Aye, my friend. I'd be retching if there was anything left in me," responded Michael as grim in tone as Henri looked.

"But they deserved to die, every one of them," Henri said in a suddenly hardened voice. Michael, his euphoric feelings of accomplishment and relief having faded completely as they moved through the battlefield, now felt a numbness of spirit, as death, brutally swift death, surrounded him. Each arrow he retrieved was a reminder that they had killed. Yes, God willed it, but they had actually done the deed—cut short the life of another.

Michael and Henri continued to retrieve arrows, while Baints, having tired considerably, told Michael and Henri he was returning to the staging area for water and to rest. He warned them to be careful and stay together as they moved through the battlefield. Eventually, they found the three riders Michael had killed. They lay alone from the others, with no horses or camels near or underneath them, the marking on Michael's arrows distinct and their lances lying nearby. All were young men and, up close, hardly had the look of veteran fighters. Their outer white robes, *jabalas*, bore the smear, splatter, and stain of blood. Underneath their robes each also wore a vest of finely woven, intricately patterned brocade or damask, over a tunic with curved daggers in sheaths tied around their waists. Their tightly wrapped white headpieces remarkably remained on the heads of the slain Muslims. Beneath their tunics they wore *battas,* loose pants that ballooned out at the legs and were bound tightly at their ankles.

When Michael attempted to pull out his arrow, just above the heart of the first one he thought dead, the lancer suddenly moaned in agony and opened his eyes, causing Michael to jump back in fright and Henri to draw a readied arrow to full tension. The Saracen was still alive, although his robe, vest, and the sand under it was soaked with an enormous amount of blood. Henri moved closer, ready to shoot.

"No, don't. He can't harm us," Michael said, curious and approaching warily.

When the mortally wounded Muslim reached into his tunic, Michael quickly drew his dagger, while Henri again drew back his arrow to full tension.

But all that the Muslim warrior pulled from under his tunic was a small rolled sheath of leather tied with a thin gold cord, with silk tassels on the ends and stained with blood. His dark eyes pleaded in desperation as he tried to speak, but the strange syllables he uttered were rendered even more unintelligible by the gurgling sound that accompanied his attempt, followed by red foam bubbles and drips of blood from the side of his mouth.

Michael was reluctant to draw nearer. Then the young lancer's hand dropped to the ground, and his head fell back to the sand, his eyes opened wide, unmoving toward the sky. They realized he was probably dead and finally approached. Michael knelt over him, putting his palm against the end of the protruding arrow to be certain there was no pulse. He looked at the outstretched hand and took from it the rolled parchment with the gold tie string.

"What could it be?" Henri asked, more to himself than his friend.

Michael carefully untied the cord and unrolled the leather, discovering it was the covering of an expensive-looking and feeling parchment, rolled up inside the leather to protect it and trimmed with a gold border and strange writing, which Michael assumed was Arabic. He'd never seen anything like it. It fascinated him, and it looked valuable. "I don't know," he finally answered. "Maybe it's a prayer or—"

"Or maybe heathen evil spells," Henri interrupted, hatred accenting every word as he suspiciously looked around them.

"What?"

"Leave it, my friend. It can only bring ill omen. Let's depart. I have disturbed feelings here."

Michael stood, re-rolled the parchment, tied it, but instead of returning it to the body or discarding it, he put it inside his jerkin under his waist tunic, despite Henri's distress. It would make the perfect souvenir for his beloved Mary upon his return, if God allowed him to do so. They moved away and hurried on, though Henri continued to warn him boyishly of a multitude of imagined evil consequences of keeping the heathen scroll.

******

Saladin was impressed with the reports the surviving riders brought back of the speed with which Richard's Crusaders had reacted to his small probing attack, and was especially awed by the descriptions of the deadly skill of this new group of English archers. Saladin, when learning of the arrival of Richard's army, had held back the bulk of his force and decided to limit his activity to harassing them, as a tactic to slow the progress of their siege. This would give him the opportunity to amass an overwhelmingly superior force with the expected arrival of reinforcements. He also wanted to test the famous English King, The Lionheart, and the effectiveness of his much-heralded English fighters, especially his archers.

Fully reinforced now, and with Richard and Philip by his side, Guy's siege on Acre swiftly began to tighten. The city and its defenders were alarmed that the end was near. They could no longer count on merchant ships getting through with supplies, not with Richard's fleet patrolling the coast. Signal fires atop Acre's tallest tower were not answered with any encouragement from the Muslim camp. Saladin, now outnumbered and with the anticipated reinforcements unexpectedly delayed, was unwilling to risk his army for Acre, a minor stronghold. He wisely withdrew, leaving a sizable force encamped around and within view of the doomed fortress to provide alert in the event of movement, planning to fight another day, at a time and place of his own choosing. He would turn instead to the reinforcement of Jerusalem, which he knew, of course, was the real objective of the Crusaders.

Acre finally sued for peace. Emissaries of Saladin were allowed safe passage through the Crusader lines to join the negotiations. Surrender terms were drawn up and agreed to within the week, and included Acre's peaceful, intact capitulation, with its civilian inhabitants allowed to depart unharmed, with all the possessions they could carry, except for gold, silver, or precious gems. The military defenders of Acre, who greatly outnumbered civilians, would also be allowed to leave, except for those who commanded, with their weapons, horses, and camels remaining behind. In return, Acre would also make an immediate payment of a huge sum in gold and, more importantly to Richard, Saladin would return the Relics of the True Cross, captured by Saladin's forces four years earlier when they retook Jerusalem.

Richard the Lionheart, King Philip, and Guy of Lusignan entered the surrendered city fortress triumphantly on magnificent white stallions given as gifts by the Caliph of Acre. In deference to the oppressive desert heat, the kings wore no armor or mail, and were dressed only in leggings, codpiece, and jerkin shirt under their regally embroidered Crusader tunics, tied at their waists with thick gold-covered corded belts. Richard did wear a neck cover and fitted hood, on top of which was a gold crown, while Philip, preferring not to have his head completely covered, wore only a simple gold laurel leaf crown for comfort.

Behind them, in recognition of having fought and won the "battle" against Saladin, were Godfrey and Gerard, each holding aloft colorful embroidered banners displaying their individual coat of arms. They were followed by their archers, who had put on the awesome display of lethal marksmanship.

Although a knight of King Philip, Gerard was allowed to remain with Richard as a temporary vassal, in honor of his participation in the battle and in a spirit of fraternity among the armies. In actuality, Philip considered Richard, once a close friend in childhood and young adulthood, a rival and enemy because of his occupation of most of northwestern France and indications prior to the Crusade to expand his holdings there, even though Philip had supported Richard in his fight with his father over the English throne. Their building conflict had only been put in abeyance because of the admonitions of Pope Gregory and their agreement to support the Crusade together. If they were in the Holy Land at the same time, with the bulk of their knights and armies, there could be no mischief at their borders in France. Even then, Philip did not trust the English monarch, detested his egotistical, pompous manner, while grudgingly admiring his prowess on the battlefield, and hoped to use Gerard to his advantage, as his eyes and ears in the English camp.

"How will we protect two hundred thousand dinars of gold while we campaign against Jerusalem?" Richard asked Philip as they rode through the long, vaulted archway, next to what had been the palace church and had been converted to one of four mosques now within the walls of the fortress-city.

The archway led to the palace's huge inner courtyard. In the middle was a massive, magnificently constructed pool, ornately decorated with thousands of tiny, colorful mosaic tiles, and filled to its very brim with clear, shimmering water, around which were palm and date trees in an oasis-like setting.

Ebony-skinned Muslim servants stood at attention, ready to assist the conquerors. Only Godfrey, Gerard, and Guy accompanied them, while the others remained in the outer courtyard, primed to rush in if called. The knights were in awe of the sight before them.

"Split it between us here, and each can send it back with the galleys returning for provisions, yours to Cyprus and mine to Tripoli," answered Philip casually. They spoke French. Richard considered himself a Frenchman rather than English, and Philip actually spoke English better than Richard and was fluent in three other languages, soon to be four, once he learned the infidel tongue.

"We'll each need to send a knight's company to protect it. Can we spare the force now?" Richard questioned, obviously unsure himself exactly how to proceed.

"We could send it under Papal protection," Philip offered with a sly smile to Richard.

"Better to give it back to the Saracens now! Either way, we would not see a dinar again," Richard answered in disgust.

Philip laughed out loud. It was true. Once the gold was in the Papal treasury, not even kings could pry it loose. "We'll devise a solution later," Philip replied.

They reached the edge of the oasis garden, and the two kings and three knights dismounted, instantly assisted by the Caliph's retainers. At the pool's end farthest from them were a row of small, covered pavilions and large tent-like structures, out of which, a moment later, emerged the Caliph, the city's military commanders, and Salah Bin Madah, the emissary of Saladin.

The Caliph, a man of medium build, wore a white, flowing tunic, trimmed with thin lines of embroidered gold thread, and a large turban with a white feather plume attached to the front. His face was tanned dark brown, he had a neatly trimmed, long beard but no mustache, and his dark eyes blinked nervously.

The officers were dressed in trim, efficient tunics, brocaded vests, partial shoulder armor, and the conical helmets peculiar to Muslim military leaders, but their impassive faces bore no facial hair. They did not seem at all pleased to be in attendance.

Salah also wore a white tunic, which revealed a rotund body beneath, but plain in comparison to the Caliph's, and covering his head was a much smaller turban, which displayed the distinctive golden imprimatur of Saladin on the front, a scimitar over a crescent. His face and eyes were quite expressive and friendly, but also revealed an alert intelligence that quickly took in all that transpired. A mustache curved around his mouth to a short beard that only covered his chin. They bowed stiffly. Salah served as interpreter. He spoke, surprisingly, in Latin.

"I will address you in Latin, so as not to offend. I've mastered French but struggle with English. Forgive me," said Salah in the most congenial and deferential tone possible.

"Thank you, but I'm far more comfortable with French than Latin or English," Richard replied.

"So am I," Philip added, half-laughing.

Godfrey, Gerard, and Guy nodded when Salah looked their way.

"Very well, then. I must confess, Latin remains somewhat of a challenge for my stubborn tongue also. I will, when necessary, translate for the Caliph and his advisers, who have had no need for mastery of any but our native tongue. In the name of Saladin Salah ed-Din Yusef, we welcome you most noble and exalted ones. Come. Sit. Rest, and refresh yourselves as we entreaty," Salah said with great respect in nearly perfect French, and pointed to the largest of the tents. He spoke the language slower than he had the ability to, in deference to the English king and knight, still thinking he was helping their understanding. The fact was, most of the English nobility spoke French as their first language. Something about the Caliph's manner and facial expression, though, led Godfrey to suspect the Caliph understood everything that was being said, as the group proceeded into the tent.

Inside they found it surprisingly cool. Dark-skinned male servants brought them drinks of exotic nectar cooled with snow from great wooden casks, to the utter amazement of the Crusaders.

"It is snow brought down from Mt. Herman in great chests packed heavy with straw and chips of wood, especially for you."

"Thank you, Salah. It is most wonderful in the heat of summer here," Philip responded, and then yawned uncontrollably. Philip was tired and, if truth be known, not well. He had caught a fever shortly after landing near Tripoli, and it alternated between mild and severe. At the moment, he felt it getting worse.

The knights delighted in the refreshment and were surprised by the atmosphere of civility and luxury afforded them.

Platters of nuts, dates, olives, and fruits with bowls of honey were laid before them, this time by striking, young slave girls with skin as black as flint. Unlike Muslim women, they wore thin robes, tightly bound at the waist, that didn't totally obscure the voluptuous form of their bodies underneath. Although they were veiled, it was done with the sheerest cotton possible, and without the accompanying head scarves, so their unusual, tightly curled black hair was visible and added greatly to their overwhelming exotic allure.

The slave girls provided Salah with the hoped-for distraction among the Crusaders while they ate and drank, allowing him to control the conversation and dispel the initial level of tension, and perhaps to even allow him to use the women in his bargaining later, or as gifts if the opportunity presented itself. Salah tried to engage the kings in discussions of science, astronomy, even Greek and Roman philosophy, but found them unresponsive and soon realized they were uneducated in such matters.

Growing impatient, Richard tried to direct the conversation to the terms of surrender and progress made thus far. Philip, though, seemed more interested in enjoying the relaxing atmosphere and Salah's educated commentary about the wonders of the classical world to the point of nodding off, until Richard loudly and pointedly pressed Salah for answers.

"The gold is here, Your Highness. Forgive me for not mentioning it sooner," Salah answered Richard in a dramatic, exceedingly deferential tone, followed by loud clapping.

Instantly, as if prearranged, ebony-skinned slaves once again entered, this time in fours, each group carrying, with great effort, ten ornately carved and gilded chests. They set them down close by, and Salah himself opened each with a magician's flourish, to the wonderment of Philip and the knights. Only Richard was unimpressed.

"I doubted not your ability to produce gold. It is the remnants, the precious Relics of the True Cross, that we deem the real treasure to be delivered, and why our treaty terms were so generous."

"Ah, yes, I understand. It is with great embarrassment and apology I must report that it will take some time for that great and holy treasure to be delivered safely," Salah said without any trace of hesitation or discomfort, although Godfrey noticed an uneasy stirring among the silent Caliph and his advisers.

"What say you? This was not our agreement! No mention was uttered, or even indicated in the slightest manner, of the possibility of delay!" Richard said loudly, becoming increasingly upset. The atmosphere of forced cordiality had evaporated like the snow in their drinks, replaced by a sudden tension that brought the knights and Muslim officers to a heightened state of readiness. Salah held up a steady hand to calm the situation.

"Forgive me again. I should have explained first the reason. Saladin, as well as I, was unaware that the priceless, irreplaceable relics—revered by us also, for we consider your Christ a great prophet—had been transported to Damascus for safekeeping. The situation at the time we, ah, resumed responsibility for Jerusalem was, how would one say, volatile. I assure you, all necessary preparations are being made to ensure their safe transport here."

Philip responded quickly, sensing Richard did not at all believe Salah's explanation. He, too, felt it was an excuse, a delaying tactic, and didn't understand the reason, but wanted to defuse Richard's infamous temper.

"Of course, the safety of the relics is of utmost importance. And we appreciate the care you've exercised over their safekeeping, but this comes as a surprise. We must know how long it will be before they will be in our possession," Philip said, in a firm yet calm tone.

Richard, fuming inside at what he believed was duplicity on the part of the Muslims, didn't wait for Salah's answer. "There will be no release of Muslims from Acre until the Holy Relics are delivered."

For the first time, Salah looked over at the Caliph. There was fear in his eyes. Richard's look was enough to inspire it. Salah responded, "Holding innocents with the responsibility to feed and care for them is not necessary. Fighting men, yes, we understand that, but—"

"No!" Richard thundered and jumped to his feet, the sudden shock of which caused hands on both sides to clutch sword hilts in reflexive response.

"Go back, Salah, and tell your great Saladin that if I do not have the precious Relics of the True Cross within three days, I will put to the sword *all* Saracen who dwell here, as God is my witness, and to Whom I make a vow this day!"

Chapter III

Salah Bin Madah left Acre immediately after The Lionheart had stormed out of the Caliph's tent, followed by a tired and disappointed King Philip. He had heard the English king's voice call out to the three knights who waited outside the tent, angrily yelling they should summon all liege lords together, so he and Philip could meet with them immediately. Philip, a hard edge to his voice, had countered that they should counsel alone first, before issuing commands. Salah had moved quickly to the tent flap to look and listen, and saw Richard give Philip a hardened stare, but remain silent and still, as if trying to regain his composure, then he nodded and grudgingly voiced his agreement.

This was the last of the information and scenes of description Salah excitedly and expertly provided Saladin Salah ed-Din Yusuf as they met in the royal palace in Jerusalem. The palace was connected to the eighth-century Al-Aqsa mosque, behind which was one of the most revered sites in the Muslim world, the Dome of the Rock. This huge, stunning, perfectly symmetrical golden-colored domed mosque was built in the seventh century, over the rock on which it was said Abraham prepared to sacrifice his son, and from which Muhammad ascended into heaven. It was located in a separate walled-off temple area just inside the Gate of Siloam, one of five gates in the nine-foot-thick, recently reinforced, inner fortress walls that surrounded the entire magnificent and ancient city.

Salah and Saladin sat on thick, velvety cushions in an anteroom above the formal great hall of court. They were positioned directly in front of a large, exquisitely grated and angled window.

It provided a sweeping view of the hilly countryside to the east, now bathed in the tranquil glow of the setting sun, so that the sand, the barren hills, and the mountains beyond all seemed the exact same color. It also allowed a strategic view of the battlement walls branching out from the gate for hundreds of paces in each direction that angled repeatedly to eventually envelop the entire city and the revered holy sites and shrines of the world's three great religions.

Salah was out of breath and sweating profusely, having ridden two horses to exhaustion without the slightest rest. He had raced straight through his own army's lines, still camped on the outskirts of Acre, sending lounging soldiers scurrying to get out of his way, and had stopped only long enough to exchange horses at the Jahfida oasis and gulp down some water. He wanted to get to Saladin's court as quickly as possible and convey the unthinkable development to his master in person, thereby ensuring there would be absolutely no misunderstanding.

It was only now, having finished his news, that he even took refreshment. He first washed his hands, and then eagerly drank the cold water in a large goblet, water pumped from a well that tapped an underground spring beneath the city and was stored in a vast underground cistern below the palace. His hands shook as he did so.

Saladin remained silent, allowing his long-time, faithful royal representative to quench his thirst. The great leader and defender of the Muslim world had dressed simply for his meeting with his trusted adviser and emissary, Salah, an Egyptian of great learning, who had been a teacher at the School of Phonetics in Alexandria, directing the ongoing work of translating ancient Greek and Roman texts, when Saladin first met him.

Saladin wore a loose white tunic that did not accentuate his powerful chest and arms, trimmed at the cuffs, and embroidered in the front from the neck to the waist with gold thread interlaced with pearls. It extended to mid-thigh, below which were billowing pants tied at the ankles with gold cord, and on his feet were pointed silk slippers. On his head he wore a large, two-tiered turban with a gold emblem of a crescent and scimitar exactly like Salah's but twice as large.

His face was broad and full, with features that were considered quite handsome. His eyes expressed his personality and mood more than any feature and could calm or terrorize at a glance. He had a trimmed mustache that curved down to a short beard that, like Salah's, only covered his chin.

Salah lowered the cup, saw Saladin thoughtfully watching him, and added gravely, "I believe the English king will not break the vow made to his god before others, Great One."

"He will slaughter women and children in the name of their Christ for tiny fragments of wood?" Saladin asked Salah Bin Madah in an incredulous tone, but one that did not completely mask the fact that he knew without question what the answer was.

Saladin, whose name meant Protector of the Faith, had come to power when his uncle, Shirkuh, died after conquering Egypt, and the reins of power passed to him. He was neither Arab, Turk, nor Egyptian, but was of Kurdish descent and born in Mesopotamia and called Yusef, meaning Joseph, for his people would bestow a Hebrew name when a boy was circumcised. As a youth he lived and studied in a monastery. Saladin gradually expanded the domain of his uncle with the conquest of Syria, and eventually united all the Arab and Muslim factions under his banner for the purpose of recapturing Jerusalem and destroying all other Crusader kingdoms throughout their lands.

In 1187 at Hattin, Saladin annihilated the vast army the Crusaders formed to stop him and proceeded to besiege Jerusalem, which fell shortly after. In marked contrast to the Crusaders, who captured the city in 1099, there was no massacre. After the city surrendered, none of the Christian occupants were harmed, no buildings were looted or destroyed. He released most of the captives, sold many others back for modest sums, allowed Syrian Christians to retain their churches, and encouraged Jews, who had been persecuted and driven out previously, to return. Although his advisers urged him to destroy the Church of the Holy Sepulcher, Saladin did not, and reopened it to pilgrimage shortly after he had secured the city.

Saladin was not only a great general of armies but also a brilliant statesman, skillful ruler, and adept administrator of captured lands. He was a towering figure of the times, and although he was capable of great ruthlessness in battle—he did behead the knights captured at Hattin who refused to surrender, and could be merciless in dealing with enemies, Christian and Muslim alike—he was unusually compassionate and honest in his wielding of power, and even earned the respect of many in the West, including Christian kings and nobles.

Salah played along with Saladin's charade, the purpose of which puzzled him. "They are as crude as is their religion that treats all nonbelievers as animals to be slaughtered in sacrifice to their God. When they took Jerusalem from us nearly a century ago blood flowed from every doorway, down every passageway. They killed thousands of Christians on their journey to these lands, and even the Christians who lived here in peace with us. And even those on pilgrimage and trapped here, who pleaded for their lives in the name of their Christ!" answered Salah venomously, then added, "Forgive my emotion, but they are not civilized, Great One."

"Those old Crusaders *were* barbarians, especially Chantilion, who I killed with my own hands for his evil. The English and French Kings who have returned are not like them."

"Forgive me for my words in respectful disagreement, Wise One, but I have looked into their eyes and souls. The one they call Lionheart is crazed and obsessed with these relics. He will keep his vow."

"The French King, and his vassal, Guy, will not allow it," Saladin forcefully responded. "And Richard will not go against them. There is no logic or profit in that. Not one drop of blood flowed after we recaptured Jerusalem. They know that. I have never purposely put to the sword the innocents of conquest. Some have become slaves, yes, but thousands have been given their freedom, even their knights for minor ransom, and we allowed all access to the Holy City under the banner of pilgrimage, whether accompanied by Templars or not."

There was silence then. Salah wondered if Saladin actually believed the barbaric Crusaders capable of mercy, but noticed as he observed his master that he was uncharacteristically emotional and troubled. He felt he was leading up to something, something he was reluctant to reveal immediately. And then the words came; words Salah had, for some reason, started to fear might be forthcoming.

"If we give their precious slivers of wood back now, we have nothing to bargain with later. The Caliph was wrong to have agreed," Saladin said, suddenly standing and motioning Salah to remain seated.

"I-we-we misunderstood . . . your instructions, Great One," Salah replied hoarsely, with fear in his expression and voice.

"Salah, Salah. Oh, my faithful Salah." Saladin continued moving to the window and looking out to the east, in the direction of Acre. "We find ourselves faced with great challenge. I have had enormous difficulty, since the sickness swept Cairo and the cities to the west and south, in getting reinforcements. I have learned few, if any, will come now. We must defend Damascus and, of course, Baghdad at all cost, thus we are vulnerable here. The bits of cedar the Christians revere may be crucial to our strategy. And, I fear, at the head of the Crusader army, these relics may provide courage and strength beyond what they really possess. On such could turn the tide of battle. When we captured the relics at Hattin, two hundred surviving knights and five hundred bowmen fought furiously against five thousand of our best to protect the chest of gold that held them. It took two thousand more fighters to finally overwhelm and slaughter them, for they readily offered up their lives rather than surrender what they fervently believed to be that which their Christ bled and died upon." Saladin paused and looked at Salah.

"I-I see. I understand now, Wise One. I would not have had such insight nor could make such decisions."

"But do not fear for the innocents at Acre, Salah. To harm them would make each of our warriors like that of ten. The Christian kings know such things."

"Were the relics, as I told the kings, in Damascus, and now on their way here?"

"Yes, the vizier brings the chest. But I will have it sent back."

With great apprehension still in his voice and eyes, Salah asked, "What will you have me do, Great One?"

"I must, regrettably, go to Baghdad, but you, Salah, you will go back to the kings of these Crusaders, have the Caliph prepare two more chests of gold, and you shall ask for the release of only women and children, after you tell them of the unfortunate change in terms."

Salah's face filled with despair, and his eyes now stared off as he pondered what he knew was most likely a death sentence for all the hostages as well as himself. Saladin gently prodded him from his reverie.

"Salah, I know there is much at stake for you in these negotiations, and will also provide something else, to hopefully use to advantage with the French king."

******

Richard and Philip had met privately immediately after the meeting with Salah had abruptly ended and Richard's order to assemble the liege knights was put in abeyance. The liege knights were those of the highest noble rank, earls, dukes, and barons, with direct royal fealty to a monarch. Out of five hundred fifty knights at the scene, there were sixty-one nobles, split two to one in favor of the French, including Godfrey and Gerard, who, although minor nobles, were both under the direct command of their respective kings.

Philip found Richard intractable in his position, something of a religious fanatic, a side of The Lionheart he had not seen before. But Philip felt Richard's deadline arbitrary, more a ploy to hasten completion of the terms of surrender than an actual time limit fixed in stone, that would never stand as long as negotiations were proceeding.

Philip, irritated at proclamations being made without his agreement or consultation, reminded the impetuous English king of this, and Richard surprisingly apologized.

Although not at all used to having decisions made by consensus, or even at times with much forethought—especially in battle, where the difference between victory and defeat often hung on instant decisions and orders—Richard was no fool. Although he thought Philip a weak leader, his frail build, short stature, and high-pitched voice hardly an inspiration on the battlefield, he did fully understand the fact that he needed Philip as an ally if they were ever to retake Jerusalem. His army was much larger. Only together could they crush the Saracen forever by marching on Damascus after Jerusalem, and then on to Baghdad, destroying the very heart of Saladin's seat of power.

Although Philip felt exhausted, with his illness exacerbated by the increasing heat, he agreed to Richard's request for an assembly that evening with the liege knights. He saw no reason not to do so, and was certain they would never announce the order to slaughter all the Muslim inhabitants of Acre in any event.

Meanwhile, archers from the two honored companies relaxed in a large tented area in the middle of the outer courtyard, which was central to what amounted to a small village unto itself, one of many contained in the vast interior of the fortress-city. It was where the wives and family of many of the merchants, administrators of the nearby port, and Muslim military officers lived in various-sized dwellings made out of stone, covered with a mixture of mud and sand that had a uniform beige color. These modest homes occupied the area under the ramparts on the outer wall, and across from larger and more elaborate dwellings at the base of and adjoining the inner wall.

Beyond the inner wall was the magnificent inner courtyard, where Richard, Philip, and the Muslim leaders had met, which was central to what amounted to a small hidden city, with streets, shops, residences of the nobles, and a mosque, which had been originally built as a Christian church, since Acre had been built as a city-fortress by French Templar knights of the first Crusade. The outer and inner walls were massive, ten feet thick, nearly twenty feet high, and ran in a rough oval pattern from the arched entrance and huge, double-thick entry doors for over a league in either direction, until they finally became joined, in effect making Acre a double-walled fortress-city.

The outer courtyard area was also where the less prosperous merchants had partially tented stalls and tables and displayed their wares and foodstuffs, around which there was regular activity, even though their stocks of goods were meager. Some were noticeably empty and unattended. A few enterprising Muslim merchants, though, eagerly stood vigil by other hastily erected tables filled with what amounted to souvenirs and crude trinkets, and constantly eyed the Crusaders lounging nearby on reed mats under open tents. They hoped they would walk nearby and engage in haggling, even if in the end they bought nothing, just to allay their boredom.

Michael sat leaning against a tent pole, a reed mat rolled up as a cushion for his back, and reworked the loop bindings on the ends of an extra bowstring. He observed the merchants who huddled together in idle conversation in front of some of the stalls, and the activity of others who moved about in performance of daily chores. Most of them, to his surprise, paid little attention to the lounging group of archers.

There was a noticeable absence of the presence of any women, who, when they did appear, were so completely covered from head to toe that only the obviousness or their veils brought attention to their sex. The rest of the Crusader Army remained camped outside the walls until the terms of surrender were fulfilled and the Muslim inhabitants and former defenders, in effect hostages, were allowed to leave.

Baints stood nearby, silently surveying the sky, his eye on a falcon circling above the city-fortress. The bird was being exercised from a perch somewhere on top of one of the walls by the Caliph, for the entertainment of King Philip, who had been given the magnificent predator as a gift.

Most of the others were strolling around the market area or engaged in gambling games with dice in a tent at the end of their makeshift compound. Baints had relaxed the normal regimen of exercises and practices for the English archers, since the size of their camp in the courtyard made it impractical. The French had done likewise, following Baints's lead, and also since their sergeant, DeGraise, and several of their number remained at the beach area infirmary, still incapacitated from the journey and lingering fever caught in Marseilles.

Cletis Merriman and Two-String Jack patrolled their compound nearby. Because they were still suffering the aftereffects of seasickness and couldn't take part in the battle and other subsequent labor once they were well, they served twice the normal sentry duty, along with some of the French archers, who had also been sick, namely Robere and Gesault the Mason. A small group of French archers, as well as a few of the English, stayed to themselves, choosing not to mix with any others. Baints told Michael this was due to relatives or friends who had died in skirmishes against each other in the more recent, ongoing border disputes between them in Normandy and other Frankish lands.

Merriman was an archer of twenty-eight, had left a wife and six children behind, and worried constantly about their welfare. He had also been an expert cobbler in Hampstead and was in much demand since they landed. Godfrey had tried to reassure him that his own wife would look in on Merriman's family, as she would the families of all who served under him, but that didn't seem to stop his constant comments and concern about their well-being.

Two-String Jack, on the other hand, was a widower of thirty, who had lost his wife and two children to pestilence while he was away fighting with another knight and had returned heartbroken to Hampstead from his wife's village. He had been given the nickname because he used two strings woven together on his bow and extra wide notches on his arrows, for what he insisted was greater accuracy.

Others in the company were lured by the tented make-shift village just behind the low hills on the coast, near the port and erected by Genoese traders, which housed boatloads of prostitutes from Cyprus, whom the nobles, and even clerics, tolerated. It was part of the agreement with the Genoese to build and provide a fleet of galleys for King Richard, and a necessary evil associated with amassing a large army, although both monarchs and their clergy shared in a tax levied on the brisk commerce in flesh.

Baints turned and looked over at Michael. "Lad, get up. Let us stretch our limbs and walk the courtyard and see the sights confined within the inner wall."

Michael looked up and readily put the string aside, bored by the work and welcoming the offer. "Aye, I do need to move about, or I will acquire the gait of an old man, like you."

"Is that so, young whelp?" Baints smiled and answered Michael's often joking refrain about his age. "Let us see if ye can keep pace, then. I agree I start slow, but it is endurance and intellect that win the race."

"Aye, I am well-equipped, then." Michael accepted Baints's outstretched hand, attached to an arm so muscled and powerful that the old sergeant literally pulled him up so forcefully that his feet left the ground momentarily. This caused them both to laugh, enjoying the jesting.

Baints led the way, and they walked away from the sun, through the long, open courtyard between the outer and inner walls, toward where a magnificent palace and its entrance anchored the east corner of the inner wall. It was where King Richard and his entourage of royal knights, guards, archers, and other men-at-arms had taken up residence.

In the opposite direction the west corner was anchored by the towering structure of turrets and ramparts of what had been the old Templar fortress, and was occupied by King Philip and his retainers. Philip had graciously insisted that Richard occupy the palace in honor of his defeat of Saladin's attack.

The pair entered a narrow, covered passageway that ran between the inner wall and the palace wall, and eventually exited into a square so large that it could have been that of any good-sized English village and, a few years previous, had, in fact, resembled one. Here the ground was a pavement of fitted stone, and there were numerous merchant stalls and tented pavilions surrounding the perimeter. In the center was a large, intricately tiled fountain, surrounded by an oval pool, though no water flowed from the fountain, and the pool itself was completely dry. Beyond the stalls and pavilions was a row of smoothly chiseled mud and sandstone dwellings. They continued on into the distance along the wall, and well beyond the great square.

Across from these dwellings was another mosque, which had originally been the church of St. Laurence and soon would be converted back to such, and many other two and three-story buildings of distinctly Arabic design. They had curved archway entrances, porticoes, balustrades, and covered walkways, contained apartments and businesses, and also stretched all the way to the north wall, giving the area between, where they walked, the appearance and feeling of a narrow roadway not entirely unlike what could be found in a large city such as London.

They were struck by pleasant, pungent aromas that hung in the air now, especially that of cooked or warming mutton. Lamb was a basic meat in England also, but it had never tasted or smelled as wonderful as it did here. Michael had remarked about this to Baints, who praised the power of exotic spices that were plentiful among the Saracen but beyond the purse of even most knights and nobles in England.

As Baints and Michael silently walked this corridor there was activity all around them, although they noticed those on the street ahead of them thinned considerably as they moved forward. They began to realize it was the women and children who were moving out of sight, back into their homes and behind the camel-skin doors that shielded the insides.

Michael took in all the sights with great interest. Muslim women and children and, for that matter, Muslim men, fascinated him. What a contrast to the stories of savage infidels he had been told about by others, especially priests and clergy. The women were covered completely in robes, with scarves over their heads, fashioned in such a way that only their eyes betrayed their humanity. The children and old men wore loosely fitted white robes, with the men also wearing plain turbans or loosely twisted white cloth wrapped on their heads and around their necks.

"They hardly seem the savage infidel described by our priests, Baints," Michael finally said, breaking the leisurely silence and giving voice to his thoughts.

"What are you saying, lad?"

"The people here, the common ones, the women, children, and the old men, they are not that different from us," Michael said, motioning around him at the scenes of daily life he saw playing out before him.

"That is a keen observation, for in my experience too, except for the savage Scots, I've not found humanity elsewhere all that much different in their daily existence." Baints put his hand on Michael's shoulder as they walked. "What you say also was my feeling when I was last here so many years ago, another lifetime for me."

"You've spoken very little of your experiences, no matter how I prodded," Michael responded.

"That is true, I have not."

"I would like to hear of them."

Baints was silent for a moment, considering the request. "I was your age then," Baints began as they walked at a leisurely pace through the Muslim area. "I served in the Jerusalem garrison in the company of the great knight John of Andover, God rest his pious soul."

"You've *seen* Jerusalem," Michael interrupted, awe in his voice.

"Yes, lad, and all its holy sites. There was little battle then. There were occasional skirmishes with Saracen groups, bandits, really, rather than men-at-arms, and if truth be known, more mischief and intrigues between Crusader nobles and Templars, than with the Saracen. As it turned out, I ended up spending most of my time assisting Hospitaliers in their infirmaries."

"Hospitaliers?" Michael questioned, frowning.

"Monks, who were also knights like the Templars, but they built and administered hospitals all over the Holy Land, to aid those on pilgrimage. Ferocious fighters when provoked. My involvement came as a result of contracting an inner malady of the bowel that nearly drained me of life. I was saved through the saintly dedication of one of their order, a humble, gentle soul named Peter. He had faced a horrific experience on the field of battle, of which he would not talk in detail. After that, he disavowed his knightly rank for the simplicity of solely living as a celibate, and devoted his life to administering to the worst of the sick and dying. I came to know him, and with little to do at times, I helped him, so as to repay the debt I fervently felt I owed because of his long vigils over me during my sickness. For without them, I would have surely become a permanent part of this landscape." Baints hesitated, as if lost in his recollections of the kindly, devoted monk.

"What happened to him, Baints?" Michael asked, breaking the spell of distant memories.

"I know not. Most likely succumbed to the very ills he attended in others, or was swallowed up by the Saracen conquests; although Muslims, even the Turks, are known for their tolerance of those who administer to the infirm and bore no weapons. Over time, it was from this saint I learned privately, in hushed tones, much in truth about the Saracen and his religion. I even managed to learn the Saracen tongue from him and captive nobles under his care, and those being held for ransom. Heathens they are not. And, I say this only to you, Michael, for I know it will not go further, there is much about them and their beliefs that is shared by us, and much about what the anointed of our church tell us that is cruelly wrong, even evil in its intent."

"Really? Can you share your knowledge with me, Baints, teach me what you still know of the language?"

"Oh, lad. I-I fear I've said too much. It may be better that you keep your feelings simple, and do not complicate them with contradictions. In the coming battles, pure hate such as Henri's, and a blind belief that we are doing God's Will, is far better than dealing with the pangs of a conscience that will only trouble thee and give rise to hesitation, which can spell death in battle. I have already babbled on far too much. Being here gives rise to such powerful memories and stirs me to wanting, finally, after all these years, to share them. Your comments gave them voice in me, but I've provoked a curiosity that I now regret."

"Baints, you've nothing to fear with me. I want to know all opinions. Whether I will make them my own I cannot say. But I do not fear what one thinks is the truth. No matter, my goal here is resolute. As our knight has also said in example, I will kill only those who threaten me on the field of battle, regardless of the justness of our cause here, and seize the opportunity, no matter how impossible, to rise from humble rank to fulfill my heart's desire. Nothing will change that."

Baints was moved by the power of Michael's words, and the eloquence with which he expressed them. There was so much more to this young man that he was only just learning. He had been impressed with his quickness in learning the Frankish tongue. If the boy could be schooled in a monastery, he would, to be sure, become a scholar of note. Yes, he would share all his knowledge with the boy. Who knew how long he had left to do so? And the lad was right, he was sufficient in years to determine for himself what truths he would embrace or not. He just hoped it wouldn't bring a torment of the soul that the knowing of truth so often produced.

"Aye, lad. You express yourself well. There should be no fear from ideas and knowledge. Just remember, we are of a people and church in which that view is remarkably absent and provokes fear, the cry of heresy, excommunication, and death."

"I understand the seriousness of your warning. You are my closest friend, Baints. Even more than that, I feel as if we share kinship. Rest assured, what we speak will be ours alone. I have found I enjoy the challenge of a new language. And, there are so many things I wish to question but never knew there was anyone with whom I could, and all along, unbeknownst, you were the one."

"I would welcome such discussion, but understand, my recollection of the Saracen language has been dimmed by time. I understand many words that I hear spoken amongst them, but have lost the ability to speak it without the labor of much thought."

Suddenly, a screeching, giggling little child, a boy, barefoot and dressed only in a short, loose white tunic, ran out from one of the dwellings into the passageway directly in front of them. A few moments later the veiled, robed figure of a woman dashed out after the mischievous child.

At this exact time, a cart, loaded with the possessions of a noble or merchant in preparation for when they would be allowed to leave the city, was being pushed along swiftly by slaves. It picked up speed on the downward slope of the pathway, unable to see clearly ahead, totally unaware of the child running wildly and directly into its path. It was clear the woman would not catch up to the child in time.

Michael immediately reacted, took two running strides, jumped straight out, and, in one motion, grabbed the child and rolled out of the way of the heavy, wide-wheeled cart that would have surely crushed the life out of the little boy. Michael struck his head on the cobblestone pavement, but held the child to his chest as he rolled. Although frightened and crying, the boy was unharmed.

The woman yelled out in alarm. The cart continued unimpeded on its way, with the pushers not even giving the scene a sideways glance. The woman rushed forward. She was swift and graceful in her movements, and as Michael watched her run toward him, with only her eyes visible above the veil, he was sure she was young. She quickly scooped up the frightened child, who had been frantically trying to pull free of Michael's hold and now struggled against her grip and tried to twist free. In doing so, the child grasped out wildly and pulled her veil and headscarf completely off.

Revealed was a young woman, just as Michael had thought. Her loosely tied black hair, olive skin, and doe-shaped dark eyes combined to make her so strikingly beautiful that Michael was frozen where he lay, unaware of the blood oozing from a gash above his eye and across his forehead. He was utterly captivated by the sight of her, to the point that he hardly acknowledged Baints's efforts to help him up.

The young woman tried to grab her head and face covering from the child's hand, while also trying to hold on to the boy, but he flung the garment away, and it landed next to Michael. Michael reached for it with one hand, while Baints took hold of the other and pulled him to his feet. Michael tried to offer the veil back to her. But she was frozen in place with indecision and surprise at the gesture, and when she stood up completely with the struggling, wailing child in her grasp, their eyes met, and their gazes lingered upon each other for several moments before shock replaced her curiosity. She immediately backed away and panicked, and turned, frantically running back through the camel skin partition of the dwelling from which she and the child had emerged.

Michael stood unmoving, staring at the entrance. Baints started to move him away when a youth, who appeared barely of age, rushed out the doorway brandishing a huge scimitar. Seeing the veil in Michael's hand, he swung wildly at him, with Baints just able to pull Michael out of the way of the polished blade.

Before the boy could swing the heavy sword back, Baints grabbed his wrist and quickly twisted the sword free. But the youth wouldn't give up and rushed Michael, who dropped the veil and grabbed his wildly flailing fists and held him at bay, while trying to explain in vain what had happened, his words not understood.

A crowd began to form. An old man emerged from the camel-skin doorway and began yelling at Michael and trying to pull the boy from his grasp. "You-you don't understand," Michael tried to explain.

Baints intervened, alarmed. "Lad, lad! Leave him go. We *must* leave."

The beautiful young woman reemerged, one hand over her face, the other firmly holding the wailing, struggling child by a hand. She was shaking her head and yelling out frantically to the old man and the youth.

Michael let go of the boy, and the old man nearly fell backward at the sudden release. Baints forcefully pushed Michael away down the street and tossed the sword aside.

"Baints, they didn't understand what—"

"Never mind, lad. We must hurry away! It is *forbidden* to look upon the unveiled face of a Muslim woman."

Michael was still entranced by the beauty he had seen. "Baints, she was the most beautiful—"

"I know, lad," Baints said as he continued to lead Michael away by the arm, as the crowd dissipated and the woman, the young boy, and the old man returned inside their dwelling.

"I often felt that women of this area were indeed uncommonly exotic, no doubt also enhanced in one's mind by distance from home and the passions of youth."

"She held my gaze as I held hers, and—"

"Lad, we may be in mortal danger now. We must hurry back to our camp."

"What a world exists here, Baints. What other revelations about this land lie ahead, I wonder?"

"From my experience, lad, most are best left unknown."

******

The Caliph's own banquet hall was appropriated for the assembly of the liege knights, and the Caliph ordered his personal staff to prepare it for the two monarchs and their lords.

Once the preparations were finished, Richard asked those in his royal entourage to thoroughly check the halls and entryways and station themselves in positions to ensure their complete privacy.

When the knights arrived, they found they had to unbelt their scabbards and swords to sit on the large, damask-covered and embroidered cushions in the Muslim fashion, although a raised platform had been quickly constructed with throne-like chairs to accommodate Richard and Philip. It was becoming increasingly apparent from his look and manner that Philip's illness was getting worse.

Richard leaned over to Philip and whispered, "Do you wish to also address the group, or should I just speak for both of us and proceed to the heart of the matter and try to finish this quickly?"

"By all means," Philip said weakly, waving his hand in agreement, content to rest back in his cushioned chair and look as regal as possible. "Proceed. The quicker the better by me."

Richard surveyed the assemblage. Most of the knights were Philip's, and the two groups sat pretty much with their own, separated, except, he noticed, for Godfrey and Gerard, who remained together roughly in the middle area between the groups. In addition, four high-ranking representatives of the church were present, Pope Gregory's anointed, Archbishop Caudinier, Archbishop Mendini, and two bishops of Palestine in exile, all nobles in their own right. Two other of the pope's bishops remained seriously ill from the journey, had yet to show signs of recovering, and had been moved to the palace, where Richard's own physicians administered to them.

Godfrey and Gerard talked as they waited for the proceedings to begin. Their expressions matched the seriousness of their discussion, which had been a continuation of grave issues they had talked about at length after the meeting with Salah had abruptly ended.

Gerard couldn't believe the vow to God that King Richard had made, and he told Godfrey that if it came to pass that the vow had to be honored, it would not be he, nor, he was sure, his countrymen who did so. His king would never give such a command, he told Godfrey vehemently. Unlike Crusaders of the past campaigns, whose barbarity did not distinguish between Infidel, Jew, or Christian residents in the lands they marched through, they would not debase themselves with such acts of depravity.

Godfrey also was shocked at Richard's pronouncement and felt sure it would have the intended effect on the Muslims and quickly produce the relics, as promised and agreed upon. There would be no need for the sacred vow of a king to be honored, as Godfrey knew it most assuredly would have to be.

Richard was confident that regardless of the composition of the group in favor of Philip, they would still be no less sympathetic to the seriousness of the development he would explain to them, and his decisive manner of dealing with it. He especially counted on the support of the papal representatives, who were far more bloodthirsty in the pursuit of plunder and holy artifacts than any noble present in the hall.

Richard stood, and the room quieted. There was no doubt his was a regal and imposing presence.

"King Philip and I have gathered all here to inform of developments of grave concern. The infidel leader, Saladin, has not fulfilled the terms of surrender, and has yet to deliver to us the sacred Relics of the True Cross."

This caused the reaction Richard had anticipated, and a murmur of unrest and anger began to build and echo in the great hall. He continued louder, above the din.

"Tonight, you will send men among all the hostages and search their belongings and dwellings, including all the nobles and officers, regardless of rank, and confiscate all weapons."

Philip looked up, surprised by the command. They had not discussed this when they had met earlier. It violated the terms of the surrender, but, of course, so had Saladin. From a security standpoint, it also made sense at this point, thought Philip, and anyway, he was just too fatigued to question and argue Richard's proclaimed course of action.

Richard continued, "I—we—we have also informed Saladin's representative of other consequences, the most extreme and *dire* of consequences . . . "

Chapter IV

Salah, again traveling under the banner of Saladin, carried by one of two royal horsemen, left Jerusalem long before the sun rose, determined to arrive in Acre as early in the morning as possible. The horsemen trailed extra horses behind them, which they would use after the stop at the Jahfida oasis halfway to Acre and heavily guarded by rear elements of Saladin's army still encamped within sight of the castle-fortress.

Not only was it much cooler in the early hours and more hospitable to travel, but his experience as a negotiator had taught him that bad news was best delivered in the morning. People, especially nobility of any origin, who were rested, had plenty of time to talk and vent their feelings, and time to think and sleep before acting and making decisions, seldom made rash ones. Bad news delivered late in the day could, and often did, lead to decisions suddenly made in the heat of emotion while tired, and invariably resulted in greater anger and far harsher, and usually irrevocable, proclamations. He realized, though, with the news he now carried, time of day delivered would probably make no difference whatsoever in the outcome. But he needed to utilize every possible advantage his experience had taught him. He also needed time, immediately upon his arrival, to initiate a carefully developed plan that was crucial to have in place before any meeting involving the English king could take place.

They rode at a swift pace, but not at the fevered rush of the day before, and covered the distance in seven hours, passing through the fortress gates of Acre at mid-morning.

Salah was immediately told of the nighttime search and the disarming of all within the fortress. Although unexpected news, it was not exactly surprising, since he had been the first to raise the specter of violating the terms of surrender. Salah, in a rare display of anger, stopped all questioning of him by the Caliph and his advisers concerning the delivery of the relics, and ordered that a sealed note from him be immediately delivered to King Philip, requesting they first meet in secret, before summoning others on both sides. Salah also told them to fill two more chests with gold coin and left them murmuring angrily among themselves as he freshened up before meeting with the French king.

Philip agreed to Salah's request, responding with a return note. Arrangements were made, and they met in private in Philip's quarters, in the former Templar fortress adjoining the inner courtyard, which anchored the western fortress wall, just as the royal palace and castle where Richard was lodged anchored the eastern wall. Salah used a secret passageway, shown to him by the Caliph, to gain entry, hoping that none other than those closest to Philip would know.

Philip asked his retainers to leave the room and offered Salah refreshment and a seat in an antechamber, away from the doorway. Salah bowed his head respectfully and followed Philip into the secluded side room containing a small, oval-shaped writing table and two elaborately carved and cushioned chairs. It was obvious to Philip from Salah's anxious mannerisms that he was nervous, and further accentuated in graveness by his mood and facial expression. The moment they sat, Salah didn't hesitate to speak.

"I cannot deliver the Relics as agreed," Salah said tersely, avoiding eye contact with Philip, whose expression instantly changed to one of utter disbelief.

"What do you mean, you *cannot*!"

"After they were captured at Hattin, there was much confusion," Salah answered rapidly in explanation, trying to keep his extreme anxiety out of his voice. "Jerusalem surrendered to us shortly after, and they were transported there, then taken to Damascus with many other valuables and an enormous amount of plunder. We know they are there somewhere, but have been unable to locate—"

"Cease this babble, Salah!" Philip yelled, and jumped up, slamming his fist on the table. "I believe not a word of it!"

Salah instantly rose in deference to the monarch, cowed by his anger, and decided silence was the best response at the moment. "You asked to meet with me alone to insult me with lies!"

When Salah looked up, Philip saw shame in his eyes, and also fear. Philip calmed himself. The abrupt action seemed to have exhausted the weakened monarch, and he reached down to the table with both hands to steady himself.

Salah, alarmed at the sight of the wavering king, quickly moved to help him, but Philip held a hand up in abeyance. "I am all right. Just drained by this unrelenting heat! Hell's fire could not be much worse."

"Permit me to say, Sire, you should take relaxation and sleep in one of the subterranean levels, where the air keeps the water in a secret cistern cool," Salah said, his voice quivering with apprehension.

Philip sat back down, motioning Salah to do the same, noticing the fear was even more apparent in his expression now. "A most welcomed revelation. Sit now, Salah. Fear not. Unlike others, I am not inclined to kill the messenger."

"It-it is not for myself I fear, Majesty," Salah said as he slowly lowered himself onto the chair, fatigue more evident now in his manner, and his discomfort sitting in the Western fashion obvious.

"For what reason I do not know, but it must be of the utmost seriousness for your great Saladin to renege on an agreement with kings," Philip said as he eyed Salah, who met his gaze and quickly looked away.

"What could be of such importance to allow the sacrifice of three thousand of his faithful?" Philip asked rhetorically, pausing in thought, leaning back in the intricately carved chair. Salah remained silent and looked downward. A few moments later, Philip continued, giving his thoughts voice.

"I suspect he possibly worries about his ability to defend Jerusalem from our larger-than-expected force here."

Salah's eyes slowly moved up and met Philip's.

"Perhaps he wants to retain the Relics to bargain with later," the king next suggested.

Salah, although expert at hiding his emotions, was unable to do so now, and his expression betrayed him and confirmed to Philip he had hit upon the truth.

"Tell me, Salah, why did you bring your news to me first, in private?"

"I felt I could reason with you, Majesty; that you could intercede with the English king. Nothing is to be gained with the slaughter of the unarmed and innocent."

"That may be true, but Richard is a king and made a solemn, royal vow witnessed by others and announced to many."

"Two more chests of gold are being prepared here. We hope you will, at the very least, consider releasing the women, the wives and children, while negotiations over the fate of the men continue."

"Two *more* chests, very impressive. How many more chests remain, I wonder?"

Salah studied Philip. Was his question asked expecting an answer? Was this an opening to further negotiation? Could a reasonable outcome be obtained through just the payment of more gold? Could the French king even prevail in a contest of wills with The Lionheart? He knew Philip and Richard were rivals and enemies, and that the Crusade had provided the only cause that could have produced a truce between them and created their tentative alliance against a common enemy. But Saladin was certain that, like past Crusader alliances, it would most certainly fracture in time, and the prospect of battles at the doorsteps of their homelands would eventually take priority.

"With great effort, more could possibly be gathered together, Majesty. Could that influence the renunciation of a sacred vow?"

"Salah, unless you deliver the Holy Relics of the True Cross intact within its unique chest adorned with the ancient gold and emeralds of St. Helena, you cannot possibly avoid the horrible outcome we both fear."

"You, of course, fully understand now why it is impossible to do so," Salah said, slumping back in the chair, thinking that now the time had come to produce the document from Saladin that he had bound to his waist inside his robe.

"The King of France, though, and all under him are not bound by the vow of an English king. Is that not true, Majesty?"

Philip's eyes narrowed, and they met Salah's, who looked back at him now with a determination he had not seen before.

"Unless a vow is also voiced in agreement, that is true, Salah. But Richard has more than enough of a force here to easily execute all hostages himself. Nothing could cause one to raise a sword in defiance to save, excuse me, 'savage infidels' who have despoiled the Holy Land and refuse to return the Holy Relics, even to prevent the senseless slaughter of innocents."

Salah's eyes never left Philip's. "I have something from my master for you. It is inside my robe, bound to my body. Can I remove it?" Salah's request was wise, so a hand inside his robe would not appear threatening. Philip hesitated a moment, then nodded.

"You may," Philip answered tersely, his eyes alert and his hands moving to the edge of the table to push out if necessary.

Salah slowly and carefully removed a thin leather pouch with long cloth strings that had secured it around his ample belly. It was stained with sweat. He opened it and produced an elaborately folded parchment secured with the seal of Saladin. He handed it to an intently curious Philip and said, "If we cannot save all, perhaps we can save some."

****

"So, you chose to meet alone with Philip first, Salah! What intent compelled you? To what purpose did you think that would serve, I wonder?"

There was silence. Richard's direct, angry pronouncement upon entering the tent produced the intended response, surprise. He had arrived last and late, having told Godfrey and Gerard to proceed without him. Other than Philip, everyone else stood, including Guy of Lusignan, when Richard entered the tent. Two of Richard's royal guards remained outside.

The knights looked at each other in puzzlement. The Caliph gave a surprised look to Salah, who, in turn, looked at Philip. Salah wasn't really shocked that Richard had learned of the meeting. He knew with the rivalry that existed between the two kings, spies could be everywhere. He was ready with an explanation when Philip unexpectedly responded first, calmly and directly.

"Yes, Salah did request to meet with me in the most urgent way. I agreed because of the grave manner and insistence he conveyed. The moment after he spoke, I understood. The news he brings from Saladin is not—well, it is not good. He greatly feared your reaction, Richard, and wanted my counsel in how he might approach imploring you to forsake the vow you made previously. I could offer him no encouragement or advice in the matter."

Richard's gaze lingered on Philip for a moment, as if he was deciding whether or not to believe the words he'd spoken. There was logic to what he said, and Philip did not at all betray anxiety, or even the slightest discomfort as he spoke. He turned back to Salah with a look of piercing intensity. Richard said nothing, but his expression demanded a response.

"I am unable to return the Relics as agreed," Salah said directly.

The Caliph and his associates gasped out loud in shock, the knights were stunned, and Richard was enraged beyond belief.

"You wretched, filthy, God-forsaken Infidel vermin! May you be damned in hell for all eternity, together with your blaspheming prophet Muhammad, for I swear I will send you there myself with my own hand to be followed by your vile Saladin, the devil himself!"

Tempers erupted at Richard's ranting words. Regardless of the attempt at disarming the Muslims, the Caliph's military advisers had drawn daggers from inside their robes and were ready to die to avenge the insults. The knights drew their swords and moved to protect their kings. Although Richard and Philip did not carry swords in such a situation, Richard did have a dagger he instantly withdrew and moved to fight the Muslims.

Philip forced himself to his feet and quickly moved in front of the livid Richard, and Salah did the same with the Caliph's officers. The Caliph stood helpless, as if in a stupor. Richard nearly pushed the smaller Philip aside, but Philip yelled in his face, "Do not, Richard!"

And The Lionheart stopped and, for a brief moment, there was the incredible uncertainty in the air about whom he might actually use the dagger in his hand on. But he quickly got control of his emotions, froze in place, and gradually lowered the weapon, much to everyone's relief.

Richard, still red with rage, turned and moved to the entrance, then stopped, turned back to them, and spoke. The tone of his voice was chilling. His words came slow and measured for effect. His eyes narrowed and were piercing in their gaze, fixed directly on Salah.

"Tomorrow morning at sunrise . . . *all infidel here will die!*"

"No, Sire!" Godfrey blurted out, immediately realizing his mistake at doing so in front of others.

"*You* say *no*, to me!" Richard yelled back in enraged disbelief.

"I beg forgiveness, Sire. I gave voice to my inner alarm and thoughts and should not have." Richard's fury and reddening face were not abated in the least. He left the tent, and the stunned knights followed him out.

Richard walked fast, barely restraining his anger. Godfrey tried to keep pace, as did the guards, but then Godfrey noticed Gerard and Guy had stopped and realized they were waiting for King Philip, who'd not yet exited.

Philip, easily exhausted by the strain of the confrontation with Richard, had lain back down on the cushions to rest. He realized the others had left, but also realized this was the best time and place to finalize the plan proposed by Salah at the end of their earlier meeting.

Richard took notice that Godfrey had not kept pace, stopped, and, further enraged by the delay, yelled as loud as he was capable of.

"Follow me, Godfrey, damn you!"

"Sire, King Philip has not come out of the tent," Godfrey replied to the command screamed to him.

"He can go to hell! Who knows what treachery he plots in there against me!" screamed Richard venomously, to which Gerard instantly responded with restrained anger. King or not, he would not allow the shocking insult of his own king to go unchallenged.

"There is no reason for such insult, *Majesty*. I take great issue with your ill-tempered words," Gerard yelled back in response, shocking Godfrey and leaving Guy speechless, totally befuddled at what had so quickly transpired, and at a loss for how he should react.

Richard knew he had spoken in error, but the words could not be unsaid. To be challenged in front of others by a minor French noble was more than he could take. If he had a sword at his hip, he would have drawn it instantly and cut down the impudent knight where he stood, regardless of his size and reputation with a sword.

Richard's face, now as red as his hair, turned ugly with hatred. Godfrey was now the one to move in front of Richard, which seemed to break the spell of his fury with Gerard. The guards were unsure what to do without any order from the king. Richard spoke to Godfrey in a slow, halting manner, the restrained rage inside him sending a ripple of fear through him.

"We leave *now*, Godfrey. There is *much* to attend to."

Richard turned. Godfrey gave Gerard a long, serious look, nodded his head as if conveying some signal, then turned and tried to match the furious pace of his king.

Gerard and an immensely relieved Guy quickly went back to the tent to find the reason for Philip's delay. When Philip saw the tent flap open and their faces peer inside, he immediately motioned them all the way in.

"What of Richard and Godfrey?" he asked, lounging now on his side, his face pale and drawn, as if not having heard the yelling outside the tent.

Gerard and Guy exchanged a brief look. "They left, Sire," Gerard replied, deciding to keep his response simple as he surveyed the Muslims now also lounging on cushions, but with faces as revealing of despair as any he had ever seen.

"Good. Sit. Join us. We have little time left to plan what must be done, and surprisingly, this is now the place most secure for us to do so."

At the end of the day, when all the archers came together to eat their evening meal, cooked and served by Muslim women, which had been arranged through the Caliph by Godfrey and Gerard when they had first arrived, Michael noticed the French seemed unusually quiet and more to themselves than normal.

Earlier that afternoon, Baints had pointed out to him, as they both lay in the shade reworking the last of the arrows retrieved from the battlefield, that he had observed the French archers slipping off one by one, including their sentries.

They had casually worked their way to the entrance of the Templar fortress at the far end of market area. It appeared they did so purposefully, as if trying not to attract attention. Whittler Will had also related to them that, in the afternoon, when he was trading carvings of horses and camels for raw wood at a Muslim carpentry shop near the Royal Palace, he had observed large groups of English knights entering the royal palace entrance.

"Something's definitely astir in the air, and we've not seen our knight since Mass and services this morning," Baints whispered to Michael as they ate.

Michael could easily feel the change in mood and atmosphere. And when he was getting his food, Henri had uncharacteristically hurried by without even stopping to talk, and left immediately after eating, as did the others in Gerard's company. Most, though, in their group ate greedily, uninterested in even taking note of any change in atmosphere or eating arrangement. They were interested only in resuming their games of chance, or returning with winnings to the Genoese tents of pleasure on the coast.

"They seem to avoid us, purposely, Baints. Why?" Michael asked, puzzled and concerned by the goings-on.

"Don't know for sure, lad. Could be a falling out between nobles. Saw it many times before when I served here. Let us leave now and take our evening walk a bit earlier today."

Baints's suspicion was confirmed when they returned to their tent. The French archers were in the process of packing up their belongings. Michael approached Henri, who was on his knees rolling up the mats of reed and coarse cloth that served as his bed.

"Henri, what has happened? Where do you go?"

Henri faced Michael reluctantly, then looked around, unsure of his response. Then he motioned Michael to kneel down as if to help him. He lingered for a bit, unrolling the mats, then re-rolling them to allow others nearby to leave first, then whispered to Michael, "Walk through the courtyard area beyond the Templar fortress when it becomes twilight. I will find you there."

Henri promptly stood up, slung his three covered quivers of arrows around his head and shoulder, then hoisted his bedroll and his other bag of gear onto his shoulders. Michael helped him and picked up and handed him his two un-slung bows. Henri quickly left the tent, joining the others of his company who had already done so, and headed off toward the fortress.

Michael just stood there, watching his friend walk away, wondering what in God's name was going on, when he felt Baints's presence next to him. Michael turned and saw his look of eager curiosity about his brief encounter with the young French archer, but unfortunately, he had nothing of use to share.

******

King Philip was exhausted. Servants had bathed him in the cool water kept in a secret cistern below the courtyard fountain and made available by the Caliph after their plan had been finalized. This had soothed him and abated his fever somewhat. His appetite had also stirred, and he ate with increasing enthusiasm the roasted, heavily spiced and peppered lamb and the glistening dates soaked in honey, which had been sent by Salah. He even managed to consume nearly an entire bottle of wine, which greatly relaxed his troubled mind. If their plan was successful, Salah, his many relatives in service at the garrison and their families, the Caliph and his family, and over three hundred other women and children would escape and be spared horrible slaughter. Regardless, nearly twenty-seven hundred hostages, mostly soldiers, would die after sunrise at the hands of Richard, his English knights, and ax-wielding footmen.

Philip had absolutely no doubt that Richard, as the first rays of sun shone in the east, would begin rounding up hostages, hundreds at a time, taking them out beyond the fortress-city walls, and in clear view of the Muslim army encampment, line them up in the glow of the rising sun, and slaughter each and every one, until, as Richard vowed, no Saracen remained alive in Acre. He had been told Richard had met with his knights immediately after the encounter in the Caliph's tent.

Philip, though, had absolute trust in Gerard and his archers to do everything in their power to carry out the plan and thereby honor and, hopefully, successfully fulfill his agreement with Salah and Saladin, for which great reward had already been granted. His loyal knight had also obtained the crucial assistance of the conscience-stricken English knight, Godfrey. With the presence of a renowned English knight at the head, escaping innocents could be provided safe passage should they be detected unexpectedly by English patrols outside the fortress walls.

Philip drained what remained of the wine in his goblet. His intoxicated thoughts drifted back to Richard the Lionheart . . . the exalted one. Richard the Despicable, more like! He detested the English king more than ever. Earlier that afternoon Richard had come to meet with him again, in an attempt, Philip interpreted, at a reconciliation of sort, to soothe things over after his accusatory remarks with Salah. Richard left even more incensed when Philip flatly refused to give the order to have his knights or soldiers involved in the executions the next morning. Richard's cold, steely stare at him before he left did unnerve him, but his feelings of discomfort quickly turned to a consuming anger when The Lionheart left. Their time together in the Holy Land had only confirmed the characterization by others to him that the King of England, during the long journey to the Holy Land, had become increasingly obsessed and fanatical about the Crusade and his goals. He had become more unpredictable in his moods, therefore more dangerous—perhaps, Philip feared, even deranged.

Well, Philip thought further, what he himself may have lacked in physical prowess and the warrior's skills with weapons, he made up for in cunning and intellect. Richard's ill-spoken vow of revenge would work to his favor. Not only would he and his army have no complicity with the coming barbaric slaughter of hostages, which could benefit the French if the battles of Jerusalem and Damascus went badly for them, but he now had a promise, in return for helping some hostages escape, that the French fiefdom of Tripoli and all lands and castles north to Antioch would not be put under siege, or otherwise challenged in Saladin's lifetime.

Tripoli would then serve as the exclusive port of Muslim trade with the West, a protected city, with the French earning an enormous fortune every year from contracts with Genoese or Venetian merchant sea traders, depending on who paid the highest tariff to the King of France. A restocked treasury containing such wealth could easily mean the difference in waging and winning future battles against the English, of which he was certain there would be many, until they were pushed off the continent entirely.

The urgent rapping at his bedroom door interrupted his wine-induced daydreams of victory and empire, greatly irritating him. "Yes! Yes! What is it?" he yelled at the noise.

"I'm sorry to disturb, Sire," said an intimidated royal guard, his voice muted by the massive door between them, "but the Knight Gerard presses that it's urgent to see thee immediately, Sire." There was desperation in the guard's words.

"Send him in, then!" Philip said, forcing himself up on the end of the bed as Gerard entered in a rush.

Gerard was so agitated he forgot the royal address and just blurted out the shocking news he brought, "Godfrey's been arrested!"

Slaughter

Chapter V

Michael waited anxiously for the sun to begin its final descent and bring the twilight that would send him walking toward the Templar fortress and his meeting with Henri.

He had told Baints about what Henri had told him to do. Baints didn't say much, but he could tell the elder man was concerned. Most of the others, except Portius Bundage and Mighty Morgan, were away from the camp. It was the cousins' turn as sentries, so they had stayed close by.

"Be vigilant, lad. Things feel disturbed tonight," Baints said to Michael as darkness began to settle and he was about to set out.

"Worry not, Baints. I'll not be long," Michael said with a boyish smile toward his unsettled and concerned friend. He moved into the courtyard path between the now-empty market stalls.

Sunset became twilight, then faded to night, seeming to happen more suddenly in the desert, along with the transformation from the oppressive heat of day to a remarkable coldness that brought a person to shivers. Michael thought about this as he walked toward the Templar fortress area. There was little activity in the Muslim rooms he moved past under the outer wall. An occasional candle spilled light into the courtyard walkway, but most Muslims retired for the night immediately after their evening prayers. The moon had yet to rise, but when it did, since it had become cloudy with the setting sun, it would be blocked and not cast the shadows that gave the courtyards, fortress walls, castle, all of Acre, an eerie, foreboding atmosphere at night. At the same time, it would become so dark he'd almost need a torch to see.

He had barely crossed from the end of the Muslim living and market area to what he thought was the beginning of the Templar corridor when he heard Henri call to him in a hushed voice. He looked to his left under the wall and saw Henri quickly show himself and move back into the darkness. Michael moved directly toward where Henri had been and felt a hand grab him and pull him into the darkness.

"We've not much time, Michael," said a heavily accented voice that was not Henri's, and it took only a moment to realize it was Henri's lord and knight, Gerard.

"My-my Lord, wha—", Michael stammered but was instantly interrupted by Gerard.

"Listen carefully. Your lord, Godfrey, has been arrested and will be executed tomorrow morning," Gerard said in hushed, halting English.

"What? Why—How—"

"Calm thyself and listen," Gerard whispered harshly.

Michael quieted, but his mind was racing.

"I need you, and the archers you trust, to help me secure Godfrey's escape. I have a plan in mind, but it cannot succeed without English involved. Are there those among your company, thyself included, who would risk all to save your lord?"

Michael still couldn't comprehend what Gerard had so suddenly told him. For the first time, he became aware of Henri's presence.

"Our knight came to me, because he knew of our friendship, wanting to arrange to meet you and your sergeant. I told him I had already planned to bid you a proper farewell this night," Henri explained solemnly.

Michael's eyes had adjusted somewhat to the darkness, and he could see the forms that were Gerard and Henri.

"Why has this happened?" Michael asked, unable to decide what he would or could do, and unsure of speaking for the other archers. He needed to know more of what had happened, to buy some time to think.

"Godfrey, your lord and my friend, resisted the vow from your king to slaughter all Saracens, at first light, including women and children."

"Slaughter them . . . but why?" Michael asked in shock.

"It matters not. Your king has vowed it will be done," Gerard said with finality.

"We are going to help the women and children escape after midnight," Henri added with pride.

"You, Henri?" Michael said, even more confused.

"Yes, my friend. Although I hate the Saracen more than most, I never vowed to kill innocents, or even the unarmed," Henri said with determination in his voice. Michael was stunned to silence, desperately trying to think.

Gerard spoke.

"King Philip never made or agreed to such a vow. It is he who has commanded us to help the innocents escape such an abomination to the God that walked this ground, and why I ordered my company to move from your camp. Our king will provide sanctuary and protect you all when we get to Tripoli, then to France. Will you and others help to save the life of your knight?"

Michael looked up at the French knight's scarred face that was furrowed with concern. It appeared even more intimidating with its rigid determination accentuated in fixed eyes and clenched jaw.

Michael still had a dazed look in his eyes from the incomprehensible turn of events.

"Will you help, lad?" Gerard sternly pressed him, impatient with Michael's lack of response.

"We must—we, we have to save our knight and lord."

"Go back to your camp," Gerard began, with a firm grip now on Michael's shoulder. "Seek out those you trust above all others, but not too large a group, and tell them of what I've revealed to you. Then, when only one of the two torches at the entrance of the Templar fortress still burns, move in the dark shadows along the outer wall and, carefully, one at a time, enter through the open doorway. Pack for travel, but only necessaries. Bring all bows and quivers."

Gerard pointed at the entrance a short distance away. "I will meet you there and tell you details of how you will assist me. Do you understand?"

It finally began to dawn on Michael exactly what was being asked of him and the other archers—*treason*! But what of their lord and knight, Godfrey? How could they not go to his aid in his most desperate time of need? Did they not pledge their fealty, swear a holy oath on their very lives to God, and vow to serve their knight without reservation or exception?

Michael's devotion transcended even oaths and vows, for his feelings were far more personal. He truly loved and admired Godfrey, as he imagined a son would love a courageous yet gentle and kind father. He would not be capable of ignoring the plight of Godfrey, no matter what peril to life or limb might await him, or what act he must commit, no matter the manner others would view it, in this case, treason against a king. But this most assuredly would mean never seeing England, his mother, his beloved Lady Mary again, if they even survived the consequences of what lay ahead! What, then, of his own dreams of winning knighthood on the field of battle at the siege of Jerusalem or Damascus? God Almighty, what reasons did He have for him to so suddenly be faced with decisions beyond his humble intellect? For the first time in his life, he felt fear of the kind that made him weak and eager to run away and hide like a coward. His knees began to tremble, and his insides churned.

"Michael. Michael!" Gerard repeated urgently and shook his shoulder, having received no response from the young archer, who was paralyzed with uncertainty.

"Will you do what I ask?" Gerard pressed, concern rising in his voice over Michael's continued silence.

There was only one among them who would know what they should do, Baints. At this thought, Michael finally answered, "Yes, my lord, I will." His voice rasped through the fear-induced dryness in his throat.

"Michael, you above all are Godfrey's most trusted and greatly admired by him. He told me that often in talks of our companies. I sense you can convince others."

The weakness Michael felt began to abate with Gerard's words, although he knew he was wrong. He couldn't convince the others. But Baints could.

"I will do my best, my lord."

"Hurry off, then, but don't run. And, remember, watch for one torch only with flame."

"I will," was all that Michael said, and immediately turned and hurried away.

His focus now was on getting to Baints with this news as fast as possible. It was a burden he could not bear alone for long. What decisions they faced. The wisdom of a Solomon was needed now. Only Baints among them could fill that role.

"Merciless bastard! Damn The Lionheart to the fires of hell!" Baints spewed a short time later, in a voice barely contained to a hard, whispered tone. Michael was shocked by the vehemence of Baints's sudden anger and treasonous insult, further taken aback as spittle flew from his lips as he cursed the king.

"Kings, popes, nobles, bishops—damn them all! They are the very scourge of the earth, more so than any plague of fever that has ever afflicted humankind."

Baints's face was red with anger, the yelling he was forced to restrain leaving his features almost purple. Michael wasn't sure what to do. Baints saw his consternation. "Apologies, lad—could not contain myself. Go on now, please. Continue."

Baints then listened as an even more apprehensive Michael somberly relayed all that Gerard had told him. Michael was surprised by how quickly a calm concentration replaced Baints's flare of anger, an intensity of which he'd never seen in him before. He never once interrupted him again as he continued relaying what Gerard had told him, and what he felt was the most shocking news and gravest situation he ever heard. He respected Baints's judgment above all others, and it was a respect that had grown over the years. Baints was his mentor, his best friend, and although old enough to be his father, their relationship was more that of equals, of older and younger brothers.

Next to Godfrey, Baints was the smartest person he knew. And even though Baints would have never referred to himself as educated, Michael gradually realized over the years that he was. Baints could read and had taught him to do so. Most of the archers couldn't. He could speak French, which he said he learned when he served in the Holy Land before the fall of Jerusalem. He had just found out he had a basic understanding of Arabic. Baints knew and possessed the skills of survival. He understood nature and weather, which he said his deceased, seafaring brother had taught him. He knew more about making medicines and healing potions than most.

Although Baints once told him, after uncharacteristically drinking far too much during a spell of malaise, that he wished he could have done something to save his wife and three children, who died of the pestilence before his eyes, while he had somehow survived the grip of the same fever. Years later, a second wife and baby had died tragically while he was away, when the thatched roof of their cottage caught fire during the night and collapsed on them before they could get out. Baints possessed wisdom, and it was readily evident to anyone who knew him. It filled his eyes, eyes that could have reflected only sadness and loneliness, brought by the tragic circumstances that had befallen him, but instead, reflected wisdom born of hardened experience and utter honesty.

Baints responded the moment it was clear that Michael had finished. "We must prepare immediately to do what is necessary. Godfrey is our lord, and more than that, our friend. We cannot stand by and let him die."

The absoluteness, determination, and utter calmness in Baints's voice put Michael at ease and lifted the enormous weight of indecision he felt. Baints had no doubt about what they must do, and even though it may ultimately lead to their death, Michael still felt relief in the certainty of their action.

Together, they identified those in the company whose loyalty to Godfrey was such that they would lay down their lives if necessary to protect him, just as they themselves would. They quickly woke them or found them about and, after the shock of their news abated, and the flurry of excited questions were answered, they took them into their complete confidence about what Gerard had told them, and where they were to meet.

Portius Bundage and Mighty Morgan were standing sentry duty nearby, so they had gotten to them first. They found Whittler Will and Basil Martin in the gambling tent next to their compound. They woke Cletis Merriman, who was fast asleep in the archers' tent, and he told them that Two-String Jack was down at the pleasure dens on the coast, having won some money gambling earlier. After Merriman was told the news, he immediately offered to go and find his friend and bring him back. They might need his skills, and there was no question of his loyalty to Godfrey, he passionately assured Baints and Michael.

This was the group they decided on, the individuals they could trust without question. Including themselves, they were eight. *Would that be enough?* Michael wondered. Gerard had said the group should not be too large. What did that mean, exactly? He should have thought to ask. But, as he told Baints, it had been clear to him that Gerard had a definite plan in mind to free Godfrey, and incredibly, somehow, also help hundreds of Muslim women and children escape undetected as well.

Deep inside himself, though, he began to feel certain he had played the key, although reluctant, role in leading them all to an inglorious traitor's death.

Chapter VI

They had made their way along the wall with their archer packs, long tubular bags on their backs, slung across a shoulder and over their head and an arm. The packs were made of rough sackcloth or heavy linen, with a thin, flat leather strap affixed at one end that tied and adjusted at the bag's other end. An extra, unstrung bow was tied on top. In one hand they carried their other strung bow, with their quivers also looped around their shoulders and chests, hanging at their hips, which, in battle, would be adjusted to fit high on their backs. Some also carried, in their other hand, reed sacks with additional belongings.

Baints had suggested that they pack right away and wait together at the base of the wall near the Templar fortress, rather than have someone stand lookout and then have to come back to get them. Baints also had Michael explain to those in the company left behind that their departure was temporary, and that Godfrey had ordered they move to another part of the city-fortress for an unexplained reason.

They waited in the darkness for well over an hour and noticed more English guards and archers taking up positions on the ramparts on both the inner and outer walls. Baints estimated that it was past midnight when one of the torches was finally extinguished.

One by one, they entered the fortress foyer as instructed. Gerard was there to meet them, and they passed the French royal guards without much attention. Once they were all assembled, Gerard led them into a large room, to the right of the foyer that originally had been one of the fortress's chapels, and had been converted to a temporary place of worship with a makeshift cedar altar at one end.

He led them to a far corner of the room, where, piled on a table, were tunics and head and neck hoods of the type worn by knights. On close examination, Michael noticed that the white Crusader cross of the English had been hurriedly stitched over the original red cross of the French. Baints pointed out to him that Gerard also wore one.

"Leave your belongings here, and put these on now," Gerard said, holding up a tunic. He continued as they dressed, with Baints helping to clarify words or sentences for the frowning, head-shaking archers when the French knight's thick accent and rapid speech were not understood.

"We will approach and enter the palace, where your king is encamped and your knight is being held prisoner. We will appear to be a group of English knights coming back from inspecting defenses outside the castle. It is very late, and a small group of knights should not arouse much interest or notice. We have learned from Saracen servants the room where your knight is being held. We believe only two guard him there. We will surprise and render all guards silent, tie and gag them, and move them out of view. We wish to injure no one. All will be done with stealth.

"Secure one bow on your back under your knight's tunic and take only three arrows, which you can secure in your waist in front, so as not to make noise with movement and draw attention. There should be no need for either, but if we are challenged and alarm is raised, just the display of eight readied bows should be enough to discourage resistance and allow escape back here."

Michael donned his tunic with a great feeling of exhilaration and imagining that his dream of knighthood was being momentarily realized, even though only as pretense. Then, the inflection of Gerard's voice broke the spell of fantasy.

"Below us, as we speak, a multitude of Saracen innocents are silently gathering throughout the vast storerooms there. After we free your lord, together, we will depart through a secret passageway revealed to us by the Caliph and built by him. It leads to the coast and was cleverly used to bring supplies and reinforcements in at night, undetected and hidden by the hills of sand and rock there."

Gerard paused, eyeing the faces of the English archers, which still reflected the lingering shock that the suddenness of unfathomable events had caused.

"Under the cover of both night and the sound of the sea against the shore, we will move with haste along the coast until out of sight of the fortress towers," Gerard said confidently. "We will turn inland then, onto the road to Tyre, where we will eventually meet one of the Saracen patrols and be permitted safe passage to Tripoli."

It all sounded simple enough, thought Michael. He turned to Baints with a questioning look. "Gerard is courageous and a true friend to our lord. He risks everything to rescue him. But to do so without incident will be quite a feat of stealth."

"Aye, lad. I hope Gerard truly knows the lay of things inside the palace," Baints whispered in response.

"The secret passage greatly relieves me, for I could not understand how we could escape through one of the gates," Michael said with great optimism.

"If it is actually secret," Baints answered with a tone of skepticism, bringing a look of apprehension to Michael's face, but he quickly added, "There is great risk, but I also believe God is with us. We are a formidable band, led by a fearless knight. We will succeed."

They were ready, and certainly did look the part of a group of knights, Michael thought. As long as no one looked too close at their leggings and boots, or at their backs, where their bows bulged their tunics noticeably, or observed that only Gerard carried a sword at his hip. But there was no reason for anyone to do so at night. Gerard had also explained that, unless they were challenged by the two guards at the palace entrance, which seemed unlikely, once inside the palace, the dimness of the minimal torchlight there would also provide a measure of protection.

The unknown was how many guards were actually milling about throughout the palace.

They left the Templar fortress and advanced to within twenty paces of the palace entrance. The guards, although alert, did not display any indication of concern or undue attention toward them. The archers tried to emulate the walk and noble bearing of Gerard. Because his French accent was so pronounced, he had asked Baints to speak if conversation became necessary when they neared the guards. Baints agreed, saying he had heard enough nobles speak in his day and could mimic them to the point of comedy.

As the two guards routinely checked each face, they seemed familiar to them, and they relaxed. But as they began to pass the royal guards, before they were through the entrance and could turn and easily disable them, one of the guards did a double-take as he looked up at the huge knight's face and recognized Gerard from Richard's galley.

"Stop!" the guard said uncertainly, lowering his lance and still trying to reconcile the white cross on his tunic with his recognition of Gerard as a French knight. Gerard reacted immediately, rushing him and pushing the lance aside. He grabbed the guard at the throat, while covering his mouth with the other hand.

Instantly, Baints, aided by Michael, did the same with the other guard, who was caught totally by surprise, as Portius Bundage moved to help Gerard. Baints and Michael struggled with the frantic and larger of the two guards, until Baints pulled his dagger and hit him twice on the head with the hilt, rendering the royal retainer unconscious. They quickly tied him up.

Gerard's size and strength easily overwhelmed the other guard, and Gerard and Bundage quickly had the guard tied and gagged with strips of his own tunic. Gerard duplicated Baints's action by knocking him unconscious with his sword hilt.

The others had reacted immediately, catching the guards' weapons before they hit the stone floor, and grabbing the guards' legs to minimize their struggles. The disabled guards were carried into the foyer area and carefully laid in the dark shadow of a corner.

The group remained perfectly quiet and motionless, difficult to discern if the disturbance aroused anyone else. The altercation, although unexpected, hadn't caused much noise, so Gerard felt confident they were still undetected. After a few anxious moments, they were reassured with the absence of hurried footsteps or yelled inquiries, although Gerard knew there were other sentries patrolling throughout the palace and guarding the hallways and rooms of the king and nobles.

Gerard's concern now was the absence of guards at the entrance and finding a more concealed place to leave the ones they had tied and gagged. They just had to hope no other knights or nobles entered the palace for a while, which was reasonable considering the hour.

As far as the guards were concerned, Two-String Jack noticed that the area to the left of the massive stone staircase in the center of the hall, directly off the foyer in front of them, was in deep shadow and shielded from the light of torches positioned primarily off the second-floor balcony. The hallways that connected off on either side of the stairway were also poorly lit. They could hide the guards without much chance of discovery should someone enter or leave the palace. Gerard agreed, and they carefully moved them to the side of the stairway.

"Baints," Gerard whispered as loud as he could to get his attention. Baints heard him and turned from watching for movement in the hallway, moving next to Gerard.

"Leave a man steady of nerve, equally skillful to wound as kill, here in the shadow with bow at the ready, to cover us if threatened when we return. Have the two men best with a blade wear the guards' swords."

Baints nodded and motioned at Bundage. "Portius, stay here, string your bow. Michael, Cletis, waist the guards' swords."

Mighty Morgan helped Bundage remove his bow from his back, while Michael and Cletis donned the guards' belts and scabbards. Bundage was the logical one to remain because of his limp, but he was also the most lethal against moving targets. Gerard moved them out from the stairway shadows and reminded them they were knights, and that they were to act as such, and walk slowly, casually.

As they ascended the stairway, the footsteps of a sentry was heard walking one of the hallways. The group stopped, but Gerard motioned them to keep going.

"The room in which they hold your knight is down the hallway to the far right," Gerard whispered to Baints. "Stay at my side now, so I can direct all just through you."

"Aye, my lord," Baints answered immediately, just as he would if it was Godfrey giving him orders, now completely comfortable with the French knight.

They continued up the stairs and into view of the sentry walking casually toward them from the center hallway, as another sentry walked in the opposite direction. The sentry took notice of them but did not appear alarmed in any way, just as Gerard predicted.

At the end of this hallway was another stairway that led up into the royal suite of rooms where King Richard slept, and where a contingent of royal guards were also on duty. Gerard raised a hand in casual acknowledgment, and the sentry returned it. They turned to the right and soon passed another hallway of rooms, where, at the far end, in the faint shadows of the dimly-lit corridor, a lone sentry walked away from them down the hall.

Gerard led them to the last hallway, where he had been told he could find the room where Godfrey was being held and guarded. Gerard stopped the group just before the hallway entrance and carefully peered around the corner. There were two sentries walking in opposite directions, and midway down the corridor on the left, two royal guards sat on cushioned benches with swords at the ready, in front of the room where Gerard was sure Godfrey was being held.

"This is it," Gerard whispered to Baints at his elbow. "But there are four, two sentries and two royal guards. We must approach quickly enough to be in position to take them all in the same swift moment, two of us to each, without arousing others. Match them up now."

Baints nodded, motioned for the others to gather around him, and whispered the plan to them. He assigned the pairs, with Michael assigned to him. Moments later he tapped Gerard's shoulder, "Ready, my lord."

Gerard led the way down the corridor. They were immediately sighted by the one sentry walking toward them. His look was curious but not threatening. Gerard raised a hand in greeting. He waved back, but hesitantly, unsure why a group of knights were in the corridor at such a late hour. Their footsteps immediately attracted the attention of the royal guards at the door, and the other sentry, who turned, then stopped. The guards rose as they approached.

Baints spoke in explanation of reassurance to buy them time, while closing the distance between them. "We've come to bid farewell to our fellow knight, treasonous though he is," Baints said in a perfect mimicry of a well-bred noble.

The gap closed further.

The guard closest to them spoke. "The prisoner is to have no visitors, by order of the king." They slowed at this, but kept moving closer.

"Thoust say that a Crusader Knight will not have benefit of a priestly visit and the last rights before meeting the Almighty?" Baints responded cleverly.

The other guard answered, "Nay, a priest will administer to him just before first light."

The first guard appeared to Baints to have sensed something was amiss and was becoming nervous. Gerard noticed this too, and as the guard slowly brought his sword up into a ready position, Gerard leapt forward with the quickness of an animal. The guard was surprised, and Gerard's weight took him against the door and down to the floor before he could even use his sword in any way. Whittler Will grabbed his legs as Gerard rendered him unconscious with a fist to the jaw.

Simultaneously, Michael and Baints took down the other shocked guard. Baints wrested the sword from the guard's hand after Michael disabled him with a blow to the stomach. Gerard sprang back up and moved to undo the metal bolt on the door. Mighty Morgan and Two-String Jack easily disarmed, tied, and gagged the sentry closest to them, but Cletis Merriman and Basil Martin had a harder time with the sentry farthest from them, down the corridor. He had his lance ready when the archers ran to him, stopping them in their tracks, and was able to repeatedly call out for help. Merriman pulled his sword, but was no match for the guard's expert use of the lance.

Gerard pushed the door open and burst into Godfrey's room, only to find another royal guard with a sword at the throat of Godfrey. Their knight's hands were bound behind him, with his head pulled back by his hair, held in the other hand of the guard. Gerard skidded to a stop on the polished stone floor.

"Advance and I'll execute the traitor now!" the guard said.

"Do so and I promise pain that will have you screaming for death until mute," Gerard said as he slowly unsheathed his sword.

Godfrey was wide-eyed with shock. He forced out words.

"Please, leave now, while you can still save yourselves."

"Not without you, my friend," Gerard said resolutely.

In the background, they heard the sounds of the scuffle with the last sentry finally end with an agonizing shriek, followed by an abrupt silence.

In the very next moment Gerard saw the eyes of the guard in front of him go wide, as did Godfrey's. Seemingly within the same instant, a buzz whizzed by Gerard's ear, and an arrow suddenly appeared in the center of the guard's forehead, simultaneous with the sound of a bone-piercing crack and dull thud. The guard and his expression seemed frozen in time, his eyes wide, his mouth agape, and the sword in his hand still at Godfrey's throat. In the next instant he collapsed in a heap, his sword dropping and banging loudly against the stone floor.

Gerard turned and saw what Godfrey continued to stare at, Michael in the doorway, still holding his bow extended, his right hand and fingers back at his ear.

"This is madness," Godfrey said with genuine agony, in a hoarse voice. Michael's arms dropped, and his head slumped. He had killed a royal guard of King Richard to save his lord. Not only was he a traitor, he was now a murderer in the eyes of his sovereign and country.

It was clear to Gerard what they had to do, and do fast. The last guard had yelled an alarm while they tried to subdue him outside Godfrey's room, and it was certain to have been heard. Gerard quickly cut Godfrey's hands free.

Godfrey turned from Michael to Gerard. "I was prepared to meet God with a clear conscience and be judged by Him. Why have you risked everything for me? Why?"

"I had to find out if-if they had suspicions, if they tortured you and learned of our plan," Gerard admitted reluctantly, then added, "and to save you."

Godfrey's eyes widened, and he nodded in understanding. "Be assured, they know nothing. I challenged Richard to renounce his vow. In anger, he ordered me to lead the executions. I refused. Enraged to the point of seizure, he ordered I would be the first to die."

There was relief in Gerard's expression, but also profound respect for the conviction of this truly noble English knight who had become his friend.

"You will not die this day, my friend."

Baints called to them from the hallway in an urgent voice. "Others are coming, my lords!"

"Michael, give me your sword," Godfrey said with authority, as if he'd decided something. Michael did as commanded, and they moved out of the room into the hall, where the others were. There, they saw Merriman, his left arm bloody, being bandaged by Whittler Will with a piece he had ripped off of his tunic. The guard lay dead against the wall, a huge pool of blood next to his slumping body, a dagger in his throat. It had been thrown by Will in desperation. The other guard and sentry lay still on the floor, tied and gagged. Will looked up at Gerard and Godfrey.

"I did not want to kill him, but he almost ran Cletis through."

"Never mind now," Gerard said, and picked up Merriman's sword. He now had one in each hand, and looked for Baints, who had gone to the end of the corridor to join Basil Martin, their lookout. Baints looked back and waved urgently for them to come. Godfrey helped Merriman to his feet and felt mentally clear now, and, to Gerard's relief, a fierce determination showed in his expression as he led the way down the corridor.

They reached Baints quickly, and he explained the situation to the two knights as the archers readied their bows behind them.

"Bundage wounded two guards with well-placed shots. They don't know he only has one arrow left, so they are reluctant to continue until they are reinforced. I fear royal archers have joined them. Martin here got the one guard coming out of the hallway opposite us. He appears mortally wounded. I feel it best we make a run for it now, and deal with whoever hides in the corridors on the run. Every moment we delay—"

"Let's go," Godfrey interrupted decisively. Gerard nodded in agreement, and the two knights led the way. The entire group left the hallway on the run to the stairway.

As they passed the first hallway, three guards moved out of doorways to challenge them, but when the archers drew down on them, they dived back in.

"Baints! Have someone protect our backsides!" Gerard called out, as they finished passing the occupied corridor.

"Martin, cover our exit! Shoot only if you have a sure shot."

"Aye, Baints. Only have two arrows left, though." Baints, his own bow at the ready with an arrow strung, reached under his tunic and gave him one of his extra arrows. They continued on and stopped just before the wider center hallway.

"We have to get archers on the other side to cover us if they have archers there," Gerard said to Godfrey and Baints.

"I agree," said Godfrey.

Baints nodded his agreement.

"Get two ready to cross over," Ge'ard instructed. "I'll draw their first volley, and they'll dart across before they re-string."

Baints motioned to Michael and Whittler Will.

"Michael, Will, get ready, lads, to dive across. Protect your bows, hold ye arrows."

The pair positioned themselves with a running start, bows in one hand, arrows in the other, so they wouldn't accidentally stab themselves when they dove.

Gerard then stepped into the corridor, and just as quickly, dove back toward them. Two arrows from anxious royal archers whizzed past, just as he had guessed, and bounced off the stone wall opposite the stairway. They dropped harmlessly to the floor below, giving Bundage two more precious arrows.

Before the arrows had even hit the wall, Michael and Will had begun their dives and slides to the other side. They made it without incident.

"We're going down to the entrance now. Don't let them take aim," Godfrey said to Michael and Will. "Then dive down the steps, and we'll cover the hallway for you from the entrance." Michael and Will nodded their heads. Godfrey looked at Gerard, and both looked at Baints and the others. All nodded they were ready.

"Go!" Godfrey yelled, and they made a mad dash down the stairway. The moment the royal archers showed themselves, Michael and Will had them sighted. Michael put an arrow through the shoulder of the archer on the right, whose arrow shot upward harmlessly into the wooden ceiling. Will's shot caught the other archer in the chest because he moved out too far, and he never even released his arrow. Immediately, the two archers dove for the stairs and purposely tumbled their length, gladly suffering the bumps and bruises to keep their bodies low and free of other archers' arrows.

In the next moment, all hell broke loose. The balcony erupted in counterattack as royal archers and guards rushed in from the center hallway. The palace archers hurried to positions behind the balcony facade railing to begin raining arrows down on all caught in the open below.

Michael and Will were just getting up to run to the entrance. Bundage saw what was happening. "Baints! Help!" he called out to the others as he shot two archers targeting the pair, but not before the first one got off a shot that hit Will in his right side, sending him sprawling to the floor in agony. The second one got his arrow off just before Bundage's shaft went clear through the middle of his chest, killing him instantly, but fortunately, it pulled the shot, sending it buzzing past Michael's head.

Bundage hit a third target on the run at the top of the stairs, as Baints and the others fanned out. Michael, and even the wounded Will, also notched arrows, and, together, they put on a swift and stunning display of lethal marksmanship. They unleashed a volley that took down five more royal archers in a single instant, and quickly scattered the remaining attackers. This gave them the moment they needed to turn and run out the entrance into the protective darkness.

They continued on the run toward the fortress, as planned. Michael soon noticed that Will was slowing and doubling over in pain.

"Will, are you—" Michael began to say.

Will quickly interrupted to assure him, "Not serious. Just through flesh."

Basil Martin pulled his friend's arm around his neck to help him move faster.

"Keep going!" Gerard urgently called out in as low a tone as he could and still be heard. He led them to the shadows along the inner wall to avoid the archers on top.

"Count off your arrows!" Baints called out twice in a muffled voice as they ran. Bundage reported none left, Two-String Jack, Cletis Merriman, and Basil Martin had one each, and Mighty Morgan had two. Baints had none and held out his hand to Morgan, who gave him one. Then he told Martin to give his to Michael and just concentrate on helping Will get back to the fortress.

"Those with arrows pair off and cover us in retreat turns. Stay close to the wall," Godfrey ordered, and the archers with arrows did so. It was a simple procedure with two archers stopping, turning, and readying their bows to stop pursuers, with two others ahead of them repeating the process, and so on, until they reached their destination, with their retreat covered all the way.

It didn't take long for their pursuers to emerge in force from the palace entrance, led by two royal knights, and take up the chase. They yelled for the guards on the walls to wake up and help. Two arrows from Michael and Baints, now taking their turn providing cover, hit their marks. Two more royal archers went down, and the others scattered to either wall or dropped to the ground. The archers on the walls were confused by the shouts from below and could not really see anything clearly, and so never became a factor in the pursuit.

One more volley from Two-String and Merriman, both of which also hit their marks, delayed their pursuers enough so they made it through the entrance of the Templar fortress with only Mighty Morgan's arrow left.

The English royal knights and their archers and footmen made it to the Templar entrance moments later. They were told by a French knight—who was backed by a reinforced guard contingent inside the entrance—that the group they pursued had continued on past them into the darkened stalls of the market area. The English knights were unconvinced, but after a tense standoff, they realized they could do nothing more. The English knights sent a small force on down toward the market area, just to make sure, and then led the rest of their men angrily away, back toward the palace.

Chapter VII

Inside the foyer and main hall, Philip's royal guards and archers had taken up positions in case of confrontation with English pursuers. Gerard quickly moved the group to the room where they had first assembled. Gerard's entire company of archers and footmen were among those gathered, and they cheered when he entered with Godfrey and the English archers. Henri excitedly greeted Michael, and the two embraced. Baints and Basil Martin carefully carried Whittler Will in and were directed by DuClaire to set him on one of the empty tables, where Will was immediately attended to by one of King Philip's own physicians.

Baints and Basil Martin held their friend in place, who now bit down on a thick piece of leather strap, and watched as the skillful surgeon scored the arrow sticking through Will's side with a knife at both ends, broke each off, and pulled the remaining shaft out. Will's bloody wound was cleaned as best it could be. The royal physician stuffed the opening with a type of yellow moss he pulled out in clumps from a leather pouch. He had Will chew the moss before he inserted it into the wound, explaining to him that a person's own saliva aided in healing. Will's face seemed to contort more from chewing the foul-tasting herb than it had when the arrow shaft was pulled out. Fortunately, no arteries were affected, blood loss was minimal, and Baints whispered a prayer to himself that the gaping but clean wound wouldn't become infected.

The physician then examined Merriman's arm wound, poured water over it, cleaned it, and had Cletis chew the same moss, which was applied over the wound before it was rebandaged.

While Baints was busy with Will, Michael sat down against a wall to rest and drink water, and while doing so, he surveyed the room. He noticed Gerard and Godfrey conferring intently with a French royal knight and saw that the French archers also wore knightly tunics, but with a red cross on the front and back of theirs. Michael noticed too that Robere was off by himself, as usual, and still looked as sickly and pale as he had in camp and on the boat.

He knew from Henri's comments that Robere was treated almost as an outcast by the French archers, especially DuClaire. The grandson of the renowned French knight DuMont of Cluremaise had been orphaned as a child. Robere's parents, and the majority of those living in nearby villages, had died of a virulent fever that swept the countryside when he was away with his grandparents.

They had taken him, their only grandchild, to the warmth of the southern Frankish lands, seeking treatment for the nine-year-old boy's chronic cough and fatigue. Robere had grown tall, but remained unusually thin and pale. His manner was noticeably effeminate, but under the loving and understanding tutelage of his grandfather, the old knight, Robere had become an archer with astounding accuracy within fifty paces, but because of his slight build, he lacked the strength to be consistently effective at longer distances. Michael, with Baints's assistance as interpreter, had tried to engage the young man in casual talk, but found him unresponsive and distrustful of even the most innocent of advances.

Michael's attention moved to Gesault the Mason, pacing nervously, talking to himself as usual, and seeming more agitated than normal, periodically gripped with the compulsion to cross himself as many as a hundred times in succession unless interrupted, which some believed was evidence of possession by the Holy Spirit. The youngest son in a family of masons, Gesault had become an archer instead of following in the family trade, but the name stuck with him, even though he never cut nor laid one piece of stone in his life. He was the best shot on the run Michael had ever seen, and even bested DuClaire at moving trick shots.

Gesault was average in height, but a lack of a visible neck—his head seemed fitted directly to his shoulders—gave the impression of a much shorter appearance. A misshapen mouth and chin, combined with his mumbling and compulsions, gave him a fearful appearance, although he was actually very kindhearted, religious to the extreme, and was always first to lend a helping hand.

The others all looked apprehensive and serious, even Henri, who was now intently reworking the stitching on one of his boots, and Michael realized that the night's adventure was just starting for the French, and was still far from over for them. Moments later, having had hardly enough time to catch their breath, Gerard called all to readiness.

"Quickly gather up your packs! Wear them over your knightly tunics. It's to our advantage we all appear as knights. You will be given your skins of water in the storerooms below where we proceed now."

Gerard and Godfrey led them out into the main hall and to a small corridor that led to an area behind the main stairway, where a small, circular stairway connected, which led to huge subterranean storerooms. They descended by torchlight, and Michael counted over thirty stairs before they reached another corridor that took them into a storeroom, where they began to hear muffled voices and the cries of babies.

Gradually, their torches revealed the presence of the nearly three hundred Saracen innocents, including the Caliph and his entire family and Salah, and the families of two of his nephews, who were officers in the garrison. His nephews, of course, chose to remain with their men, even though they knew it most likely meant certain death. The fear and desperation covering the faces of the innocents was reflected in the torchlight. Thankfully, many of the children remained asleep in the arms of their mothers.

As Michael passed the huddled group, he thought he saw among them in the torchlight the child who had run out in front of him, awake and wide-eyed and being held by the girl whose remarkable beauty had been revealed to him by accident. The eyes above the veil were hers, he was sure, and they locked on his as he walked past with a look he was also sure had initially gone wide with surprise.

Salah immediately approached Gerard and Godfrey.

"I am greatly relieved your rescue was successful," Salah said with genuine sincerity to Godfrey.

"The important thing is, our plan remains secret," Gerard responded. He added with great pride, "Godfrey refused The Lionheart's command to lead the executions at dawn and was willing to be the first to go under the sword as a result."

Salah was visibly moved by this news and took Godfrey's right hand into his own.

"Allah will reward your noble action. I thank you and your archers for helping innocents, and still pray your king relents."

Godfrey shook his head. "Your desperate plight is ours now. We have no choice but to flee with you to survive my king's madness," Godfrey answered as the Caliph put his hand on Salah's shoulder, signaling they must go.

"The Caliph will show you the underground passage to the sea. Follow him. I will remain to calm the others, until it is safe to continue on," Salah said urgently.

Gerard turned to Godfrey. "We will proceed first with our archers and footmen and secure the beach ahead of the others. Leave any extra sacks or belongings here, and they will be brought forward by the women."

They followed the Caliph to the farthest corner of the storeroom. "Usually this space is filled so full it would be difficult to move through unimpeded," the Caliph said as they moved through the vast cavern quickly. Once they reached the end, the Caliph pointed to and then traced with his finger a section of the wall.

"If your strongest could assist, we will push on this section of block to open the passageway," the Caliph said in French, surprising Godfrey and confirming his earlier suspicion from their first meeting in the tent, that he could understand their conversations with Salah.

Godfrey summoned Mighty Morgan, who joined Gerard and himself, and together, they pushed on the precise part of the stone wall the Caliph had indicated and, as if by sorcery, a large section, over ten feet in length, pivoted open. Godfrey and the Caliph immediately entered, and their torches revealed a passageway large enough to accommodate the largest of wheeled carts, even beasts of burden laden with provisions.

Gerard called to all the bowmen and footmen, "Archers, string your bows and gather here. Men-at-arms, ready your lance, unsheathe your sword, and join with us. We shall all go through first and secure the beach area in advance of those we lead."

Gerard and Godfrey led them at a near run the length of the long passageway, the sooty smoke from their torches hanging in the air against the ceiling. They were surprised at how long they traveled before they reached the end. When they finally arrived, a fatigued Caliph pointed to the rings of iron embedded in the twin wooden beam doors of the exit, with two massive timbers wedged against them. He explained they had to lift the log barriers out of the way, put them up into the areas carved in the stone walls, then pull the doorway of stone toward them to open it. He explained further that before doing so, they had to put all the torches out, except one, to be extinguished just before the door was completely opened.

Godfrey, Baints, Gerard, Michael, Henri, and DuClaire proceeded to implement the Caliph's instructions. When they pulled the doors partially open, with the help of Mighty Morgan, sand spilled in behind them, obviously used to hide the entrance on the beach. The pent-up sand wall continued spilling in as the doors were pulled farther open. Simultaneously, they felt the rush of cooler air, heavy with humidity, and were instantly aware of the smell of the nighttime sea and the sound of waves spilling onto the beach.

Henri immediately put out the last torch. The doors were pulled completely back. Bows at the ready, Michael, Duclaire, Baints, and Henri, together with the small company of footmen and other archers behind them, were led out by Godfrey and Gerard over the huge mound of sand at the entrance and across the adjoining dune, then finally, onto the beach. With drawn swords, the two knights served as vigilant sentries as they moved as far out onto the beach as they could. Enveloped by the darkness of night, the archers carefully fanned out, with each succeeding pair of archers moving farther outward to cover the next pair who emerged from the secret passageway. The footmen took up positions behind the archers, ready to move in front of them if attacked close in. The outline of sand dunes and beach were barely visible, but became more distinguishable as their eyes adjusted to moonlight made faint by clouds.

The deployment was completed without incident. Once all of the Crusaders had taken up defensive positions, Gerard sent one footman back to bring out the first of the Saracens, while Godfrey took Michael and Baints on a reconnaissance of the shore route they would take to the northeast. After a short distance, Baints held up his hand to stop them.

"My lord, I-I suggest extreme vigilance and—"

They stopped. Baints had Godfrey's full attention. "What troubles thee, Baints?"

"I fear for unexpected patrols, or even unknown encampments much farther out than we could check, especially on the other side of these hills, of which we are woefully ignorant. There will be much noise when the entire group proceeds here. Babies and children are not silent by nature. We could rouse detection without knowing, only to confront a larger, alerted force when we finally turn inland."

Godfrey had listened with serious interest that conveyed the respect he had for Baints, whose intelligence and advice he'd come to value greatly since the death of his longtime sergeant, Thomas Curry.

"What is it you would do, Baints?"

"Have Michael here strip down to jerkin and shirt to ensure stealth"—Michael looked up in surprise—"since the lad is exceptionally swift of foot, and he can quickly cover a far greater area than we can together. Have him run far ahead, two hundred paces, then turn inland and return along the base of the hills, where he would be hard to detect in the dark shadows. He would run an equal pace, then turn back to the sea, staying low over the hills to avoid showing profile, and end up back here to report."

"That is a wise plan, Baints. You stay here for Michael's return. I'll go back and tell Gerard of what we do and briefly delay the assembly of the innocents on the beach."

Michael handed Baints his bow, then took off his pack, quivers, water skin, and tunic, anything that would slow him, make noise, or flap in the wind. Michael was ready to run, and Baints put his hand on his shoulder, his role now as sergeant rather than friend.

"When you turn inland to the other side of the hills, rub earth on your arms and face to darken them, and . . . and if-if, by chance, you are detected—" Michael understood and cut him off.

"Don't worry, I won't be, but if so, I will lead them astray." Michael didn't give Baints a chance to say anything further and was instantly on the run along the beach and disappeared into the night. Baints said a silent prayer for the brave lad's return and put Michael's bow and quivers around his head and arm to be ready to move quickly and still draw string if necessary.

Michael ran as fast as he could in the soft sand of the beach, counting off his strides as he went. He could have run faster without his boots, but he would need them when he turned inland and ran along the base of the rock-strewn limestone hills. His eyes were fully adjusted to the faint moonlight, and he did not detect significant movement or the forms of men, noticing only the scurrying of nocturnal crabs scavenging the beach as he passed near them.

He covered two hundred strides so quickly that he decided to run fifty more for good measure. Quickly done, he turned inland and was slowed considerably as he struggled up and down the adjacent sand dunes, then began to labor on the steep incline of the thin strip of low coastal hills. He stopped halfway up, remembering Baints's suggestion to rub his exposed skin with the strange-colored, reddish-brown granular dirt under his feet, to lessen any reflection from his body should the clouds suddenly allow more moonlight through.

While on his knees cupping soil, spitting into it, then rubbing the semi-mud on his arms, he heard a sound on the other side of the hill farther inland. It was the faint clang of metal against metal. He instantly dropped to the ground and lay prone. He heard more noise, this time metal sliding against metal, the distinctive sound made by a sword being withdrawn from or returned to a scabbard.

Michael rolled over and frantically finished applying the dirt to his face, neck, and arms. He became aware of his rising panic and tried to force calm on his heart, pounding like a fist inside his chest trying to punch its way out. He managed some control over his fear and began slowly inching his way up the hill with his elbows and knees. As he neared the top, he moved even slower, until he was just able to put his head and eyes above the rise.

It took several moments before he discerned the outline of the forms of men-at-arms, with lances and bows at the ready, no more than ten paces to the right of his position. The one detail that stood out, in the faint intermittent moonlight, were the white crosses on their short tunics! He forced his eyes over the hilltop again, to try to get an impression of numbers. What he saw weren't sentries, a small encampment, or a routine patrol, but a force of at least thirty footmen, archers, and knights, and probably far more, ready and waiting in the shadows, waiting to act out a planned ambush, waiting for them! He had to get back to the group, and fast.

Michael cautiously edged his way backward down the hill. He suddenly was aware of how cool the humid coastal air was and felt chilled—or was it fear that gripped him? He stayed even lower now, as he made his way slowly and carefully back over the sand dunes. As much as he wanted to commit every fiber of his muscles into the effort, he had to hold back until he could be sure he was on the beach and in the clear. Once he crossed the crest of a sand dune, he rolled down the other side and repeated the maneuver three times until he reached the beach, where he quickly removed his boots. Gripping them in his hands, he began running, determined to push himself to the absolute limit of his speed.

He emerged out of the darkness so quickly he took the squatting Baints by surprise—even though he'd been eyeing the beach for any trace of movement—and nearly ran over him. Michael saw Baints at the last moment and jumped to avoid him and skidded and tumbled to a stop, dropping his boots, and then scrambled frantically back to his startled friend, gasping for breath as he tried to speak.

"Michael! Lad, what—"

"Baints—oh, God . . . ambush—"

"Ambush? Where? Are they coming? How many?"

Michael shook his head as he coughed and spit up, wheezing noticeably as he desperately tried to catch his breath and speak at the same time.

"They're waiting . . . up ahead . . . behind, behind the hills— too many. There's too many!" Michael forced out the words. His gasps for air began to ease into more normal breaths.

"How many, lad!"

"Many that I could see, but, but there must be more in the shadows beyond my sight. I fear it's a large force," Michael said frantically, his breathing more under control now. "They were stretched a fair distance to where I saw them, and only by providence did I not move right into their midst. They are not in camp or on patrol, but wait ready in arms to charge over the hills. They bear the white cross. They wait for *us*, Baints. They *know* we are coming!"

Baints let the alarm he was holding back inside himself come now. It was the worst possible news. But neither his words nor manner revealed his inward panic. He helped Michael to his feet, then hurriedly pulled the youth's bow and quivers from around his neck and handed them over. Then he pointed to Michael's clothes, pack, and water skin.

"Dress quickly. Remain here to shout the alarm. I must tell the knights to hold the Saracens back until we can decide our course. You did well, lad. Stay vigilant."

Baints was off in a run the short distance back to Godfrey, only to find the two knights with Salah, his relatives, the Caliph and his family, and a long stream of women and children emerging from the passageway onto the beach behind them.

"My lords!" Baints called in a restrained but loud muffled tone as he approached on the run. Godfrey immediately assumed the alarm in Baints's hurried manner and tone was over the congregation swelling onto the beach.

"We decided it was best not to delay and bring them—" Godfrey began to explain, but Baints totally ignored what he was saying and blurted out the shocking news.

"Michael discovered a large force waiting in ambush behind the hills!"

Godfrey was dumbfounded. Gerard was shocked. Salah's eyes closed as if in agony. The Caliph's eyes went wide with horror. Godfrey responded first.

"Are you certain?"

"Yes. Michael was nigh a breath away. And he saw white crosses clearly upon their chests."

"Richard knows!" Godfrey said hatefully, spitting out the words.

"How-how could he!" Gerard exclaimed haltingly, as if in a daze.

It was Salah who recovered first and quickly approached the knights. "We must go south instead."

"How do we know they don't also wait for us that way?" Gerard said, more lucid now.

"We do not, but we've little choice, and there are Muslim encampments to the southwest," Salah answered with the calmness under stress that an experienced diplomat learns to display regardless of circumstance. He continued, "If the English king somehow learned of our exact plan, then he knows we will head northeast to Tripoli. If he has any force to the south, it would be reasonable to assume it is the smaller of the two. In any case, our fate is perilous. We die inside for sure, or take what chance to live there is and die out here."

"The Genoese pleasure tents lie south near the water's edge," responded Godfrey.

"It's late. Only a few drunken lingerers would be left," Gerard interjected. "The Genoese would not impede knights, archers, and footmen and risk destruction of their lucrative den of sin over an affair of no consequence to them."

"My lords," Baints interjected, and he immediately had their attention. "Time runs short. I agree we must go south. I would suggest sending a few lads immediately to scout ahead, especially around the Genoese camp and alert us of treachery, so we can be prepared to fight our way through, which we would most surely have to do."

The two knights nodded in agreement, as did Salah. "Do so immediately, Baints," Godfrey answered.

Baints quickly assembled Mighty Morgan, Bundage, Henri, and DuClaire, explained the desperate situation, reminding them their knightly tunics would no doubt impress the Genoese in any encounter that might arise, and sent them south.

The group on the beach continued to expand around them and became congested and noisy. Gerard turned to the Caliph. "Begin leading them south, so they do not overcrowd here. If an attack comes suddenly, panic here would prevent our archers and footmen from defending properly."

"Salah will lead. The men and I will not be going," the Caliph said.

The knights were shocked.

"Why not? Your family—" Godfrey was cut short.

"They are in your hands now. We have decided we must stay with the others, and I have sons who remain. They are commanders and would not leave their men. It is my fate."

There was a brief moment of silence, but there was no time to ponder or discuss the matter further. Salah embraced the Caliph and his male relatives, who could not on their honor leave, and, together, they gave instructions to the expanding crowd emerging from the passageway. Salah turned and began to lead them south on the beach, along the path the four archers had just taken.

Gerard turned to Godfrey. "We will need to have two archers on the left flank at the base of the hills as we move, and a small force to protect from behind. The rest need to be around the middle, to move in whatever direction attack might spring from."

"I agree, we should—" Godfrey began to reply but didn't get a chance to finish as Michael ran up to them.

Baints had seen him run in and hurried over to listen to what he knew would be urgent news.

"I heard the noise of movement from the other side of the hills. I hurried over the dunes and up a hill and glimpsed over. They are coming this way, my lords," Michael said, trying to hold back panic, his bow in his hands with an arrow readied across it.

"We have to slow them as long as we can," Godfrey said immediately, and turned to Baints and Michael. "Gather the archers left here, and follow me."

Baints didn't say anything. He and Michael hurried away to carry out the order.

"Take the footmen, and Whittler Will. He can still shoot if he's on steady ground," Godfrey said to Gerard. "Begin moving with the Saracens down the beach. We will not be able to save them all. We'll do what we can to delay them and will fall back and join you."

Godfrey didn't wait for an answer as he quickly moved to join Baints and the archers.

Gerard hesitated. The Caliph interrupted in an urgent tone, "He is right. But there's one more thing that must be done now. I will take those that still remain and go north, as they anticipate."

The Caliph immediately went to the passageway and stopped the exit of innocents going south, told the others inside to follow him, and he calmly began to lead this smaller of the two groups north, to almost certain death, but one that would provide the diversion that could mean the others might survive. This galvanized Gerard to action, and he did as Godfrey suggested. Will had already joined him, a trickle of blood noticeable from his side down his leg. Gerard called to the footmen left standing sentry around the entrance area and moved out, becoming the accompanying rear guard of the last of the innocents the Caliph had sent south.

Godfrey, sword unsheathed, led the archers over the dunes toward the hills made up of Baints, Michael, Basil Martin, Two-String, Merriman, Robere, Gesault, and three other French archers, who hesitated at first, then reluctantly agreed when confronted by an angry Baints. Godfrey quickly broke into a run to the hills behind the passageway entrance.

The closer they got to the hills the more noise they heard on the other side. Michael was the first to arrive, and crawled to the top of the hill closest to them and saw footmen, archers, and knights massing for an attack. All bore the white cross on their chests. Godfrey huddled them together and gave the plan. Baints interpreted for the French.

"We'll climb to the top and shoot three volleys. That should cause panic and force a temporary retreat. You know this, but I'll repeat it. Go for the archers first. Spread your shots so you don't hit the same target."

Godfrey looked at the faces of the men as he talked. All were apprehensive, but his men also had looks of profound distress and uncertainty. He was telling them to shoot at their countrymen again. Most had already done so in the palace when they rescued him, but they were being attacked at that time.

"I understand the torment in thy souls, but there is no turning back now. It is the immorality of a king that has placed us here, but you are all skillful, indeed. Aim not to kill, but to render ineffective against us, if possible."

The archers' eyes locked on his. "After you loose your arrows, we'll pull back to the first dune and wait and catch them as they come over the top of this hill. One thing more, do not, I implore you, do *not* purposely draw down on knights. Let's go." After Godfrey's last comment, the archers looked at each other in surprise, and the three unknown French archers gave an obvious look of disgust after Baints translated. They moved carefully up the hill, got in place, and sprang up instantly when Godfrey shouted the order to shoot.

They caught the would-be attackers completely by surprise. Ten of them, including two knights, took arrows in the shoulders or thighs. The French had targeted the knights. Those hit yelled out in agony. The others panicked and tried to run or dropped to the ground, unsure of the direction of the attack. Another volley caught eight of those fleeing and two more knights, who had courageously remained standing, trying to see their attackers. Those knights took shafts in the chest. The third volley caught several archers, who had recovered and were trying to take aim at them.

Godfrey yelled for them to fall back, and they quickly scrambled to the protection of the dunes and awaited the counterattack. Moments later, as they lay in wait, they heard from the north the shocking sounds of the agonizing, distinctive screams of the women and children led by the Caliph as they were attacked and slaughtered by waiting Crusaders. They now knew for sure that the group that had moved toward them wasn't the entire force hiding in ambush.

Godfrey's surprise attack appeared devastating, but they were unaware of the actual size of the force hidden in the shadows and darkness. When it emerged at the top of the hills, their next volley slowed them but didn't stop them, even though all ten arrows hit their marks, and this time, the majority were lethal. The force they faced was still substantial. Godfrey frantically yelled a retreat to the beach and, on the run, led them southward to join the rear guard. Their pursuers stopped momentarily at the open passageway entrance, appearing uncertain about which way to go, or if they should even pursue their attackers. They had lost nearly a third of their men.

Edward of Leichester, a royal knight and cousin of King Richard, made his way to the head of the swelling ranks on the beach. He was livid, shaking with anger over the outrage he had witnessed—Crusaders, including what appeared to be mostly knights—having actually killed their own, including, unthinkably, other fellow knights, in apparent defense of heathen infidels. He was not about to let this outrage pass without revenge.

Enraged, he led his remaining force south in pursuit of the traitorous, murdering Crusaders, knowing the bulk of the force that had been waiting in ambush were now dealing with the escaped infidel hostages on the beach to the north. Even if defended by other renegade Crusaders, they had more than enough strength in numbers to easily annihilate all of them. They would catch these vile murderers and, with the sword in his hand and strength in his arm, he would deliver upon them the wrath of the Almighty and personally send them to the fires of everlasting hell and eternal damnation.

The archers who were sent ahead to patrol to the south, especially around the Genoese makeshift pleasure village of tents and crudely constructed storage and living quarters, found the area clear of any force waiting in ambush.

They had quickly but carefully circled the area to make sure there weren't any encampments, patrols, or large contingents hidden behind the hills near the area. Only then did Morgan, Bundage, Henri, and DuClaire enter the makeshift village of carnal delights.

Baints had been right about the effect appearing as knights would have on others. They were easily able to clear out the Crusader stragglers, mostly drunk or half-asleep, still lingering in the tents with prostitutes desperate to extract the last of their money, and immediately quiet the protests of the harlots and their Genoese pimps. The women tried to tempt the archers, but Bundage instantly brandished a sword taken from one of their drunken customers and ordered them to their living quarters for the rest of the night, with angry threats of bodily harm if any of them, including the Genoese, showed themselves before morning.

They went through the camp and extinguished the large, tightly wound reed torches that had been soaked in tar to make them burn longer. They needed to mask their presence in case of attack.

It was only a short time later that Salah, breathlessly leading the escaped hostages, slowed, to apprehensively approach the camp. He made contact with Bundage, who was waiting for them near the beach just outside the village. He informed the archer that he had heard the cries of battle not far behind him. Bundage advised him to continue with his followers quietly through the camp and keep moving along the beach, until they reached the archer guarding the area on its southern end, then wait until he could bring further instructions from the knights.

Bundage hurried as quickly as his limp would allow to the end of the hostage line, to check with the Crusader rear guard. Salah motioned to his followers to be especially quiet as he guided them through the area, while Bundage's fellow archers stood sentry at the north, east, and south approaches to the camp.

Bundage reached Gerard and the rear guard, moving slowly a short distance behind the last of the Saracens.

"There were the cries of an engagement, but it was brief," Gerard confirmed to Bundage, and continued, "I'm sure Godfrey and the archers were successful in delaying those poised for ambush, and they will be catching up to us soon. Tell Salah not to stop now for anything, and we will catch up with him shortly."

Bundage limped away as fast as he could to give Salah Gerard's instructions, but not before noticing Whittler Will was doing worse and was being helped to walk by two of the French men-at-arms. The stain of blood along his leg had widened considerably.

Godfrey, Baints, Michael, and the other archers reached Gerard and his rear guard a short time later. Godfrey was out of breath, and his words to Gerard had a frantic, desperate sound to them. "I'm sure they pursue. We took down many, but it is a large force and led by a royal knight known for all manner of viciousness. He will seek revenge. We must keep moving. Gather our small force together to make a stand on high ground inland, before we get too close to the dock and landing area where reinforcements are."

"You are right, my friend. Let's hurry," Gerard answered, but their attention was drawn to the urgent voice of Whittler Will.

"My lords, hear me. I am not to survive this wound. Leave me here. I can still draw string straight and true. I will gain you time, and perhaps even slay the knight you speak of, if he leads them."

Gerard hesitated, finding the offer compelling, and looked to Godfrey for an answer.

"As long as you draw breath, I will not abandon you. You bleed because of me. If any is to stay behind it will be I. We must hurry now!"

The entire group began to move as fast as they could. Basil Martin and Two-String Jack helped the two French carrying Will by taking hold of his legs so that the four of them now carried the severely weakened archer and kept pace with the rest of the group.

The entire group finally came together on the beach. Michael had run to bring the other sentries in, and, once joined, they moved as one force for the first time and proceeded inland due south, away from the beach. They acted in accordance with Godfrey's desperate plan and Salah's insistence that if they kept going south now, they would soon find a Saracen patrol or encampment. Salah even sent the swiftest of the maidens ahead in desperation, hoping they could quickly make contact and bring help.

The knights realized they could not outrun the force that pursued them. They had to make it to the short hills inland and prepare a defense, so Salah could continue on with the innocents and escape far enough into the desert to be found and rescued by a Saracen patrol. They all moved together now, as fast as they could. When they were within a hundred yards of the hills, beyond which was a plateau-like escarpment, a frantic voice suddenly called out an alarm that their pursuers had already caught up to them.

Godfrey asked Michael, being the fastest among them, to run ahead and position himself on the highest of the hills and provide whatever cover he could with his longbow until joined by others. Henri offered to carry his pack and gave him one of his extra quivers. Michael took off. Gerard yelled out for everyone to keep running to the ridge of the hills directly in front of them, where they could make the best defense. It was their only chance now. They knew they would be quickly wiped out in the lower area.

Knights, archers, men-at-arms, women, children, and Salah ran for their lives to the protection of the ridge. The Saracen innocents quickly fell behind, as did Salah. The pursuing Crusader archers began brutally and efficiently picking them off, one by one. The screams of mothers who had fallen behind and saw their children next to them skewered by the powerful arrows from a longbow made them crazy with grief. Those who survived the first volley began to hurl themselves back against the attackers and were quickly killed, often with several arrows each.

Salah stopped to help a young woman who had dropped her baby in panic and was frantically trying to pick it up. The woman was immediately shot through the back and fell dead. Salah tried to reach down for the baby and just as suddenly took two arrows in his back. Unbelieving, he turned in shock to look his murderers in the eye and was hit by three more shafts, as if he was nothing more than a target stuffed with hay. He collapsed dead on the spot with the cries and screams of the baby next to him piercing the night in vain.

Their pursuers moved closer. Innocents and fleeing Crusaders alike took arrows now, except for Godfrey and Gerard, who were not targeted on the repeated order of Edward. Only they wielded battle swords and were recognized by Edward as knights. Enraged, he had pushed his men to the limit of their endurance in trying to catch up to the renegade Crusaders and fleeing hostages. He was so consumed with hatred that only the act of slaying the knights himself could quell his anger and satisfy his blind fury for revenge, one of whom he was shocked to have recognized, a man he thought was imprisoned by Richard in the royal palace.

Michael had made it to the top of the ridge first and instantly dropped to one knee and began furiously unloosing arrows at their attackers without the slightest hesitation now to kill his own. He saw a woman holding a child and trying to outrun two footmen. It could have been that same woman he encountered, he thought, and instantly put his next two arrows in the chests of her pursuers. He saw her stumble then and lose the grip on her child, and he began to concentrate on saving her, unleashing arrows on any attackers nearby. When an arrow hit the ground next to her, he quickly found its source and killed the archer—who was readying another shot—with an arrow through his throat.

Suddenly, from behind, Michael heard the thundering sound of hoofs, the clanging of metal, and strange cries of warriors, which he suspected—then saw for sure when he turned—were horse-mounted Saracen archers and swordsmen! He yelled down to Baints repeatedly that Saracens were coming and tried to move back down the hill, out of the way of the onrushing horses, when he felt a glancing blow to the side of his head. He was propelled forward with amazing force, tumbling down the side of the hill. As he lost consciousness, he was certain that he had been slain, and his last thoughts were of trying to remember the words of contrition to God as the whirling specks of flashing lights he saw were suddenly engulfed by a black void.

Capture

Chapter VIII

He was in a great sea during a storm and drowning! Then Michael was startled awake by water splashing on his face. Was it the sea washing over the ship? His head pulsed with pain and was spinning. His eyes refused to focus. His arms flailed out as terror took hold, and he felt hands restraining him. He made sounds but not words. He began to relax, instantly relieved by the reassuring sight of Baints's face as it came into focus, but it was faint and seemed to revolve in a slow, constant spinning motion. He heard Baints's voice—it was distant, but he was further comforted by the familiarity of the sound. The spinning slowed, and then stopped. He realized he was not on a ship at sea. It was night, but he could still make out that Baints had a horrible gash on his cheek that slowly oozed blood as he spoke.

"Michael, lad, it is I, Baints. Can you hear me?"

Michael could only nod his head. His throat was clogged with dust. He could move his lips, but the sounds were rasps of words. Baints helped him sit up and held the water bag to his mouth. Michael gagged initially, gradually became coherent, gained strength, and then remembered where he had been before the blackness. He became frantic, clutching Baints as he forced out his first words.

"Wh-what happened? The others, where are the others? What—"

Baints cut him off with a desperate, urgent tone in his voice.

"You have to get up immediately, lad. We're prisoners. They're taking us to their camp."

"Prisoners? They caught us?" Michael said haltingly, as Baints pulled him up on his feet. The spinning started again, and he felt sharp pain from the side of his head as he moved and barely heard Baints as he corrected the young archer.

"The Saracens, lad. They, they saved us, at least some of us."

"The Saracens?" Michael repeated, utterly confused.

"You've taken the flat of a blade to your head, from the look of it, and are a bit senseless, but listen to me, force yourself to walk now. If you don't walk, you'll be run through and left," Baints said with heightened urgency in his voice.

Michael forced himself to move forward, step by step, with the encouragement and aid of his friend. Michael became aware then of others around them, Saracen guards behind and to the sides, and Crusaders in front, some of whom had their hands bound in front of them with rope that also linked them together in a chain. These were men he did not recognize, and who did not wear the tunic or headpiece of a knight.

"What happened, Baints? Where is Godfrey, Gerard, our friends?"

"Those-those that survived are well ahead, lad. Their appearance as knights, like us, gives them freedom of movement."

"Survived. Who, who—"

"It was a vicious but quick battle. I got the men to ground when I heard your cry, then the sound of horses. Your warning saved many of us, Michael. We were mixed with the innocents, and the Saracens went around us to repel our attackers."

Michael was still in a state of confusion as they walked with no suggestion at the horizon that morning would soon emerge to displace the night.

"Who was . . . not saved?" Michael asked with a profound sense of foreboding, not really wanting Baints to answer, but still desperately wanting to know the truth. There was a long silence, and Michael didn't press for an answer. He was steady now to the point of walking on his own without Baints's hands on his arm and shoulder to guide and steady him.

Michael reflexively touched the side of his head above his ear when a sharp pain struck. His headpiece was still on, and he felt it soaked through with blood and ripped at the ear, which hurt severely when he probed there. Unlike Baints, he wore no pack, remembering he had given it to Henri when he had run ahead, so he had nothing to use for the wound on his head. All he had was an empty quiver at his hip. He looked over at Baints, who had stayed close at his side. Baints stared down at the ground, shoulders and head slumped forward, as they trudged on. It was as close to defeated as he had ever seen the steady, unflappable veteran.

"Did our lord, Godfrey—", Michael began to ask again, but Baints cut him off as he straightened up and put a hand on his shoulder.

"God be thanked that He spared our knight. He is up ahead, helping others who were also spared by Him. But many ascended to Judgment this night, lad." Baints paused as if gathering the strength to continue. "Michael, thy young friend, Henri, is wounded but survives and can walk, but others have departed us. Whittler Will, who covered a mother and her baby with his body and saved them, Cletis Merriman, Two-String, Gesault, poor Gesault, many of the other French archers and footmen—"

"Dear God in heaven!" Michael responded, with profound agony evident in every syllable of every word, reflecting the fact that he had never lost friends in battle before. He continued somberly, "So many, Baints. Will, Cletis, Two-String . . . so hard to believe. I do thank Him that, in His mercy, He spared you. I truly know not what I'd do if you were not here beside me, or if I could carry on at all."

"Yes, you would, lad. Yes, you would. You'd go on, that's what you would do."

Michael shook his head in doubt and paused before continuing, "What of the women and children, and the Saracen noble, their leader?"

"Some survived, so very few from all those that departed with us. They are up ahead. Salah, who led them, was slain. His body is being carried back by the Crusader captives who slew him. So many were slaughtered, Michael, by those whom I'm ashamed to call countrymen. But the innocents were so numerous as targets around us, and this is why I believe many of us still draw breath."

Michael's only response was to slowly shake his head in bewilderment.

"One other departed this life, one I had come to greatly respect for his courage and daring and could have given allegiance, the French knight, Gerard, who risked all to save our lord."

"My God, no! Of all among us, he truly seemed invincible to me, to everyone. My God," Michael said, shocked by the additional news. Was there no end to this tragedy? He was quiet then, stunned to silence as he tried to make sense of it all.

After some moments, Baints added, "Gerard had been engulfed in a fury of madness and fought ferociously against the attacking Crusaders on one side and the Saracens on the other. He'd taken three English arrows when I briefly caught sight of him early on, and then a multitude more from the Saracens, who knew not his valor on their behalf, and finally brought the great knight down."

Michael began weeping quietly. When he regained his composure somewhat, the young archer spoke, but so softly that Baints strained to hear his words.

"How did we end up thus? It was no more than a day past we slept peacefully, and everything was glorious and hopeful. In scarcely a score of hours, the lives of friends, our world, are no more. No country, no family, dare I think we still have a God? I know not what is right or wrong any longer. "

There was nothing more that Baints could say, for he realized Michael put into words exactly his own thoughts and feelings.

Evidence of dawn was not yet present in the east, as more Saracen horsemen arrived to escort them the rest of the way to the Muslim camp, just in case other Crusaders had been sent to make an attempt to free the captives. Saracens took over transporting Salah's body the rest of the way to the camp. They were more concerned about a Crusader attack from the northwest, where the English dock and unloading area was located on the coast not that far away, and heavily guarded.

Baints and Michael remained at the end of the line, herded forward by their Muslim captors. Although fully coherent now, Michael was still unsteady on his feet at times, and combined with the distressing news from Baints, he moved slowly, provoking angry, unintelligible yells and frantic hand motions that forced them to speed up. Ahead, they saw the fires of the Muslim encampment they were headed to, beyond which, in the distance, were other clusters of fires, indicating other Saracen camps as well.

To the northeast the city fortress and castle of Acre was becoming increasingly visible as fewer clouds obscured the waning moonlight. Baints turned and looked back over his left shoulder and marveled at the sight of hundreds of fires that dotted the landscape in a semicircle outside the castle, where the majority of the two Crusader armies remained. Dozens of galleys brought wood and charcoal regularly from Cyprus to provide fuel for the encamped Crusaders, since the countryside had long since been scoured of fuel.

The Saracen camp was surprisingly close by, and Baints could clearly see Acre's fortress walls. There appeared to be more activity than normal around the entrance area for such an early hour, and the possible reason for which brought a sickening feeling to his body and spirit such as he'd never felt before.

The front of the stretched line of survivors finally entered the outskirts of the Saracen camp just as dawn began to confirm its promise, and those in the camp were stirring and immediately performing the first of five daily rituals of prayer to Allah by spreading out their small rugs, kneeling and bowing to the south, toward Mecca. A fire nearby, fueled primarily by glowing chunks of coal, over which hung a huge cauldron, sent the pungent scent of mutton and spices through the air in a tantalizing form of torture for the hungry Crusaders.

As they approached the camp, they saw Salah's wrapped body being taken ahead to a tent, where they assumed it would be prepared for burial. The surviving innocents, with the sporadic, muffled sounds of babies and children crying, were huddled around another fire and given food and drink by slaves attending the Muslim army. It was impossible to determine with certainty, but Michael saw several of the women whose forms and bearing could have been that of the young woman he met in the courtyard and desperately tried to save from the ridge.

The Crusaders were stopped and then forcefully herded back twenty paces or so away from the camp itself and motioned to remain standing. When DuClaire dropped down to rest in defiance, he was brutally kicked by three guards, until Basil Martin helped him back to his feet and restrained him from fighting back and being instantly killed. They would not have the benefit of the warmth of a fire in the chilled, early morning desert air.

Michael and Baints, as were all the others, were immediately and roughly relieved of whatever they still carried on their person, but were allowed to keep their water pouches. They maneuvered through the group until they stood among their surviving friends: Godfrey, Mighty Morgan, Bundage, DuClaire, Henri, and Basil Martin.

Robere, another French archer, Claude—a brutish-looking young man, who'd been wounded in the shoulder, although not seriously, and who disliked the English and had not associated with them from the very beginning in Marsailles—and two other unremarkable-looking French men-at-arms, Andre, and Monet, stood grouped together and slightly apart from the others.

They all also confronted the angry, bitter stares of the leader of their attackers, Edward of Liecster, and two of his vassal knights, William of Hargrove and the other, known only as Black Simon. They were among a small group of Edward's force who had been captured alive.

Edward, unlike all who appeared to be knights, had his hands bound behind him. The other attackers, two archers and three footmen, clearly not dressed as knights, had their hands bound and linked in a chain, like slaves, and were kept apart into what became a fourth group and were held closest to the camp. Godfrey gradually maneuvered next to Michael and Baints, limping slightly from an injury to his right ankle, and spoke quietly. "I'm glad you recover from your injury, Michael. Your warning saved many, including myself."

"Sire, too many were still lost." Michael's weary reply was made in a whispered tone.

"Aye, and I wish I could have aided more as well, especially our friend and brave knight, Gerard. He became possessed and blinded by rage during battle—I'm sure, from seeing so many women and children slaughtered. He did not heed, or perhaps even hear, my call to go to ground, and then Baints was upon me . . . What a loss, what a pity. There will be no other like him."

The archers were utterly exhausted, bloodied, and beyond despair, especially DuClaire and Basil Martin, who had also lost their partners. They stared out blankly without the energy or inclination to even offer words or looks of greeting.

A Muslim commander approached, Ibn al-Athir, his high rank evident in his manner of dress, which was elaborate in every detail. He spoke out in Arabic with an angry tone of authority, asking two nearby cavalry officers responsible for the capture whether the Crusaders were all from Acre. They answered, saying they were unsure, but Baints had understood and raised a hand to get the commander's attention and nodded his head and spoke the Arabic word *adiz*, for 'yes.'

This surprised the Muslim commander, who took note of Baints, his gaze lingering on him for a moment, until he motioned to the Crusaders to sit down where they were, while saying the same in Arabic. Baints repeated the simple, one-word command in English and French, and they all gratefully dropped to the ground. Godfrey and the archers, except for Michael, were surprised at Baints's ability to understand and converse with the Muslim commander, even though he only uttered one word.

The commander retreated, while several well-armed Saracen guards remained around them, but now at a distance.

Godfrey bent in front of Michael to question Baints.

"You speak the Saracen tongue, Baints?"

"Nay, my lord. I can understand many words from previous service here, but am humbled in the skill to form the words, other than a few simple ones, into speech."

Godfrey lay back, breathing hard just from the effort to lean over. He was disappointed, but responded positively, "It is still good. Your understanding may of itself prove vital."

Michael watched the commander leave them and move the short distance through the camp to his tent, one larger than any of the others. Colorfully woven rugs lay over the sand at its entrance, and it was further distinguished by silk banners that bore the Muslim crescent, on the tops of the two poles that framed the entranceway.

As Ibn al-Athir was about to enter the tent, Michael saw a veiled woman approach him from the shadows, momentarily taking the commander by surprise, but he quickly motioned for her to come closer. She became animated as she spoke and looked and pointed repeatedly in Michael's direction as she did so. The form of the woman was familiar enough to instantly provoke excitement within him. Could this be the same woman he knew and had tried to save, along with her child, with his arrows from the ridge? She held no child, though, and none appeared nearby. The commander also looked back and forth in his direction as the woman talked and finally held up his hand, said something that ended the conversation, and the woman moved away back into the shadows, with Ibn remaining in thoughtful contemplation as he watched her leave. He gave a look in the direction of the Crusaders. Michael felt that he had looked directly at him and their eyes had met. The commander abruptly looked away then and entered his tent.

Michael's attention turned back to his group. Baints and Godfrey lay on their backs, still awake, staring up at the stars.

"My lord, Baints, I just saw a woman approach the commander and talk with him, while pointing toward us. I think it was one of whom we saved, and she may have explained our noble efforts on behalf of the innocents."

"I hope that is true. Somehow, our captors must know what some of us tried to do," Godfrey said with effort, his increasingly labored breaths giving audible evidence of his extreme exhaustion.

"It is our only hope," Baints said softly, lying motionless now, eyes closed and trying to rest. "Alas, with the Saracen noble who knew of the plan now dead, I doubt, even if I could converse in Arabic at length, that I would be believed."

Michael, energized by the scene he had witnessed and what he hoped it represented—and stirred with unexplained emotion by the possibility that the young woman from the courtyard had somehow survived and was trying to help them—lay awake, kept so with thoughts of their brief encounters. He sat upright, pondering all that had happened, while surveying the scene around him and focusing on the groups of captured Crusaders nearby.

He noticed Godfrey was still awake too, and he motioned to the group of three knights, whose red tunics, although dirty and torn, were clearly luxurious, befitting their position as King Richard's royal knights. All had bloodstains on their faces, and the one who was bound also had a torn and bloodied headpiece similar to Michael's. "My lord, why does the one knight have his hands tied behind him?" Michael asked Godfrey.

"That is the royal knight, Edward of Liecster. He led the attack on us. The Saracens purposely tried not to kill those who appeared to be knights for reasons, I am sure, of ransom or prisoner exchange. Gerard's ruse to dress you all as knights saved many. It is why you were struck on the head with the blunt side of a sword, as was Edward there. Upon regaining his senses, while being led away, he attacked me in a rage. The confused Saracens pulled him off me. I was in no condition to defend myself so suddenly and could barely move my leg then. They tied his hands to prevent further outbursts."

"Bastard son of a whore, murderer of—" Baints muttered to himself, but was overheard by Godfrey, who stopped him.

"Thy mustn't judge, dear friend. To them, we are traitors, murderers of the king's men, our countrymen. Would we not think the same in positions reversed?"

"Forgive me, Sire. Their contempt for us I understand, even attempts to slay us I do not quarrel with. It's putting a shaft through the heart of a child, their mothers, babies even, that I can't abide."

"Aye, you speak truth. It is what separates us in our hearts, why we are even here. Alas, Edward and I were friends as young knights, fighting our first wars together at Richard's side—"

They became suddenly silent when they were startled with the realization that the Saracen commander was standing over them. He pointed to Baints.

"Cadiz tameh," Ibn al-Athir said, and Baints nodded in understanding and promptly forced himself up. The commander then began speaking to Baints rapidly and at length. Baints was quickly lost and held up a hand and shook his head, trying to indicate that he couldn't understand the language spoken so fast. Al-Athir stopped and acknowledged Baints's gestures. Baints then pointed to his own ear and nodded, pointed to his mouth, and shook his head. The Saracen frowned at first, but a moment later, a look of understanding filled his face.

The commander began speaking again, this time slower and pronouncing each word carefully. Baints would listen and nod in agreement and reply with a single word, "adiz," meaning 'yes' in Arabic. Finally, Baints pointed to Godfrey, the archers that made up his group, and even to the four French archers and footmen who sat apart. The Saracen looked over where Baints pointed and looked at the faces of each man in the two groups, where the looks of despair in some briefly changed to hopeful expectation.

Then he pointed at the separated group of royal knights, and Baints's expression turned hard, and he shook his head and said, "Nez," which meant 'no.' The Saracen looked over at that group for a moment and was met only with a look of sullen defiance. Baints's reaction was the same when the commander finally pointed at the remaining group of men-at-arms with their hands bound.

He looked back at Baints, into his eyes, and studied him for a few moments. The woman had told him a story that defied belief and greatly troubled him, forcing him out of his tent to try to question the Crusader who seemed to understand Arabic.

Al-Athir left as suddenly as he had appeared and returned to his tent. The moment Baints laid back down, Godfrey was eager for an explanation, as was Michael. The others were already asleep, or too demoralized to be curious.

"What just transpired, Baints?" Godfrey whispered.

"Michael was right. He questioned me about what one of the women we saved had told him, that Crusaders—and she had pointed directly at us—aided their escape."

"Thank God," Michael said with an enormous sense of relief.

Baints continued, "He asked me to point out those who aided the escape and those that attacked."

Godfrey nodded sadly and said nothing further.

"What do you think they will do?" Michael quietly asked Baints, but before he could answer, loud and angry voices erupted in the camp not far from them and instantly drew their attention.

A group of Saracens brandishing swords seemed to be arguing. Then, alarmingly, they began advancing toward them. The leader didn't hold a sword but instead, in one hand, he held a rolled leather scroll tied with a thin gold cord with tassels, and in the other held a backpack exactly like those taken from the English Crusaders who had helped the innocents escape.

Alarmed, the trio started to stand. Michael whispered urgently to Baints as he stood up, "That's the scroll from my pack."

Baints was confused by Michael's comment. "What?" he asked in surprise.

"What's happening, Baints?" Godfrey asked anxiously.

The leader of the mob had quickly approached Henri and waved the scroll angrily in his face, while shouting in Arabic, backed by the angry shouts of the others behind him. Henri was shaking his head, as if to say he knew nothing about the scroll that was being waved at him. Suddenly, without warning, two of the Saracens grabbed Henri by the arms and forced him down on his knees. In a blur of motion, without warning, another of the mob flashed a sword in a circle over his head and brought it down on Henri's neck, beheading him instantly.

Blood squirted out like a fountain from the severed neck as the body fell limp and the head lay facedown in the sand, eyes frozen wide in horror.

Michael was horrified. He had seen Henri beheaded right before his eyes without warning. His friend had died because of the scroll they found in his pack, thinking it belonged to Henri, because he had carried it for Michael. He tried to run at the Saracen who had killed his friend but was tripped by Baints and held to the ground by him, and then by Godfrey, who didn't at all understand the reason for the act of brutality and sudden execution that had taken place before them.

DuClaire had been awakened by the commotion and loud, angry shouts and was stunned at first by the shockingly swift tragedy, then went berserk and also had to be restrained by Basil Martin, Bundage, as well as Mighty Morgan.

At that moment, the Saracen commander pushed through the crowd of Muslim men-at-arms, saw the slain Crusader who appeared to be a knight, and became enraged and immediately ordered the execution of the one who was responsible, made obvious by the bloody sword he was holding. The guard standing next to the man obeyed and plunged his sword through the offender's heart, killing him instantly. The terrified leader of the group frantically dropped to his knees and showed the prayer scroll to the commander and explained that he found it in the slain Crusader's pack. Baints began to stand as Michael continued to lie in place, in shock and moaning in agony over what had happened, and his responsibility for it.

Godfrey continued to kneel next to Michael, just in case he suddenly tried to lash out again. Al-Athir turned to Baints and asked how the dead knight had come to possess a Muslim warrior's prayer scroll. Baints strained to try to understand the question and, surmising the meaning, shook his head and raised his hands with a genuine look of puzzlement and shock. Al-Athir stared at him, unbelieving, then turned disgustedly and shouted orders to his men gathered around the Crusaders. They carefully removed the body of their own swiftly executed friend and moved off.

Al-Athir gave Baints an angry look and told him, and motioned, that they must immediately bury the body of the Crusader away from the camp. He was increasingly frustrated and further angered by having to repeat his words slowly enough for Baints to understand. He concluded, in a noticeably louder voice, by saying guards would accompany them while they dug the grave in the sandy soil, using only their hands. He called out to the nearest guards, gave the orders, and returned to his tent, viciously swatting aside the entrance flap as he re-entered.

The sunrise had spread the glow of its warm, now-golden light across the sky and land. The shock of what happened to Henri had eased into a profound silent, inner sadness and eventually the Crusaders, except for Michael and Baints, had fallen fast asleep from exhaustion and the exertion from burying the remains of their young friend.

A tearful Michael told Baints the entire story about the scroll, and how Henri begged him not to take it, saying it was evil. Then he confessed that he had kept it as a souvenir to give to Mary, to impress her upon his return. He had killed Henri as surely as if he had wielded the Saracen sword himself.

Baints tried to console him and told him it was God's Will, as difficult as that was to understand. It was Henri's fate. He could have just as easily died at the ridge. Michael finally could no longer stay awake, as his grief had only added to his exhaustion, and he finally drifted off, mumbling to God and Henri for forgiveness.

Baints alone remained awake and vigilant, lying with his arms under his chin in a position that relieved the soreness of his back, which he had strained during the attack and had only now started to bother him. The constant pain from his facial wound and troubled thoughts had prevented deep sleep. He stared out across the vast expanse of desolate landscape, and then looked away from the sun and down to the left onto the city fortress of Acre, seeming so unbelievably close now in the morning light. If not for Saracen guards and archers, they could have run the distance easily and quickly, although, he realized hopelessly, most of them were now considered traitors and could not return, even if there were no guards or if easy escape presented itself.

Then, the activity at the Crusader camps just outside the gates of the fortress caught Baints's attention, and he slowly rose up on his arms, both curious and concerned about what may be happening. Saracens also started to gather in small groups behind him, having begun to take notice of the unusual activity. They started to murmur amongst themselves about the meaning of the spectacle unfolding not far away. *Were the Crusaders massing for an attack?*

Crusaders, footmen with swords and pikes, archers and knights, were hurrying out of the camps, on either side of the entrance area, and fanning out in a semicircle. Following them out of the entrance, other Crusaders emerged leading a procession of hostages, male civilians in the more elaborate robes of merchants or nobles, with their hands tied in back of them. The terrified wailing of some carried on the wind, blowing in their direction.

Baints woke Godfrey and Michael on either side of him and said only, "Look," and pointed to Acre.

The hostages came out in an endless stream, bound and linked together by rope. Those who resisted were pushed or beaten to force them forward. Eventually, nearly two hundred hostages were lined up in front of the fanned-out Crusaders, some standing stoically, others whimpering and weak from fear and unable to stand, and some on their knees, but bowing repeatedly as they said their morning prayers. Then, the sound of a great voice seemed to boom out across the desert. It came from the battlement above the gate. It was the combined voices of the English and French clergy, shouting out in Latin. Again, the wind off the sea helped carry the voices' words toward them, making it even easier for everyone in the camp to hear clearly, but only Godfrey, Edward, and his two knights fully understood the Latin words in their entirety. But their intent was understood by everyone.

"Defilers of the Land of Christ and the Holy Sepulcher, pillagers of the Relics of the True Cross, your blood will be shed and lives offered in sacrifice. Only the fires of eternal hell will atone for the evil against Him. God wills it!"

"My God," Godfrey said to himself. "And I would have been the first led out."

Even though he could not understand all the Latin words, Baints knew their intent.

"Aye, my lord. Praise be the soul of thy courageous friend, Gerard."

"How can Christians do such evil?" Michael whispered to no one in particular.

"We are doomed," Godfrey said, anguish in every syllable. And then the horror began.

******

The slaughter exceeded in brutality, gore, and depravity even the atrocities of previous Crusader armies. Saracen hostages dressed as civilians, merchants, holy men, and nobles alike were the first to die. They were held in check and kept on their feet by two Crusaders on either side of them, while a third slit their bellies, spilling entrails and vital organs onto the ground as they screamed in agony and terror. The victims' throats were then slashed, and the Crusaders poked through the bloody mess until they found what they were looking for, the gold coins and precious stones the victims had swallowed, thinking they were being released.

Once the first presence of treasure was confirmed and yelled out in triumph, an incredible frenzy of mass slaughter followed and would continue unabated for hours, until all twenty-seven hundred hostages were gutted and murdered.

Silence gripped the Saracen camp as the guards and others who were already awake and whose attention was drawn to Acre by the sound of unrelenting screams of agony watched in disbelief. The screams seemed to merge into one continuous outcry of pain and suffering. The initial shock began to be replaced by building outcries of anger. Some were so enraged they ran from the camp toward the carnage, waving their swords over their heads. Halfway there they were skewered with arrows from longbow archers on the ramparts above the scene.

At the same time, vengeful looks were cast toward the Crusader captives. Scimitars were drawn again in anger, but this time nothing could stop one group, who suddenly lashed out at the Crusader captives closest at hand, those whose hands were bound and were clearly not knights. The Saracen swordsmen surrounded them and began cutting them to pieces.

Godfrey, Baints, and Michael were on their feet, as were most of the others now, although Mighty Morgan and DuClaire had slept so soundly they were impervious to the noise and couldn't be quickly wakened by their friends. The guards around them also began to close in now. The screams of horror from the dying captives immediately alerted the Saracen commander watching the scenes of slaughter and brought him and his guards running to the scene. His sword in hand and yelling out, he was once again enraged at the uncontrolled actions of his men. The attackers stopped and pointed repeatedly toward Acre.

Al-Athir yelled back, while pointing his scimitar at the Crusaders' slayers, angrily repeating his order to move away from the remaining Crusader captives. The even louder cries of Muslim agony froze them in place. The commander saw he might not be able to prevent retaliation against the remaining captives, although they had not killed what they thought were knights this time. He yelled again to his men.

"Hear me! I am taking the captives to Jerusalem, to the court of Saladin himself! Because his own adviser, Salah Bin Madah, was slain by these infidels, they are the property of the great Saladin. He will pass judgment on them, and these Christian infidels will be punished in ways that will bring unimaginable pain and prolonged agony before death. Those you just killed here died far too swiftly."

This had the effect the commander was hoping for. Invoking the name of the great Saladin had worked. No Muslim would knowingly violate the rights of Saladin. The mob began to disperse. Al-Athir shouted orders for attendants to hurry and administer to the Crusaders who were attacked and now lay in a bloody heap. The faint moans of some could be heard. Godfrey, Baints, Michael, and others, including Edward's group, tried to move toward the scene to help but were immediately held in check by the guards, even more numerous than before.

While this transpired, the slaughter behind them, outside the gates of Acre, continued unabated in the glorious golden glow of an indifferent sunrise. Angry shouts from the now fully awakened Saracen camp built to a continuous roar all its own, which served to, at least partially, drown out the screams of anguish from Acre.

Al-Athir moved to Baints and carefully explained he had decided to immediately take them to Jerusalem, before he lost the ability to control his angry soldiers and could no longer protect them. He promised Baints he would explain to Saladin's officials the circumstances surrounding those he had been told had heroically tried to save the innocents. What would happen then he knew not. But he was certain if they did not leave immediately they would perish.

Baints agreed, the commander left to prepare the journey, and Baints explained this to Robere and his group, with Edward overhearing and giving Godfrey a glare of even more intense hatred in the process.

Ibn also knew that those in authority in Jerusalem would want the captured Crusaders, especially the knights—some of whom he suspected were not in fact knights—brought to them immediately in any event. So, regardless of the ultimate fate that awaited the captives, he was only doing his duty by leaving the camp during such circumstances.

Al-Athir and a guard force of twenty, mounted on horses, rode up and encircled the captives. He gave orders that all of them be bound together with heavy rope. Edward, his knights, and the lone surviving royal archer from the group that had been attacked—who had been discovered alive but slightly wounded because the others who had been slain first had fallen onto him—were in the lead and tied to a cart that also carried the body of Salah, wrapped in white linen and covered with an elaborately woven rug. Next was the group with Robere, but they were not tied to the first group. At the end of the line was Godfrey's company. They were tied together, but not to the first group either, as a small concession, Baints thought, to Ibn's belief that these two groups had, in fact, tried to save the innocents.

In the background, the slaughter of Saracens continued in plain view of the camp. Sporadically, a Muslim warrior crazed with anger and grief would run from the camp, waving his scimitar above his head, and join those doomed souls who had ascended to paradise that morning.

Al-Athir then yelled orders to the remaining officers gathered nearby, to hold the men in check. If their camp attacked Acre without coordination with others and orders from high authority, they would all be wiped out for no purpose, and he himself would be executed as a result. The time for revenge would come, he assured them. He told them further he would be back quickly with orders from Saladin and his commanders as to what they would do. They immediately acknowledged the command, and Ibn al-Athir moved out ahead of the cart and started them moving out of the camp, as those who remained angrily began chanting in Arabic, "Death to the infidel devils."

As Godfrey, Baints, and Michael began the journey, with the voices of rage screaming out now in unison around them, they wondered, as did the others, what fate awaited them fifty leagues to the southeast, in Jerusalem. Jerusalem, holy Jerusalem, the city that, just barely a day before, they had all thought and dreamed they would have first glimpsed and eventually entered as triumphant, conquering Crusaders in the service of God Himself. All except George Bainty, who harbored no such illusion since the day his lord and knight Godfrey, whose reluctance he detected in the knight's manner and voice, summoned his company to the great hall in the castle to announce King Richard's call to arms in support of the Pope's declaration of The Third Crusade.

The sounds of death chants, and eventually those of the horrific slaughter itself, faded as they progressed and moved as quickly away from the camp as they could. But for most, the cries of terror and agony would be ever present in their minds, long after the actual sounds faded and could no longer be heard. Michael had even more personal demons to contend with, as he would never be able to erase in his mind the look of terror on Henri's face the moment he was killed. His depression was visibly apparent to Baints, who was beginning to feel the effects of the wound on his face that was becoming corrupted.

A short time later, it was Baints who first noticed something odd within the group of horsemen that Ibn had brought to accompany them. The rider next to the commander was not dressed as a warrior and stood out distinctly because of it. This rider wore the unmistakable robes of a woman and rode upon the camel as a female did.

Al-Athir had brought a woman along with them. Perhaps the woman whom Michael had seen talking with Ibn on their behalf, perhaps the very woman whose child Michael had saved in the courtyard passageway. He tried to tell Michael this to console him, but Michael's grief and guilt was not lightened by it, and the look in his eyes barely registered acknowledgment.

Once they reached the windswept, barren, rock-strewn landscape beyond the camp, they struggled and slowed considerably as they trudged on. Eventually, each of them in their own way came to share a similar hope under their feelings of despair, that God in his infinite mercy would somehow, miraculously grant them quick, painless deaths. A death not unlike, surprisingly, that which had so suddenly and unexpectedly claimed the young French archer. Perhaps, Michael tried to convince himself, he had unknowingly but mercifully spared his dear friend Henri the far more agonizing death that now awaited all of them.

Chapter IX

In the distance, they could finally see the outline of Jerusalem illuminated gloriously by the golden, ethereal glow of the setting sun. The journey had taken nearly three days, but would have taken much longer if Ibn had not appropriated three large carts from a merchant caravan at the Jahfida Oasis. Three of the angry merchants followed behind on camels to get the promised payment in Jerusalem, after which they would immediately double back to the oasis that very night with their precious transports and resume their caravan journey along the ancient rutted trade route that led to Baghdad.

"If we must die, I cannot think of a more holy place to do so, and from which to ascend and meet our Lord," Godfrey said peacefully to the remnants of his company, in the cart in which they now rode. His eyes were locked on the unreal image of the ancient city in the distance. Except for Michael, whose depression had begun to lift, most gave only blank stares in response, or kept their eyes closed, trying to rest as best they could while crowded together and sitting up in the cart that jarred them with every bounce and swayed and creaked unceasingly.

"My lord," Michael interjected into the silence, "the Saracen officer told Baints he brought the woman to give testament of our actions and would try to intercede on our behalf. I'm sure it's the same woman we saw talking with him in the camp."

"I fear, lad, what our king has wrought has doomed us no matter. Best ye prepare thy mind and soul to face our end."

Sobered by Godfrey's despairing words, Michael slumped back against the low, rattling side of the cart, wondering what heaven could be like, and if his soul would even be allowed entry. Was his friend Henri now there, waiting for them? He looked down at Baints resting fitfully next to him. Michael was greatly concerned with the wound on his cheek. It had festered, and the swelling now threatened to close his right eye. At Baints's request, he had lanced the wound to release the foul puss inside, with a small knife heated in the camp's fire and loaned to him by Ibn for that purpose. But the wound had continued to worsen, and Baints had been considerably weakened by it.

Michael had removed his headpiece and washed the matted blood from his hair and head the day before, while at the oasis. Other than a missing piece from the top of his ear, he was surprised to see that his wound had not shown signs of corruption as Baints' had, and had actually started to heal.

Al-Athir had originally underestimated the toll the relatively short journey would have on the Crusaders, especially on Godfrey, Baints, and Bundage, who could not walk at the pace necessary and had to be helped by others taking turns to support them. This had slowed the entire group considerably. Since al-Athir was convinced many among them had actually tried to save the innocents, he decided he must keep them alive until they reached the court of Saladin. As a result, he commandeered three large carts from a caravan resting at the oasis and used horses from his riders to pull them, instead of the slaves the merchants used, to speed their arrival to Jerusalem.

Several times, while resting at the oasis, Ibn had to disperse angry mobs that had formed around the Crusaders as a result of the news about the barbaric slaughter at Acre, which had traveled swiftly throughout the area. He repeatedly used the same speech he had given at the camp, about taking Salah's body—which was now bloated grotesquely under its white coverings and close to the ritual three-day deadline for burial—and the captives to Saladin, whose property they now were. Invariably, that fact and al-Athir's look of determination to use force if necessary, quelled their thirst for immediate revenge.

The carts and their escort moved for nearly a league past and through the temporary and permanent encampments of an enormous Muslim army stationed outside the ancient biblical city. They continued up the gradual incline of Mt. Zion, upon which Jerusalem had been built. The city itself was a fortress, much like Acre, but considerably larger. Its main wall surrounded the city and was nearly three leagues in circumference, towered nearly fifty feet, and was protected by another lower outer wall to prevent nearby valleys and ravines from giving attackers protection. Between the two walls was a dry moat, twenty-three feet deep and carved from solid rock. Traffic streamed in and out of the many gates around the ancient bastion revered by three of the great religions of the world. Rows of merchant stalls displaying cloths, spices, foods, and delicacies, pottery, ornaments of jewelry, carvings of exotic birds, even caged animals, together with a variety of colorful tents and pavilions inscribed with Arabic writing, lined both sides of the roads that led directly into each of the city-fortress's five gates.

Al-Athir, with the woman still riding next to him, turned his procession of carts onto a narrower road that circled the outer wall, in order to enter from the west through the Gate of Siloam. Only the Muslim faithful, during holy days, could enter from the east through the Golden Gate that led into the holy area and passed the stunning golden Dome of the Rock, behind which was the restored and sacred Al Aqsa mosque.

As they entered the long approach, lined with merchant stalls jammed together, leading to the Gate of Siloam, people began to recognize the carts being escorted by Muslim horsemen held Crusaders. This caused much excitement and agitation, and the onlookers began to shout out, "Death to the Christian barbarians!" Even larger crowds began to gather along the route, and Ibn found that he could not move through the gate as swiftly as he had planned.

The chants escalated in volume, intensity, and anger, bringing more and more people to the road. They effectively surrounded the carts and al-Athir's horsemen, preventing their movement. Ibn tried to yell out the name of Saladin as before, but could not be heard. Enraged protesters began to try and drag the nearest of the Crusader captives from the back of the carts.

Godfrey and Michael were terrified, even Baints had summoned the energy to push himself up, concerned with what was happening around them, but it was apparent he was not coherent. He repeatedly yelled out a call to arms and fell back, exhausted and semi-conscious, muttering helplessly to himself.

Suddenly, a contingent of Muslim lancers forced their way through the crowd from inside the gate and effectively moved the crowd away from the carts. Al-Athir immediately moved his men and the carts through the gate. They continued until they were safely inside the courtyard below the royal palace, where the general of the Jerusalem garrison watched from a balcony. Al-Athir and his men promptly dismounted and straightened to attention, as Dahur ed-Jamir, accompanied by two aides, left the balcony and slowly descended the palace steps to meet him and his prisoners. He stopped halfway down, put his hands on his hips, and stood as if posed, frowning severely down upon Ibn, whose eyes, along with his men's, were fixed downward.

"You should have had the sense to send a rider ahead, Commander, and we would have dispatched an escort to meet you," General Dahur said, greatly irritated with the younger officer.

"I apologize, General. I had few horses left after using them to pull the carts, and"— al-Athir pointed to the figure standing behind his men—"transport a woman, who—"

"You brought a woman? Why?"

"She is from Acre, and—"

The general interrupted again, greatly surprised, "She escaped the slaughter?"

"Yes. And was witness to-to something unusual that concerns some of the captives," was all that Ibn said, knowing it would be impossible to explain details of the incredible circumstances in their current setting.

"Tell me of their atrocities later," the general said contemptuously, then noticed the body covered in the lead cart. "Who lies covered there?"

"It is the body of Salah bin-Madah, General."

There was a look of even more profound surprise in the general's expression, which then turned to seething anger. He spoke slowly, with every word accentuated with hate.

"Take those vile pieces of camel dung to the dungeon of the citadel, now."

"Yes, General."

"Then come back and explain to me the event of their capture." Dahur abruptly turned away, dismissing al-Athir with a wave of the back of his hand.

Also observing the scene and hearing the conversation from a partially hidden palace balcony above the steps was the Vizier of Damascus. He had several relatives among the slaughtered hostages at Acre that now included another, his brother, the slain Salah. In the absence of Saladin, who had left that morning with the Caliph of Jerusalem for a gathering of Caliphs, Emirs, and senior military leaders in Baghdad to urgently plot strategy against the Crusaders, it was he who would rule at court. It was he, Adul bin-Madah, who would decide the fate of the barbaric captured Crusaders. The moment was one he could hardly wait to arrive, he thought, while watching Ibn and his men escort the captives away.

****

Al-Athir personally made sure that the two Crusader groups were put in separate cells from each other. He looked quite concerned when Michael and Godfrey had to carry the old sergeant from the wagon and down the many steps of the ancient dungeon that lay beneath the citadel of the Tower of David. At the last moment, Michael motioned to al-Athir that Robere and his group should also be put in their cell, rather than with Edward and his knights and their lone surviving royal archer. Ibn understood and readily did as Michael requested. Robere and his friends reacted indifferently to the gesture, and just huddled together, exhausted, in a corner. Ibn left several skins of water and the one reed bag of food that remained from the journey. He also left a burning torch in a holder on the wall next to the door, so they wouldn't immediately be plunged into darkness.

The dim, dirty, and foul-smelling confinement of the dungeon did bring one benefit, relief from the oppressive sun and heat, for the subterranean depth provided a natural coolness they all welcomed. Michael surveyed the group in the flickering torchlight's yellow glow. He realized as he looked about the cell that he was probably in the best condition of anyone there. His ear and head wounds had continued to heal without any sign of festering.

Everyone, of course, suffered from sore and bloody feet and skin blistered raw by the sun. Mighty Morgan had only minor scrapes and bruises but was visibly exhausted from carrying Bundage most of the way before the Saracen commander had appropriated the carts at the oasis. Basil Martin and DuClaire both had wounds to their face and neck, and Martin also had a deep gash on his bow hand that, like Baints's wound, had festered and was swollen grotesquely. DuClaire had grown thin and even paler than usual and had recently not been able to hold down any food.

Robere, on the other hand, had not a scratch on him from the battle, but his thin, frail body had barely tolerated the harsh conditions of the march. Riding in the cart had probably saved his life. His friends, Andre and Monet, appeared exhausted but reasonably well otherwise, their wounds not serious enough to distinguish them from others, although their boots were only shreds of leather now. Michael had noticed they left bloodstains on the stone floor of the dungeon stairs when they had been moved down.

Claude, the angriest and most outwardly unfriendly of the French archers and the remaining member of Robere's small group, lay against the wall in such a way as to favor his wounded left shoulder, which had forced him to keep his arm in a sling, made from his brassard, for the last two days, in an effort to alleviate the pain.

In the cell next to them, but in total darkness, were the three royal knights and their lone archer who had survived the mob at the camp. Their condition was roughly the same as most of the others. They, too, nursed various wounds and were severely debilitated by the journey. What had not diminished within them, though, was the hatred evident in their eyes anytime their gazes had crossed with Godfrey and his group, especially the French.

Michael, his eyes closed, slumped unmoving against a wall, could not fully comprehend the fact that he now found himself in a place Christ had walked, where He had been crucified, buried, and rose from the dead. He wondered if the Saracen commander and the girl he brought to bear witness for them had been able to speak on their behalf. The more he replayed the image of the girl's robed form and veiled, covered face in his mind, the more he felt she was the young woman whose child he had saved from the cart and desperately tried to save at the plateau.

Godfrey had said he doubted their testimony would make any difference after the unspeakable slaughter at Acre. So, this land in which Christ died would likely be the very place from which their spirits would also rise soon, to be judged by Him.

Michael had never been as outwardly religious as most of the other archers, influenced, no doubt, by Baints's long-standing contempt for most clergy and a church hierarchy's cold, uncaring, institutional imperiousness that had distorted and complicated what he felt was Christ's simple and powerful teachings. But at that moment, Michael longed for the company of a priest who could hear his confession and give him the last rites. Then his thoughts turned to Baints and became troubled, and the coldness he began to feel had nothing to do with the dungeon.

Chapter X

They awoke one by one in the blackness of the windowless dungeon cell. They actually felt cold, although most had slept better than they had since the night before the events had begun. Michael had slept little, and, until the torch burnt itself out, he tried to comfort the feverish Baints, who had begun shivering. Most of the night was spent covering his friend with his tunic and giving him water as frequently as possible. Earlier, when they still had the light of the torch, Godfrey had divided the food from the bag among them, including Robere and his group, and Michael had noticed the knight had taken none for himself. Michael had offered him his meager portion, but Godfrey refused, thanked him, and had suggested he keep it for Baints, if he could do without it.

Godfrey's voice now penetrated the void, and he told the men that if they had to relieve themselves, they should stand and carefully move as if blind men, using short steps with hands outstretched to first locate the door. Once done, they should move to the left corner, where the large oval pot, made of pottery, was kept in which they could piss and defecate. Men cursed as they were stepped on and yelled to redirect the interlopers, trying desperately to find the place where they could relieve their bladders and bowels.

It was not long after they had all awakened that they heard footsteps echoing in the passageway, and the sound of the iron bars being removed. They recoiled from the intense light of the torch thrust in by two guards, followed by the sound of the heavy door banging against the wall, and the entry of four more guards armed with swords and clubs.

"Dez! Dez!" the largest and meanest of the Saracen guards yelled in Arabic, while brandishing his scimitar up and down. When some Crusaders couldn't respond immediately, two of the other guards roughly and painfully began pulling the prisoners to their feet. Claude, who was closest, screamed in excruciating pain when the guard lifted him by his injured arm and shoulder. In reflex, he tried to push the guard away with his other hand and arm and was beaten unmercifully with a club-like piece of hard, charred cedar wood that was clutched in the guard's hand.

Godfrey rushed to Claude's aid and took the last blows on his back, before the largest guard, the one in charge, stopped the beating and motioned them all out into the passageway. Michael had started to move to protect Godfrey and instantly found a scimitar at his throat, which froze him in place. The Crusaders quickly understood the order and moved as fast as their infirmities would allow, but the guards still roughly pushed them through the passageway and against the stone walls. Godfrey helped Claude to his feet. The archer looked up at the brave English knight with his face contorted in pain, but his eyes conveyed gratitude.

Michael, assisted by Basil Martin, using only his good hand, pulled Baints upright, and they carried him out of the cell. Robere, in a surprising display of compassion for the man who openly hated him, helped DuClaire stand and, with the assistance of Andre, walked him out of the cell and thereby avoided a vicious clubbing. DuClaire mumbled a barely audible, "Merci," to both of them.

Monet forced himself up slowly, but could barely walk due to weakness caused by bowels that could hold nothing in all the night. With one hand and arm around Bundage, Morgan used his other to help a grateful, sad-eyed Monet out the doorway.

They waited there in the passageway until the scene repeated with the four occupants of the adjoining cell. Each were pushed out one by one, and their appearances in the torchlight seemed worse than their own. Edward of Leichester fell to the stone floor with a coughing spasm that racked his body terribly. The lone royal archer was shaking both from the cold dampness and the fear of the prospect of torture and death.

The other two knights, William and Black Simon, even though weak and unsteady on their feet, tried to assist Edward, but the guards continued to beat on him to get up, even as they tried to help him do so. They finally managed to manhandle Edward to his feet, and the guard in charge yelled an order to all in the dungeon passageway, and then turned and led the way out.

So this is how it will all end, thought Michael as they were roughly pushed along the passage and then up the curving stairs. They would be executed in a Jerusalem courtyard with no chance to plead for mercy and have their noble, self-sacrificing efforts told to their captors. He was glad that Baints was nearly unconscious. He prayed then that they would be beheaded, as Henri had been. They'd be joining the young archer soon, he thought.

They stumbled or were pushed out into the morning sunlight, which shocked their eyes, forcing them to hold up hands or arms to shield them. All around them were congregated groups of angry Muslims, who yelled and chanted as they were led through the courtyard toward the palace. The guards kept the crowd at a distance, so their progress was not impeded, but that didn't prevent the Crusaders from being continuously pelted with rotten fruit, stones, and especially camel and horse dung.

They entered the palace through a side entranceway and moved up the steps of a narrow spiral staircase like that in a castle turret. Two lead guards had hurried up ahead of them, and the others followed behind. The narrowness actually helped them because they could lean or push on either wall, which made the ascent more manageable, although still a labor with the guards at the bottom constantly pushing the Crusaders to move faster.

Michael and Godfrey were relieved that Baints was showing signs of coherence now, asking clearly where they were and where they were going. Michael thought the forced movement had actually helped him in that regard. He was still unsteady, but they felt a sense of comfort in the fact that he had his wits about him, for his basic understanding of Arabic might be especially important now.

When they reached the top of the stairs, they exited into an open walkway similar to a castle's battlement but covered with a bright-red, pavilion-like cloth canopy. From there they moved through a series of interior rooms, until they emerged into a narrow hallway, but with a towering ceiling, at the end of which, to the right, were two massive, ornately carved and decorated, wood beam doors nearly as high as the ceiling itself. The guards pushed the captives forward until they reached the doors. The guard in charge proceeded to enter a small side door alone and disappeared.

While they waited, Michael and Godfrey became aware that Baints's alertness and renewed strength had begun to ebb. They felt his weight sag onto their arms and hands more. It became increasingly difficult for most of the Crusaders to stand, and when anyone attempted to lean against the wall they were roughly grabbed and pulled away. After a few minutes the massive doors were pulled open, revealing the grand hall and magnificently appointed court of Saladin in the palace of Jerusalem.

Originally built by Constantine the Great, the modest, spartan interior was enlarged and greatly improved in splendor by the Muslim conquerors, added to by Frankish Crusaders who recaptured the city in the first crusade, then restored it to its present grandeur after being recaptured by Saladin just four years earlier. Huge, intricately crafted mosaics decorated the walls and interior columns. Bright-colored silk banners hung between columns that formed a wide main aisle in front of them. Thin, gold-covered iron bars, fashioned into intricate geometric patterns, filled the windows. The guards prodded the Crusaders forward. A murmur of angry voices began to build as they moved into the great hall.

As Michael and Godfrey entered at the head of the procession, still supporting Baints, they looked in awe at a palace court as grand as any they had ever seen, or for most of them, could ever have imagined. As they moved forward, the open aisleway narrowed, and they passed between large groups of bearded men in richly adorned silk robes, wearing turbans or head scarves of varying sizes and styles, and affixed with gold emblems of different designs. They sat on large damask-covered pillows in two crescent-shaped rows facing each other, with an aisle only several paces in width separating them.

Crowded close in and seated a few paces directly behind them on each side were many others, lesser nobles and court retainers, also dressed in fine robes and turbans of many designs and colors. Finally, behind them, stood a formidable line of armed palace guards, distinctive in dress from the other guards, wearing gold-embroidered vests and identical jeweled daggers and scimitars in their waistbands. They stood on raised platforms in front of the columns, in order to clearly survey everyone and everything in the room.

Twenty paces or so beyond the seated gathering, at the end of the open aisle, was an elevated oval stage made of a highly polished rose-colored stone, with two rows of steps covered with layers of silk pillows, on which sat a fierce-looking, regally adorned man, the vizier, Abdul bin-Mahdah.

His outer robe was interwoven with gold and silver thread in a symmetrical pattern of subtle geometric shapes. The robe underneath was plain, but so white it seemed almost luminous. On his head was a plain white turban, the simplicity of which served to greatly accentuate the gold crossed crescent and scimitar on the front.

Standing next to him, quite odd and startling, and hardly taller than the sitting vizier, was the surprising sight of a black-skinned dwarf of a man, Mantuka, whom Godfrey and Michael assumed was a slave. He wore a plain white robe and white turban with the insignia of a single gold palm tree, all of which contrasted starkly with his skin, which was as deeply black in color as that of flint. The whites of his eyes stood out prominently and made them seem too large for his face. If his beard had not been flecked with gray it would have been difficult, because of his size and the blackness of his face, to easily tell if he was a man or a child. Yet he did not display any of the telltale traits of dwarfism. He was simply *small,* with the typically proportioned size of an older child. The fact was Mantuka was an African pygmy.

The guards remained around them as they shuffled forward amid the shouts and jeers in Arabic, from the enraged Muslim audience, who could hardly contain their fury and hatred of the Crusader captives. Those closest to them were forced to cover their noses with frantically produced perfumed cloths to partially ward off the powerful and disgusting stench the Crusader prisoners brought in with them. Godfrey asked Michael out of the side of his mouth if he saw Ibn and the woman anywhere among the crowd.

Michael stole looks from side to side, trying to spot the familiar face of the Muslim commander, who, along with the girl, could attest to their actions on behalf of the innocents. He told Godfrey he did not see him, but suggested maybe he was present somewhere out of their sight.

The Crusaders' movement was halted when they were within a few paces of the stage. The vizier raised his hand, and the hall became instantly silent, except for lingering echoes, which quickly faded, leaving in their wake an eerie sense of foreboding. Surprisingly, it was the black dwarf who spoke first, in astoundingly precise English, and in a deep voice that belied his size. It resonated clearly throughout the court area and instantly commanded attention.

"You have been brought before the most noble and powerful Abdul bin-Madah, vizier to the great Saladin. Bow to him."

Mantuka surprised them further by quickly repeating the statement in French, for the few who wore red crosses on their tunics. Fearful not to obey, everyone bowed except the defiant Edward, who was sure he would die soon anyway. A guard immediately clubbed him unmercifully to the floor, knocking him down to his hands and knees, accompanied by cries of approval from the crowd.

The vizier yelled out a command in Arabic, and the guard stopped the beating instantly. He then directed a question to his diminutive interpreter, who, in turn, directed it to the Crusaders.

"Why did he not obey?" the interpreter asked, looking at Godfrey and Michael in the front. Michael looked to Godfrey to answer.

"He-he has been deafened, and-and addled from battle, lord."

Edward didn't challenge Godfrey's surprising explanation, deciding he did not want, or could not stand, another beating. He just remained down until the guard roughly pulled him back up on his feet, at which point he did bow. The interpreter translated the answer to the vizier, who immediately asked another question, which the dimunitive Mantuka translated only in English this time and directed to Godfrey, who was now assumed to be the knight who spoke for them all.

"Are you of the vile Crusader force that occupies Acre, those who committed unspeakable crimes against Allah by slaughtering all, including innocents and men who had laid down their arms in surrender?"

Godfrey was taken aback by the directness of the question, hesitated, then answered, "We tried to help innocents escape. We did not—"

Mantuka held up his hand to stop any explanation. "Are you from Acre?"

"Yes, but—" Once again, a hand went up to stop any explanation. Godfrey tried to continue anyway, but was instantly silenced by a guard, who put a sword tip to his throat as the interpreter relayed his answer, which caused a swell of angry yells from the crowd, with many jumping to their feet, shaking their fists in the air, and yelling out for immediate executions. Alarmed and frustrated, and unafraid that a sword would again threaten him, Godfrey yelled out over the angry voices.

"We were trying to help innocents escape! Did not the commander who brought us here tell you of this?"

The interpreter, of course, was the only one who understood Godfrey's frantic plea. And he alone knew it was true.

General Dahur had not believed al-Athir's incredible report about some of the Crusaders' heroic actions on behalf of the innocents. He forbade the young commander to even talk of such ridiculousness with the vizier, telling him that doing so would end his promising career.

Then, he ordered him to return to his camp immediately that evening, though he was to first present the woman he claimed had escaped Acre and was a witness to his fantastic claims. Al-Athir was shocked by the development but could not disobey his general. He did not meet or talk to the vizier directly, but his conscience would not permit him to do nothing on behalf of the remarkable Crusaders who had so astonished him with an act of heroism he previously believed any Christian incapable of.

Ibn al-Athir wrote out a report of what had happened and what he believed the truth to be, and added that a woman who witnessed the events at Acre was being held by the general. He added that he feared for her life, for the general angrily pronounced her a liar after she immediately told her story of some of the Crusaders' heroism on behalf of the innocents, while Ibn still remained standing before the general.

Immediately afterward, and just before his departure that same night, al-Athir went to the vizier's residence in the palace and asked the attendant to summon one of the vizier's assistants, thus not violating the order of his general. He was promptly met by the assistant who happened to be available at that late hour. The unusual-looking assistant introduced himself to the commander and listened as Ibn briefly explained the contents and urgency of his note and asked that he deliver it to the vizier. He then immediately left to return to his men, as he had been ordered to do. The one who read al-Athir's letter, with great and compelling interest, was a child-sized black assistant, an interpreter, among other talents, who now stood before the Crusaders, translating for the vizier.

"What did that one say?" the vizier asked, pointing at Godfrey.

"He begged for their lives, Master," Mantuka lied matter-of-factly in Arabic.

The vizier slowly stood, and a hush immediately settled over the crowd, and they quickly sat back down to await his words. He looked directly at Godfrey, and then at the faces of each of the other Crusaders. A moment later he announced they were to be executed immediately in the palace courtyard, before all who now sat before them. A satisfied murmur of approval rippled through the hall.

The interpreter, though, was surprised by the sentence and did not translate for the Crusaders. Instead, he moved closer to the vizier, surprising him with that action, and whispered into his ear. The nobles looked on with equal surprise. "Wise and noble one, why do you treat the barbaric infidels with such mercy?"

The vizier reacted with puzzlement. "Mercy? They will lose their heads within the hour!"

"Should they not suffer as those at Acre did? Is not the Torture of the Moon appropriate, ending with slow amputation until there is nothing left of their extremities *but* their head?" The vizier listened with obvious interest, his irritation over the interruption passing. "And should it not take place in the great plaza of Damascus, where most of the relatives of the slaughtered of Acre live, so they can take some measure of satisfaction in their enemies' agony and justified deaths? I say this only for your consideration and most respectfully, Master."

Abdul bin-Madah pondered what Mantuka had said. The odd-looking black-skinned man was a slave, but he did not really think of him that way, for he valued his counsel. Mantuka called him 'wise one,' but it was the pygmy who was wise, brilliant really, a scholar, physician, speaker of many languages, trusted by Saladin himself, and there were few times in the last twenty years that he did not carefully consider and take his advice when given.

The concept of slavery was unusual in the Muslim world, for although it meant that one was the property of another, that did not restrict a slave from becoming a part of Islamic society, being educated, and rising to positions of power, wealth, and influence, as had even the oddly diminutive, black-skinned Mantuka.

Once again, the vizier realized Mantuka was right. He nodded his head in agreement and straightened up and announced the change in sentence to a greatly surprised audience, then sat down. Although disappointed they would not witness the Crusaders' immediate executions, the nobles also saw the justice in the vizier's revised sentence of death, obviously in some way influenced by his wise assistant.

Mantuka, in turn, translated for the somber Crusaders, whose puzzlement had been mixed with dread as they stood wondering what was happening. Godfrey was sure it had to do with their fate. Michael hoped it somehow had to do with the Saracen commander, Ibn, even though they had not seen him anywhere in the great hall. The black assistant spoke first in English.

"You will be taken to Damascus in the morning. There, before the families and friends of the innocents and unarmed men you slaughtered unmercifully, you will suffer and die in a way reserved for only the most vile and evil creatures of this world, and only then will justice be done before Allah."

As Mantuka repeated the sentence in French, Michael couldn't believe what he heard. The others of their group also stirred in alarm and protest. The guards brandished their scimitars at their faces, but Michael was not cowed. "We did *not* kill innocents! We tried to save them! Ask the commander who brought us here! Don't you understand?" Michael called out.

A guard was about to club Michael, but Mantuka, having finished the French version, called out and stopped the guard's action. Michael felt Baints's weight in his grip even more now, as Baints sagged down in unconsciousness. Godfrey simply appeared resigned to their fate and tried to help Michael prop Baints up as best he could.

Mantuka spoke in response. "The commander returned to his men last night. He said nothing to the vizier."

Irritated at the prolonged exchange between Mantuka and the young knight, Abdul bin-Madah angrily asked what was being said. Mantuka replied simply that he was pleading for mercy. This enraged the vizier, who stood once again, looked directly at Michael, and yelled that he could not believe the nerve they had to ask for something Christians had never shown to others, ever! Even though Michael and the others could not understand the words, they understood the hatred and finality behind them.

"Take this filth away!" the vizier commanded, having finished his tirade, and swept his hand in front of him for emphasis.

The guards immediately complied, and the pitiful-looking Crusaders, with all hope now lost for Godfrey's group, were roughly led away. Godfrey and Michael held up the unconscious Baints as well as their ebbing strength allowed, only managing to drag him along back to the dungeon. Their despair was complete. They had even been denied the quick death of beheading. They would be forced to endure another agonizingly long journey, at the end of which was not only the prospect of gruesome, unknown tortures and a horribly painful and prolonged death, but it would take place in a city that held no spiritual comfort in death, Damascus. It seemed even God had now forsaken them.

Chapter XI

It seemed a short time after they were thrown back into the blackness of their cell that they heard the sounds of activity in the corridor and the grating noise made as their door was being unbarred. Moments later they held up hands and arms to shield their eyes from the shock of the intense light from three torches thrust into their confined space by guards. Michael was instantly alert, as was Godfrey. They were surprised to see the black-skinned interpreter from the vizier's court move right up to them and look down intently at the semi-conscious Baints. The interpreter was followed in by five others, ebony-skinned like him but much taller, dressed in simple robes, tunics, and headwraps. They carried in many reed bags and covered baskets, large urns and jugs, and several unlit torches.

"My name is Mantuka Mace Sabutta," the interpreter said, his deep voice resonating, and made even more impressive by the close confines of the dungeon. He wore only a white cotton tunic, over which was a gold-embroidered vest. His head bore a simple, bowl-like covering in place of his turban. He carried, over a shoulder, a shiny silk bag on a sling. Had they not seen his face they would have thought a child stood in their midst.

He continued, "We are here to restore your health before you begin your journey to Damascus tomorrow."

"What?" Godfrey questioned, sitting more upright. Glowering, he continued, speaking out defiantly, "Why should we let you keep us alive, only to torture and kill us later?"

"They want the pleasure of seeing us suffer before they take our heads," DuClaire answered in a tone of disgust.

"And after we risked everything to help the innocents," Bundage said, shaking his head. "God has forsaken us."

"God has nothing to do with it," DuClaire responded bitterly. "It is the work of an evil king."

Godfrey gave DuClaire an angry stare, even though he was right. It was a feudal reflex of a knight and noble. No Frenchman had the right to call his lord evil, even though he now believed the words were true.

"Silence!' Mantuka ordered loudly. It was surprising how one so small of stature could possess such a powerful voice and wield authority in a manner that instantly commanded attention and obedience. He continued, reverting, in the next moment, to a calm, dignified tone.

"No one knows with certainty what the future holds, Christians. Be thankful for life, even if it may be brief," Mantuka said in response, and then said something to the guards in Arabic, who immediately gave the torches to his attendants and left, barring the door behind them, to the continued amazement of the Crusaders.

Godfrey spoke out directly to the diminutive court interpreter, "The vizier did not believe what we said in the palace, because we possessed no proof. That I can understand. But what I do not understand is why the commander who brought us here did not speak the truth about us before he left, as he promised he would."

"And he brought a witness, a woman we helped escape. What happened to her?" Michael added with great desperation in his voice.

"As God is our witness, we tried to help the innocents escape from Acre," said Bundage.

"And some did escape," Michael added in a tone that was becoming angry. "They are at the commander's camp. We risked everything for them!"

Mantuka hesitated. He surveyed each of the dirty, exhausted, blistered faces that looked at him expectantly, and then he nodded his head.

"I know," he said.

Michael, Godfrey, and the others exchanged shocked looks, unsure they heard right. "You know?" Godfrey asked in disbelief.

"Yes, Ibn al-Athir wrote a letter before he left."

"But why didn't—" Mantuka held up a hand to stop Godfrey's questions, as well as the others, who erupted at the same time.

"Stop! All will be explained in time. For now, be satisfied that you live. The vizier wanted you executed immediately. I convinced him otherwise."

The Crusaders again looked at one another in complete confusion, and nearly everyone tried to ask questions at once.

"Why?" Godfrey managed to say loudly above the others, the tone more pleading than demanding. Mantuka again raised a hand to quell the discussion.

"Time is very short. I cannot be gone long. I and my assistants must attend to you quickly. Later, in the evening, we will talk."

One of Mantuka's assistants removed the burnt-out torch in the holder next to the door and put his torch in. Then he and other assistants without torches began distributing bread and chunks of spiced mutton and odd-looking vegetables on skewers from the reed bags, to the absolute amazement of the confused but grateful Crusaders, who ate the unexpectedly delicious food greedily and noisily.

Robere actually began to sob as he ate. Another assistant set his torch down and took out large wooden cups and began to fill them with water from one of the jugs, which he also handed out to the warily appreciative Crusaders, their hands shaking from their weakness and excitement, most of whom had never seen a black-skinned person before that morning.

Mantuka moved closer to Baints. "Please, make room so I can administer to him," he said to Michael, who was staring up at him and thinking that he looked even smaller up close than he had standing next to the vizier at court.

Michael promptly scooted back out of the way, allowing Mantuka to kneel next to Baints. He took the bag from his shoulder and set it next to him, and then carefully checked the wound on the desperately ill sergeant's face, gently touching it, then slightly squeezing it. Baints winced in pain, and his arms flailed out wildly but weakly. He gave a muffled moan and opened his eyes. Michael could tell that his friend, in that brief moment of full consciousness, was totally confused by the black-bearded face in front of him, illuminated by a torch now held close to them by one of the assistants.

Mantuka gently pushed Baints's arms down and spoke calmly and reassuringly, assuring Baints that he was there to help him. He reached into his bag and removed several small boxes, a wooden plate, a short but obviously sharp dagger, a silver goblet, and ornate-looking vials containing salves, potions, and medicines. He looked over at Michael.

"You will need to watch closely, for you will have to repeat what I give him now throughout the day and night."

Michael nodded and moved closer, while he greedily bit into the bread and meat they had just handed him. Between bites of his food, as Mantuka arranged what he had taken out, Michael asked, "Are you a healer?"

"I am a skilled physic and interpreter in the court of the Vizier of Damascus."

"Can you make him well?" Michael asked hesitantly.

Mantuka looked into Michael's eyes and saw agony. "I cannot say yet. Hold up his head so I may give him water first." Michael stuffed the last of the bread into his mouth, wiped his hands on his tunic, and did as requested, while Mantuka poured water from an elegantly trimmed goat skin bladder he took from his bag, which had been sealed with a fitted wooden stopper at the end. He held the cup to Baints's lips, and he drank it, with difficulty at first, but then he quickly consumed it all.

Baints's eyes showed more alertness, although he remained too weak to talk. Mantuka refilled the goblet and gave it to Michael to continue to give to Baints in small sips, while he turned his attention to one of the small boxes. He opened it, dumped the contents, which resembled dark pieces of tree bark, onto the plate, and sliced and chopped them with the dagger until they were reduced to small pieces. He used the knife's handle to grind it into a coarse powder. He took out another odd-looking cup from his bag, which had a long, narrow handle attached, and slid the powder into it, filled it with water, and handed the cup up to the assistant, who held the torch behind him. The assistant held the cup over the torch's flame.

Michael and Godfrey watched all of this with puzzled expressions, as did the others, who now felt somewhat refreshed. No one spoke a word; they all just watched intently, as they would a magician at a fair. Michael drank down his own water, asked for more, then continued to help Baints drink as Mantuka opened another of the small boxes, which contained something wrapped in fine white cloth. He removed the wrap, revealing what looked like a large gray, oval-shaped object that looked like a smooth, dull stone. He noticed their frowns.

"You have not seen this before? Or have not used it ever upon your bodies?"

They either shook their heads or gave blank stares.

"It is called soax. It is rubbed on the body to rid skin of the dirt and the humors that cause flux and pestilence."

"How does it do that?" asked Michael.

"To be pure of mind and clean of body is the way of Islam. Do Christians ever bathe?"

Godfrey answered, "We wash in the spring. We believe the coating of dirt and the oils of meat and fowl protect us."

"You are wrong, and your odor before battle prevents stealth and precedes you on the wind," Mantuka said, while curiously pouring water over the rock in his hand.

"How is it Christians have traded with us for spices and fine silks but care not for that which protects life and health?" Mantuka asked, but in a soft voice, more to himself than to the Crusaders.

Godfrey said no more, and just thoughtfully considered the logic of Mantuka's remarks as he watched him pour more water over the rock in his hand, and then proceed to rub it gently on Baints's wound. A gray lotion rose up on Baints's skin as his hands flailed out again, but Mantuka finished quickly before Baints's weak action had any effect. He poured water over the soax, rewrapped it, and returned it to its box and opened another, the content of which was also wrapped in white cloth. When it was removed they could see it was a thick yellow ointment of some type.

"Hold your friend's hands now, while I apply this," Mantuka said to Michael, who set the goblet aside and leaned over Baints and did as he was asked.

"His name is George Bainty. We call him Baints," Michael said, feeling, for some reason, the black physician should know his friend's name.

Mantuka dipped his fingers into the ointment and applied it to Baints's face, rubbing it into the wound hard enough for him to moan in pain this time and try to use his hands and arms to stop it.

"Will that make the wound heal?" Michael asked.

"It will help. It is the tonic that I brew that will bring relief, if the corruption has not spread too far." He looked up at Michael. "Otherwise, he will die. You should pray now to our God for his help."

"*Our* God?"

"The Christian, Jew, and Muslim all worship the one and only God, the God of Abraham," Mantuka said, obviously enjoying the revealing of a startling truth to the ignorant Crusaders.

"Baints here also said that to me once," Michael said in response, which surprised Godfrey, and more so, Mantuka.

"Ah, he is a learned man?"

"Yes, he is wise and knows much about the Saracen, having served within these very walls many years ago, and he can understand the language. He is our sergeant and friend to us all, especially to me," Michael said with a mixture of pride and sadness.

"Then he is a man worth saving. I will do all that I can," Mantuka said somberly, and asked the assistant to give him the cup that had been held over the flame and which made the bubbling sounds of having been brought to a boil.

Mantuka expertly poured the liquid into another goblet, set it down, and removed some small, deep-red leaves from another box and dipped them into the hot liquid repeatedly, until the leaves broke apart in pieces from their stems. He stirred the liquid with the knife, added some cooler water, then spoke to Michael.

"Hold him up against you, so you can also hold his arms."

Michael did so, and Mantuka fed the brew to Baints, who initially spit out the bitter-tasting hot liquid. Michael quietly spoke to Baints, gently repeating that he had to drink if he was to live. Mantuka forced open his mouth and, gradually, Baints relaxed and relented in his delirium and, little by little, drank the concoction until it was gone.

"You must continue to do this throughout the day and night. I will leave you the ingredients and implements and the extra torches so you can have light until I return tonight, when I will bring more." Mantuka saw Michael's eyes go to the knife.

"Yes, I will leave the knife. Understand, I intend to help you, so there is no need for desperate actions."

"Help us in what way, exactly?" Godfrey asked pointedly, his irritation plainly evident.

"Escape along the road to Damascus?" Basil Martin asked in a blunt tone, speaking out for the first time.

"If not escape, help us by using your skill to allow us a merciful death here and now," DuClaire said chillingly.

Mantuka saw they were desperate men who had been resigned to their fate and could not tolerate the prospect of false hope dulling their despair.

"You must trust me, and let us do our work now. We will talk more of this later."

Godfrey's eyes met Mantuka's, and he saw within them determination and something else, something that said he should trust him now—not that they really had any choice. Godfrey nodded his head, and Mantuka nodded in return, then he quickly resumed his treatment of Baints. He cut a small piece of the cotton and put it over the ointment on Baints's wound.

"Does he have any other wounds or injuries?" he asked Michael.

"No, I don't think so. He didn't mention anything else."

"Good. And yourself?" Mantuka noticed his scab on his ear.

"Your ear was gouged, but it heals. Let me look closer." Mantuka carefully checked the wound and promptly applied some ointment to it and to the bruise on the side of his head, under his hair, above his ear. He then moved to Godfrey, who immediately told him he was okay and to attend to the others. Michael told Mantuka this was not true and to check his right foot. When he removed Godfrey's tattered leather boot, he found that his ankle was swollen and badly discolored. Godfrey winced as Mantuka probed the injury.

"I do not believe it is broken."

Mantuka proceeded to apply the same ointment he used on Baints, then ripped the cotton used to cover the ointment into strips, which he tightly wrapped and tied around Godfrey's ankle. He promptly moved on to treat the various injuries and wounds of the others.

The swollen gash on Basil Martin's bow hand he pierced with a hot dagger point to let the puss and blood drain, cauterized it with the same blade held over a torch flame until it was red-hot, while Morgan, Martin, and DuClaire held him still, and then repeated the treatment given Baints's wound. He applied a sweet-smelling greenish salve to the badly blistered skin on Morgan's face and hands.

After carefully probing Claude's shoulder with his fingers, Mantuka determined that it had been jarred out of its socket. He worked it back into place, while Claude was held down by Morgan, Robere, Andre, and Monet. The French archer passed out from the intense pain as he bit down on a piece of leather cut from one of Mantuka's bags. The black physician then revived him with a vial of an intense perfume, which he uncorked and held under Claude's nose.

He treated various other minor wounds, blisters, and scrapes and scratches with ointments and salves, which could have become corrupted if not attended to. To all, he gave a powdered root potion to add to their water to help their bodies heal and recover more quickly from their ordeal of the last three days. Combined with abundant food and water, this had many of the Crusaders already feeling decidedly better. They felt their strength starting to return, and were truly grateful to Mantuka, and amazed at the skill of the unlikely-looking physician who carefully returned his medicines, potions, ointments, and salves to his reed bag and left out those that Michael would need in order to continue treating Baints and others with festering wounds.

"If you could all bathe in clean, hot water scented with lemon and lavender and rub your body with soax, you would feel as if reborn," Mantuka said as he finished gathering up his things. He reviewed the instructions with Michael for preparation of the tree bark potion.

"I am leaving you enough to make and give to your friend and the others with open wounds, and also the one whom I surmise must be your lord, and the other there, whose shoulder I forced back in place. They will need this also for their pain and recovery. Will you do this?"

Michael instantly nodded his head. "Of course, but tell me one thing more, do you know what happened to the young woman, the one the commander brought to—"

"Forget her. She can no longer help you."

Michael ignored his dismissal of the issue. "What do you mean? Is she well? If she is the one I feel she may be, this young woman has probably lost her entire family."

Mantuka could see Michael's concern was genuine. *What had transpired between them?* he wondered. He had yet to question the young woman, but would soon do so, although he had learned the general was holding her as a prisoner now. He knew she would never get the chance to tell her story to anyone else.

"She will be provided for," Mantuka said tersely with obvious impatience, and immediately instructed an assistant to bang on the door for the guard to let them out.

"I go now to the others in the next cell. I will return this evening," Mantuka said, lingering at the open door after his assistants departed carrying out the empty jars and bags.

"Some food and water remains. Also, in the covered reed basket you will find lemons, figs, pomegranates, and sweet palm fruit. Make sure you all eat of them and rest and sleep as much as you can," he added.

Mantuka turned and spoke to one of the guards, while pointing at the bucket in the near corner filled with their waste. The guard yelled in Arabic down the corridor, and a slave with a huge empty bucket and a smaller one filled with water quickly appeared. He moved the filled bucket, and splashed water over the area, and Michael and the others watched as the water disappeared between the grooves between the flat rock of the floor. *That explains why Baints's piss had not collected under him,* Michael thought. The slave replaced the bucket and carried out the other, with its foul stench disgusting the guards, who saw no reason to even remove it.

Satisfied, Mantuka simply turned and left. The door was slammed closed, followed by the familiar sound of it being re-barred, and in turn, followed a moment later with the sound of the cell door next to them being opened.

It was immediately apparent most were feeling better because the room erupted in questions and conversation the moment the door was closed and they could hear the guards walk away to the next cell. What did the black dwarf mean when he said he would help them? Could they trust him?

Godfrey told them all it was useless to force hopeful meaning into his words. All that was certain is they were alive and regaining their health and strength. With that and rest, the opportunity to escape, although remote, may present itself on the way to Damascus. Their only real hope was that God would allow them the chance to die fighting for their lives as Crusaders against an armed foe. Conversations died down as they began to eat the deliciously refreshing fruit. Content for the moment with their voracious appetites sated one by one, they lay back and easily embraced sleep. Only Mighty Morgan continued to eat, but eventually, he too nodded off with a half-eaten pomegranate still in his hand.

Once Michael finished his figs, he proceeded to prepare the potion as instructed, and he and Godfrey helped Baints drink it and did the same with Martin, Claude, and Monet, who had a minor cut on his right leg. Godfrey drank last and reluctantly, still unconvinced that a potion could ever help a swollen ankle. Eventually, he couldn't resist the pull of sleep, and Michael alone remained awake, forcing himself to remain so by getting up and walking in a tight circle near the door, counting slowly to a hundred, then preparing and giving Baints and the others, including Godfrey, the potion once again.

Later that afternoon, after replacing the torch, it became increasingly evident to Michael that the medicines were, in fact, helping his friend. Baints's eyes had opened and had become active and clear, and gradually, he was even able to help himself sit up to drink the hot, bitter concoction, which greatly spurred Michael on in his battle to resist sleep. Finally, Baints spoke for the first time since lapsing into his delirium.

"What, what has . . . transpired, lad?"

"Praise unto St. George, you have returned to us!" Michael exclaimed, relieved by the sound of Baints's voice, which he had been afraid he would never hear again. "We are in Jerusalem."

"Beneath the tower of David," Baints said knowingly.

"Yes, Godfrey told us that also."

"I knew of these dungeons," Baints said, speaking slowly, haltingly. "I walked the ramparts above . . . years ago." He said this while carefully putting a hand to his face and feeling the dressing on his wound. Michael anticipated his next question.

"A strange man, black-skinned, the size of a child, the court physician and interpreter, he treated your wound and provided miraculous medicines to us all."

"That is what you've forced down my throat continuously."

Michael smiled. "Yes, and it has helped you."

"It has, lad. It has also made me piss much in me pants."

"True, you have, but I assure you, it made no difference to the odor in here."

Baints smiled slightly. "I was sure I would depart this life as did my past lord, John of Andover, within these same walls. I must thank this unusual physician."

"He may have only saved you for greater pain, torture, and death in Damascus," Godfrey said, eyes opened and observing the scene, having been awakened by Michael's excited voice.

Some of the other archers also had awakened and yelled surprised and irreverent greetings to their friend and sergeant. The food, water, tonics, and rest had returned some of their humor in spite of their plight. "If so, then, then I'm glad . . . to depart this earth . . . with my friends," Baints replied, having already tired noticeably.

"He said he would help us," Michael added seriously. "He knows we tried to save the innocents."

"What? How-how will he help?"

"We do not know," Michael answered somberly.

"Worry not, lad. It's in God's hands now," Baints said and drifted off into silence and closed his eyes, as Michael changed the dressing on his face and carefully applied more ointment.

As he did so, he thought about 'God's hands,' and that they were in the very land that he had lived, walked, and died, and so very close to the Holy Sepulcher, the sacred spot where Christ's body lay in death and rose again into heaven. He thought too about the evil that had been done by so many in His name. 'God wills it!' they had shouted often. The priests had yelled it from the walls of Acre before the slaughter of unarmed men. It was clear to him much of what had happened was the evil will of men, and to invoke God's name in such deeds was blasphemy of the most heinous kind.

Michael could no longer hold off sleep. Exhausted, he drifted off into wonderful dreams of home, his mother, and his love, beautiful Lady Mary. But then, for some reason, pleasant dreams evolved into a nightmare, and over and over, he saw the terrified look on Henri's face the moment the Saracen blade cut into his neck, with the lips of the disembodied head crying out, 'Why Michael, why?' It only ended when he was startled from his deep sleep by the sudden, alarming sound of the heavy door banging against the wall, when it was thrown open by guards, who obviously resented the extraordinary treatment given by Mantuka and his helpers. Others had replaced the torch while he slept, most likely when they had to relieve themselves, so a flickering red-and-yellow glow still illuminated the room.

Everyone else was awakened also, including Baints, whose look and manner had improved dramatically. Mantuka, with only two assistants this time, entered again, carrying reed bags filled with food and jugs of water and extra torches. They just left them on the floor in the room and didn't distribute the food. A slave with a scarf over his mouth and nose followed them in, and again replaced the overflowing waste bucket. When he left, Mantuka closed the door on the lead guard observing the scene with an expression of suspicion and disapproval. The sound of the door being barred followed. One of the assistants lit a torch to hold near Mantuka as he again administered to the Crusaders.

"I have little time. I must check your wounds quickly and ask questions that you must answer with truth," Mantuka said immediately and moved to Baints and knelt down next to him to inspect his face. Baints moved himself up on his elbows.

"You are feeling better, I see."

"Due to you, I am told. Should I thank you?" asked Baints with a smile.

"I do not require thanks," Mantuka said cleverly as he removed the covering from Baints's wound.

"It is thought by some you saved me only to face death of a worse kind."

"Perhaps. Would you have decided otherwise?"

"No, if it is to be, I'm grateful to share the fate of my friends, so I will thank you."

Mantuka smiled, the first time Michael had seen him do so, and it seemed to transform him in a way that allowed his humanity to be exposed and inspired trust and hope.

"I understand you were in Jerusalem before now."

"Many years ago, when I was young and thought England the center of the world."

"I understand. I too felt that way about my land many years ago." Mantuka became the physician then. "Your wound is much improved. You will have a great scar all warriors will envy."

"I envy those who can stand and walk to the bucket in the corner."

"Then try now."

Mantuka stood and held out his hands. Baints took them as everyone watched with interest. Michael was ready to assist, but did not need to do so, for the small black physician surprised them, especially Baints, with his strength, and pulled him up onto his feet, where he stood. Somewhat unsteadily, but he stood nonetheless.

"Your size masks the strength of one much larger, indeed."

"Appearances are often not what they seem. You'll need to remember that in the coming days," Mantuka said, as Baints took his first steps with Michael at his side and wondered what the black court assistant had meant by his last remark.

Mantuka then moved to Godfrey, who had watched and listened with great interest.

"From what distant land did you come?"

Mantuka unwrapped Godfrey's foot as he answered, and by the look in his eyes, it was evident that, for the moment, he had been transported somewhere else.

"It is not a name you would know. It is very far to the south and west, beyond even one's imagination of distance. It is a land unto itself, and different in every way from any other you have seen."

"How did you come to be here?" Godfrey probed as the others listened with rapt interest and curiosity, as they would a teller of news and tales traveling through their villages.

"I was taken as a slave after a battle that should have never taken place."

"You were a warrior?" Godfrey asked with surprise in his voice.

"No, even then, I was a healer and interpreter for my people," Mantuka answered, smiling. "Now *I* ask questions," Mantuka said with finality as he applied a sweet, but strong-smelling oil to Godfrey's ankle and rubbed it into the skin. Godfrey could feel a warmth envelope his entire foot.

Mantuka spoke while he rewrapped the ankle. "Are you all really knights, as your tunics suggest?"

The question surprised Godfrey, as well as everyone else. The cell went quiet. *At this point, it made no difference what rank they were,* Godfrey thought, *unless they would be treated cruelly during their journey or executed immediately.* But life naturally bred hope, and the food, water, and medicines had made most of them hopeful, even though, considering their circumstances, unreasonably so.

"Why do you ask?" Godfrey questioned as Mantuka finished with him and moved to check Basil Martin's hand.

"Ibn, in his letter, stated he believed you were mostly archers. When captured, regardless of the tunic, most wore the forearm leather of the archer, which many still wear, and had empty scabbards at their waist, and many longbows were gathered up."

Godfrey was silent, considering carefully if there was any advantage for his men now to try to continue their ruse. At this point, being a knight, since no ransom was to be sought, did not seem an advantage at all.

"If that is so, what difference would it make now?"

"It could make a great difference, if they were truly skillful," Mantuka answered.

A loud murmur of hope rippled through the cell. Michael was helping Baints to lie back down, and he had heard Mantuka's last comment and couldn't help interrupting Godfrey and admitting the truth. He could not see how concealing it mattered now.

"They are the best of the best, the most skillful archers in all of England"—he hesitated and looked at DuClair—"and France."

Baints eyed Godfrey, who displayed no displeasure at his announcement, and added, "And Michael here is a master archer, a champion. But why would that matter? Does the Saracen allow archers to compete for their lives, as do the Byzantines after battle? If that is so, they will win their lives for sure."

Mantuka did not answer. He concentrated on applying ointment to Martin's wound. Martin told the physician that it was feeling much better, and that was important, since it was his bow hand, and he smiled at Mantuka after admitting so.

Godfrey anxiously asked more questions, but Mantuka remained silent. After checking Claude's shoulder, he stood and finally spoke.

"I can say no more about all this now." He turned to Michael. "Continue making the potion for them as long as you can stay awake, or perhaps others can help. It would be good they continue to drink through the night."

"I will," Michael said, and Godfrey added he too would help and, surprisingly, Robere also offered to assist, as did the usually silent Andre.

Mantuka addressed them all then. "You start the long, difficult journey to Damascus tomorrow, before the sun rises. Eat, drink as much water as you can in the morning before the guards come, and get as much rest as possible now. You will need every measure of strength for what lies ahead."

Mantuka signaled with his hand, and an assistant banged on the door. It was promptly unbarred and pushed open.

They all watched the strange-looking physician leave, presumably to go to the cell next to theirs, and each pondered the meaning of his questions and comments, especially the last. Although he had answered some questions, he had given rise to far more that remained unanswered, provoked their curiosity, and seemed to spark further hope; a hope that everyone was reluctant to speak about.

Godfrey, most disturbed by the encounter, asked Michael to distribute the food. They ate in an uneasy silence, contemplating the next day, the start of the long journey to the ancient city of Damascus, and wondering if and how that would lead to the possibility of reprieve or escape. Or would it, instead, inevitably lead to what appeared the more likely prospect, that of lengthy, unimaginable torture, and a death they would scream for, but would seem to take an eternity to come.

Chapter XII

Michael awoke with a start the moment he heard the heavy footsteps of the guards approaching the cell. He had slept soundly, and much longer than he had intended. He saw that the torch had been replaced and was surprised to see that Robere was awake and in the act of grinding up pieces of bark when he, too, heard the ominous sound of the guard's camel-skin-soled boots echoing in the corridor. They exchanged looks.

"They come for us," Robere said.

"Yes. Hurry, let's gather the medicine into a bag, to take it with us."

Michael sprang forward to help Robere, and when he saw the knife in his hand, he took it from him and tucked it inside the shirt under his tunic.

The guards burst in before they could finish. They yelled in Arabic and motioned for all to get up, and proceeded to kick at those slow to respond and still groggy from sleep. Michael moved between Baints and the guard to protect him from the kick, and Godfrey, who had awoken quickly, immediately moved to help him lift Baints onto his feet. Surprisingly, Baints stood mostly on his own, and Michael and Godfrey were greatly buoyed by the sight.

"My strength is returning," he whispered as he remained standing without assistance.

When Robere stood with the reed bag in his hand, a guard grabbed it from him, yelled something in Arabic as he did so, pushed him back, and angrily threw the bag aside.

One by one, they were roughly grabbed and pushed out into and then down the corridor, along with Edward and his knights and archer from the other cell. They didn't even have a chance to drink their last fill of water. They were herded up the stairs, directly out into the cool night, and, without a moment's delay, were loaded directly into two large cages mounted on wheels, which were just high enough for them to fit inside while squatting down. The cages themselves were made from a combination of wood poles and iron supports, with a door at the back that was secured with an iron bar and latch, all of which was securely fastened to a flat wagon bed with numerous iron braces.

The haphazard manner in which they were loaded ended up putting Edward and his group with Godfrey, Michael, Baints, and DuClaire. In back and in front of the cages, a considerable force of Saracen cavalry was lined up. At the very front was another large wagon covered with white cloth in such a way that it nearly resembled a tent on wheels. In front of that was another contingent of cavalry, and a commander at the head.

Their apprehension heightened when they did not see Mantuka anywhere. Godfrey hoped he was in the tented wagon. They all did. He alone knew their sacrifice and heroism, and he had implied the possibility of help. Mantuka had kindled in them a spark of hope that kept them from the edge of utter despair. Or was it all just a cruelly devised scheme that was meant to initiate their prolonged torture?

The horseman next to the lead commander waved a torch, and the procession began to move, slowly weaving its way around the pools and fountains in the enormous courtyard lit by tall stanchions of coal fires and long, iron-handled torches. They moved past the royal palace and its alert guards, then proceeded out the gate of Siloam and continued around the outer wall, until they connected with the main road going north. They bumped along this cobbled stone roadway in ruts worn into the granite over hundreds of years of continuous use, which would eventually connect with the even older caravan route that led directly to the most ancient of all the cities of this ancient land, Damascus.

They passed merchant stalls and their sand and mud hut dwellings behind them. A few occupants, just starting to stir in preparation of the day's activity, took little notice of them as they passed by. Once they cleared the city itself, they saw that dawn had begun to displace the night in the sky behind the hills to the east, with a sun that would soon become their unrelenting tormentor.

****

The column had made only two brief stops along the way, until they finally reached the Sea of Galilee early that evening, although they were unaware of the name and knew only that it was a large inland lake. They had made efficient use of the longer period of summer daylight by traveling continuously for nearly three-quarters of an entire day. The Crusaders had been given only water and small pieces of hard, flat unleavened bread that was also eaten by the cavalry riders, although the Muslims put large globs of honey on theirs.

The sun had beat down on them unmercifully, but they had arrived at the lakeside oasis in reasonably good shape. They had taken off their tunics and used them to shade their heads and bodies as much as possible. Even Baints had held up without problem or concern, and by all accounts, those with previously treated wounds continued to notice improvement. The constant jarring of the wagon, though, had produced moans of pain from Claude, with his still-healing shoulder, in the cage behind them.

At the oasis campsite they were finally permitted to leave the cages, and, like a group of old men, after they stepped out, they remained bent over. It took a while before their muscles, ligaments, and back bones allowed them to straighten up completely. Godfrey in particular had difficulty walking. He discovered that his ankle had swollen again and stiffened up considerably.

They were given reasonable rations of bread, figs, and water after being bound in twos, at the ankles and hands, by heavy rope. Fortunately, Michael was tied with Baints, and Godfrey to DuClaire, although it seemed Edward and his two knights and archer were no longer as sullen and hateful as they had been after their capture and on the journey to Jerusalem. They said nothing to them or, for that matter, to each other. Their despair appeared complete.

After eating they were motioned by a guard to dig out a hole nearby with their hands for their waste, and after doing so they slept on the ground without covering, with four guards posted around them. Whatever spark of hope Godfrey's group had at the beginning of the journey, had dimmed considerably, for they had seen absolutely no sign of Mantuka during any of the stops. They were further dismayed at the sight of the tent-covered wagon being used by the commander as his quarters for the night, dashing any hope that Mantuka had been inside.

Michael, lying in silence next to Baints, felt for the knife inside his shirt. Then he poked at his friend to get his attention and whispered to him, "Even with my hands tied I could remove the knife and cut us free."

"Aye, lad, and then what? Even if we took weapons from the guards, the cavalry would quickly hunt us down. If it's a quick death you seek, no doubt they have orders, no matter what may happen, that we are to be kept alive."

"Without Mantuka, what hope remains?"

"I'm not sure, lad, but, the things he said, his look, I-I sense something's afoot, although I cannot fathom what."

"We have to do something, Baints."

"I overheard talking, and I believe we have another night at camp before reaching Damascus. Hold thy desperation at bay, and we will plan tomorrow."

"Quick cuts at the wrists can end this torment easily and deprive them of their revenge."

"You talk of eternal damnation, lad."

"Who is to say we aren't damned already, Baints?"

"Talk no more of this. Sleep, lad. In the 'morrow, we plan."

*****

The baying of horses as they were readied for travel stirred those who were not already awake. Michael had slept little and had carefully observed the first stirrings of the camp, noticing that their guards were hardly alert, if not asleep, even though standing. He determined this would be the best time to attempt escape and worked through in his mind various plans of action for the next night.

They were given only water before they departed, and their bindings were left on as they shuffled forward and were loaded again into the cages. Those who had been in the other cage hurried to stay together, for no one wanted to be grouped with the royal captives. Unlike the previous day, they moved through populated areas, and when the inhabitants saw the captives and realized they were Crusaders, they, like those outside Jerusalem, angrily began throwing rotted fruit, animal dung, and even stones at them. They realized the closer they got to Damascus the more people they would encounter who had friends or relatives massacred at Acre.

They eventually began a gradual climb up foothills that led into a range of higher hills, and they continued upward at a steep angle along a well-worn pathway carved out of the rock, so it was wide enough to accommodate carts and wagons. They reached the crest at mid-morning, which provided a panoramic view of the area beyond, and also gave them a slight reprieve from the heat of the lake valley. They made a brief stop, and were given water and their first food of the day, once again pieces of hard, flat bread. Michael pointed out in the distance the outline of what appeared to be a long river, unaware that it was the Tigris.

When they resumed the journey, they moved at a much faster pace down the hill, and the cavalry ahead of their cages kicked up enormous dust clouds from the rough mountain trail they followed downward. The dust choked them into fits of coughing and forced them to cover their faces with their tattered tunics or hands. After a few miles they appeared as gray ghosts, covered completely with dust and struggling to breathe.

They finally reached the base of the foothills below and connected with a less dusty, more solid but extremely rough road that jarred them relentlessly, causing Claude to moan in pain until he finally passed out. Quinta scrub trees and escadia brush became plentiful all around, and they saw numerous villages not far from the road. As obvious as their distress was, the commander did not stop and maintained the relentless pace.

Several hours later, after only a short stop for water, Michael, the only one still alert in the cage, was the first to notice in the distance the outline of the walls and towers of what looked to be a large city, and a wide river running toward it. It had to be the same river he had seen from the summit of the hills they crossed earlier. *Could this be Damascus already?*

Alarmed, he poked Baints to attention and pointed so he would turn and see also. Baints was also shocked by the sight. "I-I must have heard in error, lad. I am heartily sorry. A city of that magnificence near such a river can only be the one which we dread, Damascus."

Chapter XIII

As they approached their destination it became apparent that Damascus was the most magnificent and largest city any of them had ever seen, but it was impossible to get excited over all they saw when what it meant for them was an unimaginably prolonged torture and an agonizing death.

Once they entered the outskirts of the city that stretched far beyond the protective walls that circled Damascus, angry crowds once again began to gather along the road. They understood then why such a large cavalry force accompanied them. It took all of them to provide an effective barrier between them and the chanting, swelling mob that followed them through the old Roman west gate framed between the remains of two huge Corinthian columns, and all that remained of what had been the Roman temple of Jupiter.

As they moved through the city to the prison, the tightly packed phalanx of horses and riders around them made it difficult to see anything completely. They were only able to catch passing glimpses of market stalls, fountains, oasis-like gardens, and the top domes of huge and ornate mosques and their minarets and even, much to their surprise, a cross-topped bell tower of a Christian church.

Damascus was not the largest city within the Muslim empire, or the most magnificent—that description could only be applied to Baghdad—but it was the oldest and the longest continuously occupied city of any dating to ancient times. The schools of medicine and science were the most prestigious, and their graduates the most celebrated, and Damascus remained at the crossroads of trade with the known world.

It connected the exotic kingdoms of the Far East with Arab and Muslim lands to the west, and in turn, the Christian kingdoms and principalities to the north, which allowed those in the city access to knowledge, innovation, and new goods before others. It was enlightened in its attitude toward other cultures and religions. Jews, Christians from Muslim lands, and peoples from all over the known world lived in relative harmony and peace in a city that had been, five hundred years before, primarily Christian. The church of St. John remained as a Christian house of worship through the centuries, since its construction by Syrian monks. The schools of Damascus had provided Mantuka with his education, and although he could never shed a status that branded him a slave, it nevertheless allowed his rise to a position of importance, wealth, and influence.

The prison was located next to a huge smelting pit, where renowned Damascus steel for swords and daggers was initially made, which was then reheated, folded, and hammered hundreds of times by armorer craftsmen into near indestructibility, and polished to glistening perfection. It was located in a section of the old city surrounded by plain, stone, fortress-like merchant warehouses, one of which had been converted into a prison.

At the prison entrance the Crusaders' bindings were cut and removed, and they trudged up two floors of stairs with Michael nervously feeling for the knife under his shirt, but their movement and the presence of so many guards made it impossible to do anything that would be considered effective.

They entered the cell as the sun began to set in the west, exhausted, backs aching, covered with dust, thirsty and hungry, but still, remarkably, in better health than when they had arrived in Jerusalem. Those with wounds experienced no reversals, although Claude's shoulder had hardly improved and Godfrey still limped, but not as badly as before. Still, he had to be helped up the stairs by Michael and Baints.

The dungeon cell they found themselves in was on the top floor. It was huge, easily large enough for all of them, but since it was not subterranean, as had been the case in Jerusalem, it was stifling hot inside, even with open barred windows on two sides.

They were not the only occupants, either. They were surprised to find other Crusaders there, Germans captured months earlier during an ambush, shortly after they had departed Antioch to join the siege at Acre.

Remarkably, one of them was a prince, Otto II, Duke of Bavaria, a huge, imposing man, and was being held for ransom. In an unheard-of act of defiance, the prince had refused imprisonment in a royal apartment in the Caliph's palace. He did so as a point of honor, when those of his personal entourage who had also survived and were captured with him—a knight named Hardwick and two footmen—were not allowed to stay with him.

The Germans, surprised by their arrival and appearance, welcomed them excitedly, and immediately shared what water and crumbs of food they had. Godfrey was able to talk with the prince primarily in rudimentary Latin, combined with some basic French.

Edward joined in the discussions eventually as well, and neither of the English knights made mention of the circumstances that had actually brought them together. They had simply said they had been captured after a battle with Saracens, taken to Jerusalem, and because of the slaughter of the hostages, ordered by King Richard at Acre, they had been sentenced to torture and death in Damascus, where many of the relatives of the slain lived, so they could have the satisfaction of seeing the sentence carried out.

The fact was that Godfrey and Edward's two knights, Black Simon and William, had reached a truce of sorts on the way to Damascus. Forced together in the tight confinement of their cage, Godfrey broke the bitter silence between them and explained what had led to the events that had forced his conflict with Richard. He told the details of his escape and that he and his men at that point had no choice but to join with Gerard to protect the innocents and save themselves.

In return, Black Simon revealed that Richard had told his knights that Godfrey was a traitor and implicated in a French plot to free wealthy Saracen nobles from Acre for gold, to pay the heavy mortgages on his lands. William conceded he found it difficult to believe, but Richard was his liege lord and king. He also revealed in their talk that it had been Saracen slaves, turned spies for dinars and freedom, who had told the king of Philip's plan to help hostages escape.

176

Edward had remained silent, but obviously, from his expression, he was not pleased with Simon or William talking so freely with Godfrey. Edward was too debilitated to voice objection, but he still would not look at Godfrey directly. Godfrey revealed nothing about their previous hope, that Mantuka would somehow help them to be spared the fate that awaited them. There seemed little point anymore in even mentioning it.

Prince Otto was genuinely shocked at the fate of Godfrey and Edward and their men. He stated he would do all he could, pay gold, appeal to Saladin himself, to have their sentences reversed. They listened, knowing full well there was nothing he could do. Otto then went on to explain the circumstances of his capture and imprisonment, and that his ransom was being negotiated, in what would necessarily be a lengthy process, taking months or longer. Saladin had allowed him the courtesy of access to couriers to communicate, via Constantinople, with his kingdom.

The last call to prayer wailed out eerily from a nearby minaret and could be heard in the cell, after which dusk quickly became night, while Godfrey talked on with Prince Otto and Hardwick, with Edward joining in at times. Everyone else was exhausted from the journey and lay back against a wall or prone on the floor in their now-darkened cell.

Then they heard the sound of many footsteps in the hallway. They also saw the faint, reddish glow of torchlight through the small window on their cell door, which was crisscrossed with thin iron strips, but still open enough to allow any sound in the hallway to be easily heard or light to be seen. They immediately became silent. Monet whispered to Baints, alarm and fear in his words, as the torchlight became bright through the cell door's barred window.

"Is, is our torture to start so soon?"

Baints shook his head. "Not likely with night already upon us, lad, but—"

Baints stopped as the door was quickly unbarred and kicked open by guards. The sight before them produced a spectrum of emotions, from surprise to elation to relief, then puzzlement. Mantuka Mace Sabutta had entered their cell.

Escape

Chapter XIV

Once again, Mantuka was accompanied by several assistants carrying bags, jugs, and torches. He signaled with his hand, and the guard closed and barred the door. The shock of seeing the short, black physician again quickly wore off for those who had seen him before, replaced by their excited murmuring, but the Germans sitting up now continued to stare at Mantuka with the same amazement that the English and French Crusaders had experienced when they first saw him at the vizier's court.

Godfrey spoke English—though Prince Otto would not be able to follow the conversation—so his own men could understand what was being said, if it would affect their fate in any way, and knowing the French at this point all understood enough to comprehend the key points.

"We thought we'd never see you again!" Godfrey exclaimed with both irritation and excitement in his voice.

"I am sorry. Remember, I counseled that appearances may not be as they would seem, but I did not want to inspire false hope."

Baints looked over at Michael then, who caught his eye. *Again, Baints's wisdom may have saved them, or had it?* Michael thought. They were to find out now, he was sure.

Mantuka continued, "I had to leave immediately the night I last saw you, to determine if it was possible to make arrangements here."

"Arrangements? What kind—" Godfrey began to ask.

"Was it possible?" Baints anxiously interrupted, having a sense now that Mantuka was about to reveal something significant. He noticed, too, that he was nervous and excited at the same time. Mantuka exchanged a knowing look with Baints, the one Crusader he knew he would rely on more than any other.

"Yes. And now it is most urgent I tell you exactly what I have planned." The cell became absolutely silent, except for the occasional noises from outside and below their barred windows. Edward and his group were especially interested, a look of confusion shared by them.

"Your escape has been arranged. Even for the Germans," Mantuka said, and repeated in French and then Latin for the benefit of Prince Otto.

It was apparent the entire group couldn't believe what they heard. They were on their feet now, and they all started talking at once. Otto translated for his men, who didn't understand what was going on. Mantuka's hand shot up in an urgent motion to be quiet.

"Silence, please, and sit back down," he said above the noise. "You will raise suspicions with loud talk. Just listen to me. There's much I must yet explain, and that must be agreed to."

They quieted instantly and lowered themselves to previous positions against the walls. Prince Otto, whispering, repeated the startling news to his men, who continued to ask questions he couldn't answer. No one else said anything further, but they all wondered what he meant by 'agreed to.'

"Three groups have been provided for. Camels, weapons, water, food, and a guide—all will be ready and waiting for us outside the walls this night. The Germans will go to Antioch. From there they can proceed to Constantinople and on to their home." Mantuka turned to Prince Otto and repeated this in a halting but understandable Latin.

He turned to Edward and continued, "You and your knights will go to Tripoli. From there, you can return to Acre if you wish."

Edward's look of surprise turned to confusion, and he was about to speak, but Mantuka ignored him and abruptly turned back to Godfrey, Michael, and Baints. As Mantuka addressed them, Baints couldn't help but wonder why Mantuka had been so generous with Edward and his men.

"You and your archers are the last group, and the reason I do this and risk everything. I give you only one choice. You may die anyway, but at least not here, after being tortured one full moon to the next. The risks ahead are great, more than any you have ever faced, but, at the very least, you will live free, and if you die, you will do so fighting, as warriors."

"Anything is better than dying here," Godfrey replied, but was obviously greatly puzzled as he tried to continue, "But what—"

Mantuka stopped him, as well as Edward, who again tried to interrupt.

"Listen!," he ordered sternly, and with a tone of urgency.

Godfrey quieted, as did Edward. Mantuka moved closer to Godfrey and his group, talked directly to all of them, then, his eyes meeting each of theirs, he said, "You must agree to my conditions first and give your holy vows to God in return. I choose you, not just because of your desperate circumstance or your skill as archers, which is crucial to my plan, but because of the extraordinary honor and courage displayed on behalf of innocents," Mantuka said, galvanizing their attention now.

"To defy a king, to risk all to protect them, it is the most sacred of all tenets in your scripture and the Q'uran. It was clear you are not only men of great skill in battle, but men I could trust to keep their vow, to honor a pledge of fealty no matter what hardships are to be endured."

"A vow, a pledge of fealty, to whom?" Godfrey interrupted, even more confused, but Baints already knew and nodded to Mantuka, who answered Godfrey, as well as the others, who had the same look of mystery on their faces.

"To me."

Surprise replaced confusion, murmurs erupted again, but Mantuka held up his hand to quiet them and continued.

"You must vow to help me return to my homeland."

Again, there was the sound of surprise, except for Baints, who gave a knowing smile and placed a reassuring hand on the shoulder of an utterly confused Michael. Mantuka continued as Black Simon tried to translate for Prince Otto, who anxiously pressed him to explain what was being said.

"We must journey through the vast expanse of lands that lay to the south and west of here, over a distance measured not in leagues, for it is not known, but in the change of seasons and the solstice of the sun. It is a distance I covered on the sea when taken as slave, and took two changes of the moon, but neither you nor I could travel that way now without the certainty of capture."

"Why?" Godfrey asked. "With all you have attained here, wealth, position, why—"

"Would you not risk all to try to return to your home if you could?"

Michael answered immediately and spoke for them all, "Yes, I would," he said with determination and understanding of the power of Mantuka's motivation.

They all understood as they sat there contemplating the question. Godfrey knew, of course, they would do as Mantuka asked. Obviously anything, even death fighting to escape, was immeasurably better than their current fate. They clearly had no choice, but he could not speak for all under his command.

"The French archers who fought with us, under their fearless and great knight, Gerard, who was struck down in battle, they could freely return to Tripoli with Edward and then home, as was the promise when we left Acre with the innocents."

"We will most certainly need all the archers among you. I cannot give them that choice," Mantuka said with finality.

DuClaire spoke up immediately. "I have nothing to go back to. With Gerard gone, I'd be put back in prison to die there."

"I do not want to go back in any event," Robere' suddenly said with conviction, and DuClaire nodded to him.

Claude followed with, "In Marseilles we learned that our village"—he looked from side to side at Andre and Monet, to include them in the statement—"was swept with pestilence after we departed. It is likely there is no one for us to go back to anyway. No matter, only a fool would wish to remain here and die horribly."

His friends seemed to nod, but in an uncertain agreement. Godfrey was relieved. Mantuka appeared satisfied, but he did not underestimate human nature, and understood its frailties. He had one more inducement to ensure loyalty and inspire effort against all hardship and obstacles—greed.

"To those who survive all the dangers and hardships that lay ahead, I can also offer as reward the promise of fortunes beyond your imaginations."

And with that, he opened his two hands, and in the palm of each were objects that immediately riveted everyone's attention. In one hand was a nugget of gold, the size of a thumb, and in the other was a polished white crystal, a huge, although uneven, diamond, the size of an eyeball, polished and glistening in the torchlight. Excitement filled the room. All were instantly mesmerized by the sight, including Prince Otto, who impatiently pressed Black Simon again for an explanation, while Godfrey asked more questions.

"These come from your land?" Godfrey asked, astonished.

"Yes, it is what we used for trade at the distant posts and ports over the mountains on the coast far to the east of our land. We know the places where it can be found in abundance; they are prized for ornamentation but have little value for us otherwise."

"What is your land like?" Michael asked, enthralled with Mantuka's revelations.

"There will be time enough to tell you of it during our journey."

A question then came from DuClaire, who suddenly seemed energized at the talk of riches, hardly a surprise to anyone. "What benefit will such riches be in your land, where you say they mean little?"

"There is a possibility, although perilous, for those who survive to return to their homelands if they wish to do so. Such wealth can most assuredly buy restitution of past sins. I have learned of Muslim traders who found lands and great cities and ports on the coast to the far west and south of the great city of Timbuktu, where ships come from Iberia to trade, and passage could be secured to Frankish lands. It would be a treacherous journey, no doubt, but my people would escort you there."

The Crusaders' imaginations were electrified. There was no doubt now in their minds—life, escape, weapons, adventure, gold, and precious crystals. It was beyond belief. Where only a few moments before they had reached the depths of despair and were resigned to a fate worse than any they could have imagined, they now faced the prospect that fired men's imaginations, of which impossible dreams were made. Not only had hope been rekindled within their spirits, but now in their hearts and minds, there was the possibility of a future, a chance to return home wealthy, as nobles. No matter how slight that chance might be in actuality, they were ready to embrace any ray of hope and magnify its chances in their minds.

"This is unbelievable, Baints," Michael whispered excitedly.

"That it is, lad . . . that it is," Baints answered, but with a tinge of skepticism that went unnoticed by his excited young friend.

Baints did not understand all that Mantuka was doing, nor his reasons for it, but he felt there had to be more than he revealed. He did appreciate the brilliance of the child-sized man they all towered over, and his fearless, almost ruthless determination. He understood how he was cleverly manipulating them, and that he had to have powerful reasons for wanting to return home so desperately.

Mantuka turned back to Edward, knowing the question he had tried repeatedly to ask.

"Your archer will not go with you to Tripoli. I need every archer for what lies ahead. He will join the Knight Godfrey and his men."

The archer, Thomas Wilton, was aghast at the statement. Edward jumped to his feet in protest.

"You cannot do that!" yelled Edward.

Mantuka's assistants moved forward, and Godfrey, Baints, and Michael were on their feet, in case the enraged knight actually attacked Mantuka. William and Black Simon were instantly on either side of Edward, to restrain him if necessary. The expressions on the faces of Prince Otto and his men showed utter confusion at the sudden eruption of emotion.

"He is a royal archer in service to Richard the Lionheart himself! He would rather die than mingle with traitors and murderers!"

"You forget your position, slayer of innocents," Mantuka said sharply in a manner they had not heard before. It was the universally cold, menacing tone one in authority would use when life or death hung in the balance.

"I can, and I will, do exactly what I want. I can have *you* executed tonight if I wish. Sit down. And if this young archer wants to die this night, I will grant him his wish," Mantuka added ominously, but in a remarkably controlled manner that left no doubt that this was no idle threat. Mantuka seemed much taller now as he spoke.

Edward's ranting clearly revealed that any apparent relaxation of enmity toward Godfrey and his men had been only the result of the numbness of a hard journey, and despair over meeting a horrible death. The fire of his burning hatred may have dimmed, but it had never been extinguished. Mantuka's pronouncement forced Edward to reluctantly back off, and he and the others sat back down.

At that moment the young royal archer stood up and surprised them with a sudden pronouncement.

"I-I will accompany you. I-I do not wish to die here," he said. He spoke in English and appeared quite exhausted, his face drained of emotion, accentuating the dark hollowness around his eyes. His dusty and dirty tunic still showed the stains of blood from the slaughter of his companions at the Muslim camp.

Mantuka's tone softened. "What is your name?"

"Thom-Thomas Wilton. I—"

Godfrey interrupted to speak to Mantuka. "It is of such importance we have one more archer, especially one who may not be trustworthy?"

Mantuka answered without hesitation. "I believe the lethal skill with the longbow to be crucial to us surviving what lies ahead, Knight. Every Christian archer we have multiplies our numbers greatly versus those we might face in the battles that most certainly will come. With a score more I might even sleep peacefully as we journey."

Godfrey and Baints shared a look of skepticism about Mantuka's answer and his judgment. Wilton saw their expressions of concern and spoke to Godfrey.

"Sire, I do not want to return to Acre. I have seen the defenses of Jerusalem, as have all of us. Would you want to fight in siege against them? Most will die, if not in battle then of wounds or pestilence here, I know that. I'd likely not see England again in any event. With you, the possibility may be as little or less, but there's still the chance to return home, *but* with riches to live as nobility."

There was a murmur of conversation in the room, and Edward looked truly incensed by Wilton's remarks, as if he actually expected him to embrace execution rather than join Godfrey, whom he had proclaimed traitorous.

Godfrey surveyed the faces of his men. Baints had a knowing smile, Michael nodded, then moved to DuClaire, who first spoke in French to his countrymen, who may not have understood all Wilton had said, and then also gave Godfrey a nod. Andre, Robere, and Monet had suspicious looks but didn't respond negatively. Claude winced as he tried to adjust his position but gave a nod; Bundage did so also, and Basil Martin did likewise. Mighty Morgan just looked at Godfrey expectantly, not really understanding exactly what was happening. Godfrey looked back at Mantuka and gave a nod in agreement, to which Mantuka simply nodded in return.

With a suddenness that startled everyone, even Mantuka, Godfrey moved forward toward their child-sized deliverer and knelt before him.

"I, Godfrey of Hampstead, pledge to you the fealty of myself and company, English and French alike, and in the sight of God, vow to use every last drop of our life blood and skill at arms to protect and lead you to your homeland."

Baints immediately followed Godfrey's example and knelt down, followed by Michael, and then, all the others for whom Godfrey had given his vow. The last to do so was Thomas Wilton, who suddenly realized he had been spoken for also.

Mantuka placed his hand on Godfrey's shoulder and said only, "It is done, then."

Mantuka promptly turned and motioned to his assistants, who began handing out food and water. "Eat to your fill and refresh yourselves, for our journey, through a land that will test us all, begins this night, when I return."

In the background, Prince Otto had been explaining to his men what a greatly intrigued Black Simon had tried, as best he could, to explain to the prince, the meaning of the events unfolding before them. Noticing the lull, Otto stepped forward and spoke to Godfrey and Mantuka. He asked several questions to clarify his understanding of the still-surprising turn of events. Godfrey and Mantuka took turns patiently answering each.

Satisfied, the prince finally stated, "If I were not a prince I would join you with my men. It is a glorious, blood-stirring adventure in exploration only the truly courageous dream of. But I must proceed to my homeland. Many challenges await me there. I will pray God speeds and protects you."

He looked at Godfrey. "If you wish to write letters to loved ones, I will promise, once I return home, to arrange to eventually have them delivered for you and ensure they remain private. I have plenty of the Saracens' wonderful paper, inks, a candle for wax and seal, and quills to use."

Prince Otto's last comment and offer inspired Godfrey with an idea. "Yes, my lord, I will do so, and greatly appreciate the opportunity, for I doubt I will ever see my sickly wife and children again, but . . . but in addition, I wonder, if, Sire, I could humbly prevail upon you to grant a most unusual request."

"If it is within my power, anything," Otto said sincerely.

"It is most assuredly *only* within your power, Sire," Godfrey replied, arousing Otto's profound look of curiosity. He continued in Latin, leaving his men frowning about what was being said by their knight.

"My men are archers, although dressed as knights. Led by the greatest of French knights and my dear departed friend, Gerard de Seucre. He dressed them thus as a ruse to gain entry to where I was being held awaiting execution, as ordered by King Richard, for I refused to lead the slaughter of innocents and the unarmed," Godfrey said, as building emotion seized him, forcing him to pause momentarily.

"They were willing to fight their own and die readily for my rescue. It meant sacrificing everything they held dear in their lives. They did this out of loyalty to me, to honor their vow of fealty." Godfrey glanced at Mantuka, then back at a surprised Prince Otto, and continued with great passion building in his voice.

"I wish to honor them, both English and French, as futile as it might be, by making them knights in reality, so we go on this perilous journey truly as equals, with tunics that are true to who they are. For no group of men have done more before God to honor the rank.

"Such a document I can prepare with explanation of the circumstances of their extraordinary heroism on my behalf, but more importantly, on behalf of innocents, which will blunt the charges of treason by others. Sire, this document can only be made valid by the signature of royalty, a prince or king. I implore you to do so and arrange its deliverance into the hands of the Archbishop at Canterbury."

Godfrey paused, looked at his men, took a deep breath then continued, "If Richard survives this Crusade, he will, of course, not recognize our action, but the knightly ranks granted by you will stand in the eyes of the Archbishop, a more saintly man than ever existed, and not enamored of a king's ways. He will keep the document there in safekeeping for all to see, to the lasting honor of my men and their families."

Otto was so taken by this remarkable and impassioned request, he moved to Godfrey and put both hands on his shoulders, in the highest act of esteem a monarch can display to a vassal.

"I will be greatly honored and proud to do so. Prepare thy proclamation for my name and seal."

"Thank you, Sire, thank you," Godfrey said, greatly moved by Otto's words of agreement. Edward couldn't believe what he had heard and shouted out in protest, but was angrily dismissed by Otto.

"Silence to you! You have dishonored your knightly rank in misguided loyalty to a dishonorable king!" Otto yelled back in Latin, but with an authority that only a prince or king could command, and his words were easily understood in their tone as a rebuke by everyone in the cell. Edward slumped back down, outwardly silenced and humiliated, but inside, he was seething with an anger and hatred unlike any he had ever felt.

Shortly afterward, Mantuka announced he must leave, and his assistants handed the torches to the archers. There were no holders inside their cell, and an assistant pounded on the door. "Do not keep the torches aflame for long. Be vigilant, for when the night is darkest and all is still, I will return. Be alert and ready to move swiftly," Mantuka said hurriedly, looking at Godfrey. A moment later the guard opened the door, and Mantuka and his assistants left.

Godfrey wrote the document out of sight of the doorway, as the others proceeded to eat and drink. As he labored over the listing of names, he decided it would be right to include their newest archer, Thomas Wilton. Once completed, he gathered the company together and explained what he had done. Except for Baints, who had understood some of what Godfrey had said to Prince Otto, they were stunned, and, while still in a state of shock, he had the men kneel before the prince.

With a solemn, quiet dignity, Godfrey said the words, as best he could remember, from the knighthood ceremony, which was followed in turn by words from Prince Otto. Although they could not understand what the prince said, since it was spoken in Latin, it had the sound and tone of a profoundly sacred and important ceremony.

Without a sword, Otto instead began to use just his hand to tap the first Crusader's shoulder, but then Michael remembered he had the knife in his tunic. He quickly pulled it out and offered it to the startled prince. Otto smiled at Michael, nodded his head in approval, took the offered knife, and began again, now tapping their shoulders, one by one, while awkwardly pronouncing their names, with a distinct German accent, as best he could.

And there, in the confines of a hot Damascus prison, they all became English or French knights from the tap of a small, curved Saracen dagger and the Latin words of a German prince.

The men were subdued but genuinely sincere in their words of appreciation to Godfrey, and each bowed once again before a greatly moved Prince Otto. Wilton was brought to tears by what had happened and spoke out to the entire group, saying he was truly not deserving of such an honor but promised he would do all he could to earn it from this day forward.

Afterward, Baints came up to the young archer and put his arm around him, an act that truly made him one of them—he was now accepted as a member of Godfrey's new company of English and French archers and a newly anointed knight as well.

The scene utterly disgusted and added to the humiliation of Edward of Liecster, royal knight to King Richard the Lionheart, and even appalled his more sympathetic fellow knights. Edward's hatred was consuming him. He felt no elation over the prospect of escape. The initial feeling of relief over being spared a prolonged, tortuous death was gone. The only emotion he felt now, the one that fueled the intense thoughts that swirled in his brain, was that of revenge.

Chapter XV

Godfrey had extinguished all but one of the torches, which he positioned on the floor in a corner to restrict the light that might reach a window. The soft glow offered enough illumination that the Crusaders could eat and drink all that they could of the more than ample supply of food and water that Mantuka had left. A clever arrangement in a corner of the cell allowed their waste to be dumped from buckets into a large, plain, funnel-like bowl made from lead, with piping connected, that took it down into an underground sewer system. This, in turn, allowed it to be flushed with the city's waste directly out into the large river that ran through the western edge of the city.

No one except Mighty Morgan could sleep. The anticipation of their escape, the details about which they knew nothing, kept nerves taut and tension high, but they kept their emotions in check. Some paced nervously, others tried to rest with eyes closed, and some prayed openly, their whispered words being heard.

Edward, William, and Black Simon had withdrawn to a far corner and whispered conspiratorially among themselves while eating. At times their voices grew briefly louder, and it appeared the knights were disagreeing about something being discussed, but they would quiet immediately when they noticed heads turned their way. Prince Otto and his men sat with Godfrey and ate mostly in silence, their nervousness about events apparent in their look and manner.

Michael tried to relax, but his mind raced repeatedly over the astounding series of events that had transpired since they had arrived in Damascus. Baints's instincts about Mantuka had been correct. He was glad his mentor had trusted his feelings and knew he always would. And thank God—and Mantuka—that Baints was well again and the difficult journey hadn't caused his illness to return. Soon they would attempt escape, and hopefully succeed.

And incredibly, by some strange twist of fate, a miracle, really, he had realized his life's ambition. He had become a knight in, of all places, a Saracen dungeon! Were they *really* knights? Baints had told him they truly were, although it would change nothing among them. Would anyone other than they ever know? Godfrey said they were equals now, but what did it all really mean? His ambition to become a knight had grown solely out of his mad desire to make Lady Mary his wife. Even if, somehow, he survived, could he ever return to England and not be hanged as a traitor? His mounting anxiety could only be calmed by talking with Baints. He was nervous, but also felt a strange joyous excitement. They were about to embark on a dangerous, unimaginable journey, a great adventure to be sure, but one that would most likely remain unknown to anyone else. They would possibly be spared a horrible death, but for how long?

"The lands we travel to, do you know anything of them?" he asked Baints, who had tried to close his eyes and rest. But Michael was eager for any scrap of information his friend might know. He noticed now, as he talked with Baints, the wound on his face had scabbed over and the swelling that had closed his eye was nearly gone. His eyes opened.

"Aye, lad. I know of some things, but not the truth of them. The old monk I spoke of before, the one who tended me, had been assisted by tall, black-skinned slaves with a white scar of a cross on their foreheads. He said they were Christians that came from a vast land far distant to the south of the land of Egypt."

"Black-skinned Christians?" Michael responded in astonishment. Baints moved himself up and sat back against the wall before continuing.

"Aye, lad. He said missionaries sent by Constantine had converted them long, long ago, and that they fiercely resisted Islam and still adhered to the true faith. He said theirs was the land of legends, of gigantic, ferocious animals, strange tribes, unimaginable riches, and from where the dragon that St. George slew had come. But the monk was skilled as a teller of tales, and I doubt much of what he said was altogether known as true by him."

Michael was captivated by what Baints said, and equally with the manner in which he said it. Among his many talents, Baints was also an expert teller of tales and had kept them entertained during the many months of their travels on the way to the Holy Land. He was about to ask more questions when, suddenly, they heard the sound of the door being unbarred without the sound of footsteps announcing the action or the light of torches showing in the window of the door.

The heavy door opened carefully and, barely visible, there stood Mantuka and three assistants, who quickly entered, carrying huge piles of cloth in their arms.

"Remain quiet," he whispered. "You must all dress in these. Put them over your tunics for now."

The assistants handed the robes out to everyone, together with a head covering, which would also allow them to hide their faces. They then moved around and helped those having difficulty putting the robes and head coverings on and adjusting them correctly. Mantuka continued whispering instructions.

"You will appear to be part of a merchant caravan. They often leave from this area in the middle of the night, while it is cooler, and to move through and out of the city much quicker. It appears we are the only one to depart tonight, although it would have been better if there were others. Follow me now, make no sound, and do exactly as I instruct. Those in cells on the floor below are asleep. The guards have been dealt with. Leave their weapons exactly where they lay."

They left the cell in single file, and at the end of the corridor, by the stairs, they saw two guards, one slumped back at an odd angle against the wall, and another sprawled facedown on the floor next to their bench. But there were no stains of blood or other obvious marks of violence evident.

"Are they dead?" Michael whispered to Baints as they passed the bodies.

"It appears so, lad. I did not see the movement of taking breath."

They moved down the stairway to the second floor and once again saw several guards slumped against walls or lying awkwardly on the floor with their scimitars not even removed from scabbards. Baints could not help but wonder how it had been accomplished so stealthily, without even the slightest sound of a struggle heard by any of them before Mantuka returned.

They proceeded down the last stairway and passed what had been a heavily guarded entrance when they had arrived. There was no one in sight. Mantuka's lead assistant opened the thick, heavy wooden doors and led them out into the night.

The air was cooler than in the cell but still warm. A sliver of moon in a clear sky provided little light to see, but was apparently enough for Mantuka and his men to lead them. The smell of animals was obvious in the night air, and they understood why as they crossed a narrow street and turned into what appeared, as they approached, to be an even narrower alley.

Positioned there were one-humped camels. "Exceedingly ugly creatures," Godfrey whispered to Michael as they approached them. The animals had large reed sacks on one side tied over their humps, and more supplies on the other side, also secured by rope over the humps, but covered with a thick, plain white cloth. Behind the humps and also secured to them were what appeared to be saddles on the camels' rumps. The line of animals must have stretched the entire length of the alleyway, although they could not see them all.

The smell was powerful and awful in the confined space, but there was little noise from the beasts, other than the occasional sound of a powerful stream of urine splashing into the sand. The animal's hide was covered with a coarse wool, which was rough to the touch and produced the offensive odor. They had barely enough room to fit between the camels and their burdens and the alley wall, but Mantuka's assistants still managed to deftly squeeze between and under them in order to grab hold of the Crusaders and push each of them into position between two camels and hand them the rope rein for each of the animals behind them. They had no idea what was happening, but none of the Crusaders said a word.

Once this maneuvering was completed, Mantuka moved down the line to Baints and whispered to him, "Under the white cloth on each beast are weapons to use only upon my command. Inform your men *quietly*. I will advise your lord and the others."

Baints immediately checked under the cloth, and sure enough, there were weapons, but what weapons! English longbows and quivers of arrows held in cloth holders and secured by rope but easily and quickly accessible. Also there, tied securely just above the bow, was a scimitar and dagger with scabbards and a belt.

Baints marveled at the sight. With longbows, even ones not their own, they could escape from anywhere. They had certainly proven that in the palace in Acre. How on earth had Mantuka managed to get longbows? Baints wondered, and then immediately went up and down the line, informing the men, as Mantuka did the same with the knights. Twice he had to muffle a man's excitement at the sight of the weapons, with his hand over their mouth. Once he finished, they were on their way.

The camels began moving forward, and they followed, rein in hand, out the alley, and turned onto a wide cobblestone street that took them on a meandering route through the city. They realized Mantuka's plan was clever. They were playing the roles of Saracen merchants on a trading expedition, simply leading camels in a caravan out of the city. Guards they occasionally spotted at posts within the city, and sentries stationed on walls, took little notice of their passing, for what to them must have been a routine and commonplace occurrence and sight, apparently led by a father and his young son. Nevertheless, they were all on edge and tense to the extreme. Knowing now they had weapons, though, helped to somewhat ease their apprehension.

Mantuka's caravan wound its way through the city, up to the same gate they had entered as prisoners in cages. They held their breath as they passed unchallenged, underneath numerous sentries on the outer wall overhead, and through the massive gated entrance, where additional guards stood casually leaning against the huge open barrier doors, with numerous large torches lighting the area. Mantuka's assistant next to him in the lead waved a farewell as they passed through, which was returned by the unsuspecting guards. They had done it! It seemed so simple, so easy!

They continued on, following the main road for a considerable period of time, as the torches at the gate they passed through became faint in the distance behind them. They moved off the road then, and went left through a ravine that completely shielded them from the highest signal towers along the Damascus battlements.

But the slight moonlight was even fainter in the shadows of the deep ravine, and Mantuka was forced to light a torch to guide them in the blackness. Eventually they moved behind low hills and then into a long but narrow canyon, where they saw several torches being held by other assistants with two additional groups of camels, one of which had twice as many animals and appeared more heavily loaded than the others. Once they were all completely in the canyon, Mantuka called for them to come together.

"From here, the groups take separate paths. Askim here will lead the prince and his men to Antioch, and Tenuta there will lead the three English knights to Tripoli. You must depart immediately and move swiftly. You will be shown how to ride your beasts. Those going with me, move your animals now to join the group over there, on the right."

Mantuka pointed to the larger group of animals nearby, and then repeated an abbreviated version in Latin for Prince Otto. When Mantuka finished, Otto approached Godfrey, and they clasped arms in farewell.

"If I survive, know I will keep my pledge and get your words to your family and our document to Canterbury," the prince said emotionally.

"I know you will, Sire. I wish I'd had the privilege of serving one such as you."

"If God Almighty allows and someday distant you desire, and are able, to return to my northern lands, you shall have title, estates, and a place of honor at my side."

"I thank you, Sire, as do my noble archers. God speed, and may St. George protect you."

Godfrey and his company also waved farewell to Otto's knight Hardwick and the two footmen next to the same camels they had walked into the canyon with, and that they would now use for their departure. The animals had already been brought to their knees.

They waved back and gathered to help their prince mount his beast first, and when he had done so, their guide, Askim, tapped the animal's neck with a stick, and it lurched up with Otto maintaining his seat, hands secured on the reins and around the saddle's pummel. Otto's men did the same without encountering much difficulty.

Mantuka and Askim embraced in the Muslim fashion and said their words of farewell in Arabic. Askim mounted the lead camel, and they promptly departed through the narrow ravine they had entered from.

Next to depart were the three English knights. They were huddled together next to Edward's camel, and their discussion seemed intense. Edward was quite animated as he talked in a muffled whisper, constantly pointing at the two other knights. Their look and manner reflected defiance and outright disagreement over something they were heatedly discussing. Edward abruptly turned his back on the pair as their guide, Tenuta, approached and promptly brought Edward's camel to its knees and motioned for him to mount the beast. He repeated the procedure with the other two knights, who were obviously still upset.

Although it was the smaller of the two groups of camels that had been in the canyon when they arrived, it still had as many animals as Prince Otto's caravan. Nearby, Mantuka and Tenuta embraced, and the loyal servant mounted his kneeling lead camel and quickly began to move the second group out into the night.

Baints wondered out loud to Michael and Godfrey next to him why the two groups that departed had so many camels and supplies for so few riders, and he asked Mantuka about that when he approached them.

"Not all carry supplies," Mantuka answered. "Many bags are filled only with sand, so the track of the beast appears to be carrying a man. When their trails are found, each will appear to be a group large enough to contain all who escaped. If at least one group eludes capture and reaches their destination, it will be thought all are accounted for and had successfully escaped. There will be no reason to search further."

"They are really diversions, then. It is a clever plan, indeed," Baints said, then added, "I marvel at your ability to do this all so quickly."

"Wealth has many advantages and a ready plan, and faithful servants made it possible."

"So, you have been planning such a journey for sometime," Baints added.

"Yes, opportunity is only realized when one is ready to seize it," answered Mantuka.

Godfrey was concerned, though, with the implications. "Can both groups reach safety?"

"It is possible, especially those who go to Antioch. Their camels are healthy and swift, and they will have many hours ahead of pursuers. But there will be much rage and desperation over your escape, and the best cavalry will be sent on the swiftest of camels. Failure will mean the commander of Damascus and his officers will be executed in your place if all are not recaptured."

"Will they not pursue our trail?" Michael asked.

"The route we take from here to the south enters a land considered impossible to travel through, but we will leave no trail easily found in any event."

Michael appeared shocked by the pronouncement, but Baints knew Mantuka wouldn't take a route he hadn't prepared for. "Pursuit will be in the direction most logical, along trails that are readily found," Mantuka concluded.

"And," Godfrey added, "when they find two trails, they would have no reason to believe another even exists."

"Exactly," Mantuka replied with a slight smile. Suddenly, his attention was turned elsewhere, and they also looked in the direction of his gaze.

Two small figures emerged from the shadows. The lower part of their faces were partially hidden by their headdress scarves, but, even in the torchlight, it was clear they were black-skinned, shorter than Mantuka, and their quickness in moving suggested they were young, apparently children, and dressed as boys.

"Who are they?" Godfrey asked.

"You bring children with us?" Michael asked.

"They come with us and are of no concern to you," Mantuka said with an uncharacteristic flash of impatience and irritation, as he hurried to take them to camels near the end of the line, where an assistant had the animals already kneeling. He helped the children onto the saddles and tapped the necks of the beasts to get them up.

Behind the children another camel had a rider already mounted. Robes obscured the form, scarves covered the head, and a scimitar and dagger in scabbards were visable, tucked in a belt. But as the scarf across the face was rearranged by the rider a brief glimpse revealed striking eyes on a familiar face, that of the young woman who had told the commander about Crusaders who had fought and died to save Acre's woman and children, and unmistakably the same face *Michael had seen unveiled.*

Mantuka returned to where Godfrey, Baints and Michael still stood together and made no mention about the children. He asked Godfrey to come with him. Mantuka, holding a small torch, led Godfrey to the front of their caravan.

Meanwhile, his assistants, also holding torches, helped the wary archers mount their kneeling, grunting camels. The flickering light from the torches created pockets of ominous, undulating shadows on the craggy rock walls of the narrow canyon that comprised the staging area. Once again the loud splashing sounds of camels pissing were accentuated by their confined area, as were the offensive odors given off by the animals' puffs of breath and their dirty skins.

They passed Basil Martin, who was quietly coaxing the terrified Mighty Morgan to mount his beast. "He has always been vexed by riding atop a beast of any kind," Godfrey told Mantuka, who frowned at the sight of the giant's child-like aversion to being forced onto the back of the camel.

"Come, noble knight, there is something I wish to show you that may imbue hope for survival beyond reason and instill a fanaticism to reach journey's end no matter the consequence."

A deep frown wrinkled Godfrey's brow in reaction to the curious words as he followed behind the diminutive prince to whom he had sworn allegiance as his lord.

Upon reaching his lead camel, Mantuka withdrew a prodding stick from the saddle, tapped the front legs of the animal until it knelt, and handed his torch to Godfrey. He proceeded to loosen straps on a rectangular sack tied to the back of the saddle and hanging to the side. He opened the heavy flap covering the large, roughly made pack of scraped, sun-dried camel skin, and motioned to Godfrey.

"Look inside, Knight," Mantuka said matter-of-factly.

Godfrey moved closer with the torch held high, and he peered into the open sack. His eyes expanded with amazement, and his expression changed from frowning curiosity to stunned surprise.

"The top of a magnificently crafted chest encrusted with precious jewels that form three crosses atop the Calvary mount?" Godfrey shot an incredulous look at Mantuka. "Can-can it be in truth what I dare not believe my eyes reveal?"

"It is the revered chest of your St. Helena."

Godfrey's eyes fixed on Mantuka's. "Jesus Christ and all the saints!" Godfrey used his free hand to touch the chest's jewel-encrusted top. "Are-are *they* still inside?"

"Yes, my noble and brave friend, the reputed relics of the cross your Christ hung on still lie within. I am quite certain they have laid within undisturbed since their capture at Hattin."

Godfrey uncharacteristically found it impossible to contain himself. "I must tell everyone!" he exclaimed.

Mantuka closed the heavy flap. "No. We must first depart. We cannot afford the loss of precious time that such eruptions of emotion and distraction would bring."

"Yes. Of course. I-I agree. But I say this to you, Mantuka, my sworn prince, with these precious relics now protecting us, we may actually reach your homeland; something I had not, in my heart or very soul, ever pondered as possible."

Mantuka took hold of Godfrey's arm. "And then, if you live, this treasure would allow you a return to your home, perhaps?"

Godfrey, his eyes filled with the energy of newfound hope, looked down at Mantuka's smiling face. "If he lives, that damnable Richard himself would welcome us back!"

"I have one more revelation that may expand your heart and soul with yet more elation. Move back to the camel behind mine, the one that will now be your animal."

Mantuka took him to the camel, turned up a flap covering a large reed oblong sheath, and pointed to the large handle of a sword sticking out, tightly wrapped with thin leather, with its metal crosspiece etched with inscriptions but otherwise unadorned, absent of precious gems. Godfrey recognized it immediately.

"Gerard's sword!" Godfrey exclaimed, and slowly removed it. "How in God's name did you possibly come to have it?"

"It came from the camp of Ibn el-Athir, although I did not know for sure it was your friend's until now but knew from its appearance and markings that it was assuredly that of a knight, a French knight. It was the only one obtained. The others likely were more ornate, as I suspect yours was, and were bartered away or kept by the commander."

"Yes, his was plain by comparison. But, when-how were you able—"

"Assistants went to his camp with many swift horses while I hurried to Damascus. They traveled with my personal letter under the Vizier's seal, ordering all captured longbows, arrows, and other weapons be loaded on their horses and immediately sent with them to Damascus for use in your execution. It was vital to our survival and my plan to secure your fearsome weapons."

"I thank you. It heartens me to have the sword of such a great knight and true friend."

"We must leave. Prepare your men. My assistants will help."

Godfrey returned to Baints and Michael, as the other men gathered around them, and he explained the surprising appearance of what they recognized as Gerard's huge sword now in his hand. Godfrey told them that later, when they stopped to camp after putting distance between them and possible pursuers, they should check all the bows and knives packed with the supplies on each of the camels. He explained that they may possibly find their very own weapons, and explained how Mantuka had actually been able to obtain them.

Godfrey then added in a voice heightened by an extreme of excitement which especially drew Baints' attention because he had seldom seen such from his lord.

"I have other news to share of the most momentous import but will do so later. There is no time for its revelation now." Baints and Michael exchanged curious looks as Godfrey continued.

"Baints, tell the men we are ready to leave and they must all mount their animals quickly if they have not done so."

"Aye, my lord," Baints responded as Godfrey turned and hurried back to his camel.

Godfrey secured the huge battle sword under the cloth that covered the other weapons on his beast. He vowed silently to use it to honor his friend's memory. Baints passed the word of their immediate departure, and the archers who had not mounted their camels did so with the assistance of Mantuka's men. It was a comical scene, with most having difficulty adjusting to the unusual saddle arrangement. Mighty Morgan fell off of his and had to agonizingly remount. Most grumbled that it would be better to walk. Baints reminded them they were still in extreme danger and had to put considerable distance between themselves and possible pursuers before dawn.

When Mantuka passed by checking the caravan's readiness Baints called to him to ask a question that had been bothering him.

"Can I ask something of you, Sire?" Baints said respectfully. Since they had given a vow of fealty to Mantuka, their acknowledged prince, he was in effect their liege lord also, and should be addressed as such, a point not lost on Mantuka.

"Yes, Sergeant, quickly, though," Mantuka responded.

"I was thinking about what you said, that the group going to Antioch should make it, but what, then, of the other group if captured? Couldn't they be made to reveal our existence?"

"I do not believe that would happen."

"Torture can reveal a man's very soul and curse his own mother," Baints said.

"Tenuta, the one who leads them, will not allow himself or the three knights with him to be taken alive. It is also the case with Askim, headed for Antioch."

Baints pondered this a moment, and the calm manner in which Mantuka bluntly stated so chilling an answer. "How would they do so if-if surprised?"

"There is a way. You noticed all the dead guards throughout the dungeon. All was done swiftly, without a sound." The dispassionate, direct statement left Baints quietly pondering the fact.

"We must depart *now*," Mantuka said with authority, ending any further questions.

Mantuka returned to the head of the line, expertly mounted his kneeling camel, and Baints returned to his and was helped by one of the three Mantuka assistants who would also accompany them on their incredible journey.

Baints thought intently about what Mantuka had said. This small, brilliant man had apparently planned for every possibility and was revealing an absolute ruthlessness behind an iron will of determination to succeed in reaching his goal. He wondered then at what point they would become expendable as well.

The caravan began moving out of the canyon, and they gradually began to adjust to the swaying rhythm of the camels. One by one, the torches were extinguished before they exited the canyon and approached the road. Behind the last camel, now with an empty saddle, the rider, one of the assistants, followed on foot and moved a fan of palm branches in a wide arc over their tracks in the gravel and sand to obscure them. After their eyes adjusted, the moonlight gave them enough light to see, and when they reached the road, they were surprised when they turned right, heading back toward Damascus. But after a short distance, once they moved to the other side of the hills, they turned right again and headed southward. There was no evidence whatsoever that they followed a well-worn route, or even an occasionally used pathway, and after another short distance, the assistant who was obscuring their tracks ceased the effort and mounted his camel.

The fact was, they were headed toward one of the most desolate desert landscapes known to man. It was a route that Mantuka knew would avoid other travelers and caravans, make pursuit by a large force nearly impossible, and shorten the distance to Egypt, their initial destination. It was a route only the most desperate of men would choose, and even though it would test the limits of their endurance, he had an advantage over all others who had ever attempted crossing this forbidding land.

The pace picked up considerably then, and the Crusaders found themselves desperately learning to balance and hold on to a cantering camel. Their incredible journey had begun—a journey that none of them, except Mantuka, had even the slightest comprehension of all that it would involve. Mantuka knew it would take a miracle for them to complete it, but he had absolutely no choice but to try.

It was an opportunity he had been planning for and hoping would appear for years. Then a large Crusader army had landed and taken Acre. Saladin and other leaders were preoccupied with that development and unprepared for the initial Crusader success.

When a group of unusual Crusader archers, experts with the devastating longbow, were captured and brought to Jerusalem at the very time he was there, the last piece of his puzzle had fallen unexpectedly into place. Fate had provided the best opportunity he would ever have to put what he knew was a desperately reckless plan into motion.

And now, the future and very survival of his people depended upon it. Many challenges lay ahead, more than even he could know or anticipate. The greatest of these, he knew, lay in the lands beyond Egypt, to the far south, and marked 'unknown' even on the maps of the most renowned Arab explorers, the land referred to forbiddingly by Red Sea traders as *Alaradi Almzolm,* 'The Dark Lands.'

All Mantuka knew was that his home, their ultimate destination, lay somewhere deep within those lands, most of which he himself had never seen, a place he, his people, and their ancestors had always called . . . *Kokongo.*

TO BE CONTINUED...

If you enjoyed this book, please consider leaving a review on Amazon, Goodreads, or mentioning it on social media.

My sincerest thanks,

Curtis Burdick